Detective

book one

SIGNS

PAMELA MURRAY

ALSO BY PAMELA MURRAY

Murderland

Bloodline

Duplicity

CHAPTER ONE

'I'm not really sure about this,' Maria Turnbull said nervously, chewing hard at the skin around her thumb nail. It was a habit of hers whenever she was anxious about anything, and had started in light of what her friend had just said to her.

'What have you got to be unsure of?' Caroline Watkins laughed, looking towards the other two women in the room for support. She discreetly jerked her head in Maria's direction, hoping that they'd take the hint and back her up.

Selena Douglas was the first to pick up on it and oblige. 'It's only for a laugh and a bit of fun, Maria; it's not like we're going to take it seriously or anything. Isn't that right, Barbara?' she said, turning to the fourth person present.

'Yes ... it is.' Barbara didn't look happy being asked. She hadn't wanted to be dragged into this, or push Maria into something that she didn't want to do, but found herself now having to go along with it. 'It's only make-believe anyway. I hear there's a knack to reading those things, like the way a magician or a mind reader performs their act. How can it be anything other than a party trick, as we all know there's no such thing as real magic?'

'But you know I don't like anything supernatural like that,' Maria insisted, biting down harder on her skin with just enough pressure to draw a spot of blood.

'Listen to what Barbara and Selina have just said,' Caroline insisted. She didn't believe in that stuff either, but she'd heard interesting things about this woman online and had been wanting to go and see her for such a long time. 'It's not real, just a bit of harmless fun that's all, and it'll be a good laugh. Come on Maria, stop being such a spoilsport. Don't ruin it for the rest of us!'

Maria stopped the chewing and looked at her three friends whose eyes were now all on her, each of them waiting for a response. She couldn't let them down, she knew that; so, she finally agreed to go. 'But if I get spooked, I'm straight out of there,' she said warily.

'Good girl, that's more like it!' Caroline walked over to her and put an arm around her shoulder. 'You'll be laughing at this by the end of the night, just you mark my words.'

***

Caroline suggested they stop off at a trendy wine bar on Half Moon Street before visiting the fortune teller. It was one she'd been to on a few occasions with work colleagues and liked its atmosphere. A couple of glasses might take the edge off the tension.

'As long as I don't have too much; you know what John's like with alcohol,' Maria protested upon hearing where they were going.

'Oh, tell him to go to hell, Maria!' Caroline retorted somewhat unexpectedly. 'You've only been married for a few months and he's already got you well and truly under his thumb!'

'No, he hasn't, that's not true. How can you say that?' Maria had never heard anything untoward said about her husband before this evening, so was shocked by her friend's sudden verbal attack on him.

'You were the life and soul of the party before you met him. You were always the first to agree to a night out.'

'Well, I wouldn't say that-'

'You were, and you know it. He's cramping your style. Just let your hair down and have a good time like we all used to.'

Maria had to admit that used to be the case at one time, but she was now a married woman with new responsibilities, which didn't include going out every Friday evening and getting blind drunk and then having to sleep it off the next day. They didn't seem to realise that, as they were still free and single. However, despite feeling pressured, she eventually said, 'Well maybe just the one then,' thinking that if she agreed it would get her friend off her back.

'Good girl!' Caroline rejoiced and led them all into the wine bar. She knew Maria would come around in the end.

Despite her determination to only have one drink, Maria ended up having three glasses of Prosecco, which more than relaxed her resolve. Maybe Caroline and the others were right, she pondered mid-way through the second glass. She shouldn't have to be worried about what hubby would think or say if she returned home just a little bit intoxicated. It was her life after all, and she shouldn't stop doing the things she used to do just because she was no longer a singleton. *Yes, sod him*, she thought. By the end of their drinking session Maria was surprisingly in agreement with them. Like they'd all told her, it would be a laugh, a bit of fun, so what would be the harm in it as it was all a con anyway?

Apart from Caroline, none of the other women had heard of Madame Ortiz before that evening. And despite their lack of knowledge of her, the fortune teller was a renowned figure not only in Manchester but across the entire country, and considered by many to be the real deal. Her readings were in great demand, and Caroline was lucky in that she'd managed to secure the last available time slot for the entire month of June. She'd also expected that Maria would come around to her thinking after a few drinks, which was why she suggested the wine bar. As for the other two, they were always up for a night out whatever that entailed, despite Barbara's seemingly initial reluctance to go along with it all.

.

CHAPTER TWO

C aroline already knew what to expect of the place when she'd booked the evening out for them as the website had photographs of both the exterior and interior. However, for the others it came as a complete surprise. Maria had half-expected her to work out of a dingy room tucked away down some dimly-lit back street, but it couldn't have been further from the case. Madame Ortiz had her business premises in The Northern Quarter, which was nestled in between Piccadilly train station and the Arndale Centre, right in the middle of the city's trendiest bars, cafés and boutiques.

'Here we are,' Caroline declared as she brought the party to a halt outside a bright red half-glazed door with the name *Madame Ortiz – by appointment only* etched on the frosted glass panel.

'This is not what I expected,' Selena declared looking around her at the setting. 'I thought she'd be down a-'

'Back alley?' Maria finished her sentence.

'Yes, exactly!'

'Oh ye of little faith,' Caroline quoted before pressing a button on the intercom beside the door. After a few moments, the intercom crackled into life and a woman's voice greeted them and asked if they had an appointment. Caroline again took the lead. 'Yes,' she spoke into the device. 'Party of four for 9pm in the name of Watkins.'

'Ah yes, do come up, I've been expecting you,' the disembodied voice continued before a buzzer sounded and the red door automatically unlocked for them.

'Thank you,' Caroline replied as she pushed it open and went inside, with the others following.

'Wow!' Barbara exclaimed, stunned by the impressive décor. The passageway was decorated in an Art Nouveau style, with framed prints adorning both sides of the wall. She recognised some of the works immediately: Gustav Klimt's *The Kiss*, and others in the style of Charles Rennie Mackintosh. Having studied Art History, she was impressed by the extent of the collection, especially as this style had always been her favourite. At the top of the flight of stairs the landing led on to an open door. Upon entering they saw four seats arranged around a circular coffee table. The décor in here was a continuation, and Barbara wasn't certain if it was a genuine interest in the art itself or if it was the way Madame Ortiz had decided to market her business. In either case, she thought it had been done in a tasteful way.

Before they had time to sit, one half of a curtain at the far end of the room swished open and a woman appeared dramatically from behind it, dressed in what could easily be described as an outfit from the 1920s, complete with a sequined headband with a feather plume sticking out of it. She looked for all intent and purpose like an extra from the film *The Great Gatsby*. All that was needed to complete the scene was Leonardo DiCaprio to come through the curtain as well, with champagne glass in hand, bidding them a warm welcome. Selena managed to stifle a laugh by turning it into a cough.

'Welcome,' the very attractive brunette greeted them, bowing her head as she said it causing the feather to flutter as she dipped then rose up again. 'I am Madame Ortiz, and I will be giving you all a reading this evening.' It seemed to be the standard, well-rehearsed greeting speech for all her clients, culminating with 'And who will be the first to enter my chamber?'

Selena coughed again. Apart from it being overly dramatic in her opinion, Maria started to feel all panicky again. All this talk of psychics and the supernatural was disturbing, despite the false sense of bravado the alcohol had given her. She wasn't into it at all, if truth be told, and was a little bit concerned about meddling with things that we didn't really know anything about. This had all stemmed from a friend telling her years ago that she and her husband had been to a party, and after a few drinks a Ouija board had been brought out. Like everyone else, they'd played the game – if indeed it can be called a game – but on the way home they'd got lost on a road they regularly travelled on. They'd found themselves in a densely wooded area, which was nowhere near where they lived, with no sense of how they got there, and they both swore blind to this day that they'd lost about forty-five minutes from the start of the journey to the end. As they were both level-headed, scientifically-minded people, she had no doubt in her mind that something supernatural had happened that night after they'd used the Ouija board. So, from that day forth she avoided anything remotely to do with the unknown. For that reason, she said that she'd go last, thinking that if she chickened out at the last minute at least the others would have been in to see the clairvoyant.

Surprisingly, Caroline, the party's organiser, said that she would go either last or second from last, leaving the first slot open for either Selena or Barbara. As keen as ever to try something new, Selena put her hand up only seconds before Barbara, and by doing so won herself the chance to going in first.

While their friend went behind the red curtain with Madame Ortiz, the other three sat and wondered what would be going on in this mysterious chamber of hers – well, apart from Maria, that is. She didn't really care what nonsense the woman was spouting out, and just longed to be as far away from this place as she possibly could. Her sense of bravado after downing the three glasses of sparkling wine had now worn off, and she was back to chewing the skin around her other thumbnail this time. Fifteen minutes passed before they noticed the curtain move and Selena returned back through it on her own.

'That was crazy!' she exclaimed, rushing to her seat and sitting down. Her face was flushed with excitement.

'What did she say?' Caroline was the first to ask, eager to hear what her experience had been like.

'Well, at first when she looked into her crystal ball it didn't make any kind of sense at all, but when she dealt the Tarot cards what she told me was interesting.'

'Go on,' Barbara urged, eager to hear what she'd been told.

'She told me I'd be married by the end of the year, and have my first child the year after!'

'What a load of rubbish,' Maria spouted, finding herself unable to keep silent on the matter any longer. 'You're not even going out with anybody at the moment.'

'Well, she'd better get busy and find Mr Right,' Caroline laughed, 'Tick tock, tick tock!'

Madame Ortiz re-appeared through her dramatic entry curtain to take the next client in. Maria suspected that she may have heard her comments, but really couldn't have cared less. It was her opinion, and no second-rate fortune teller was going to make her change her mind.

Still thrilled by her prediction, Selina cried out 'Good luck,' to Barbara as she rose to make her way to the other room.

While waiting for Barbara to return, Selena continued to tell the other two what she'd been told. Maria was still less than impressed, and couldn't hide the fact from her two friends.

'Aw, come on,' Caroline said to her with more than a hint of anger in her voice. 'We all agreed it would be a bit of fun; you even said so yourself after a couple of drinks. You're no fun anymore, Maria. You've been like this ever since you got married.'

'That's unfair, Caroline.' Maria was hurt by the comment. She had her opinions, yes, and it didn't mean that she had to agree with them just for the sake of it. True, the drink was wearing off, but she wasn't going to change her opinion just to suit what her friend thought. 'Maybe I should go now then.'

'No, no, stay,' Selena begged her. 'There's no reason for us all to fall out just over something as silly as this.'

'But you believe what she told you,' Maria continued, reminding her of her reaction a few moments ago.

'Well, at the time yes, but let's face it, it is a bit far-fetched isn't it now? I mean, as you so rightly said, I'm not even seeing anyone.'

The room fell silent. Even Caroline refrained from commenting, which was most unlike her. She always had an opinion, one which the others sometimes disagreed with, and was more than likely be the first to either say or suggest anything – like this evening, for instance. None of the rest of them would have ever thought of visiting a psychic clairvoyant, but this was her idea and hers alone. *Goodness knows why she'd even thought of it,* thought Maria, but knowing in her heart that she was the one who probably wanted to go and just dragged everyone else along with her so she wouldn't be alone. She was like that.

Following the prolonged silence, with each staring down at the floor and avoiding the others' eyes, the next sound they heard was a swish, which was Barbara coming through the curtain after her session.

'Well that was a load of codswallop!' she exclaimed, face like thunder and plonking herself down heavily on a chair. Her reaction was completely the opposite of Selina's.

'Oh no, what were you told?' Caroline and Selina rose to their feet at the same time. Maria remained seated, still chewed up about what her friend had said.

'Nothing that was credible, that's for sure. It was a complete waste of time.'

Madame Ortiz had, it seemed, skillfully acquired the knack of suddenly and silently appearing out of nowhere; and if she'd heard their comments then she didn't react in any way to what had been said. She stood looking at the remaining two people who had yet to go in, waiting for the next one to join her in the room beyond.

'You sure you want to go last?' Caroline turned and asked Maria, to which she nodded sullenly. 'Okay then, my turn to go in.'

While Caroline was in, the other two tried to cheer Maria up, but to no avail. Aggrieved by the whole thing, she was now set to go home without even venturing in to see this so-called famous woman. Why Caroline even thought of it in the first place was beyond her, especially as she knew of her long-held abhorrence of anything remotely like this. It was completely out of order in her mind. While she was mulling all of this over, Caroline's sudden appearance after only a very short time took them all by surprise, especially when they saw the expression on her face. She'd turned ashen, and both her hands were shaking so much that she was holding them together in front of her in a feeble attempt to try to control the tremors. She ran unsteadily to the nearest chair and slumped down in a heap onto it.

'What the hell?' Selena rose from her seat and quickly went over to see what was wrong with her. Both Barbara and Maria joined her, horrified to see Caroline's reaction to what she must have been told. This was just the final straw, and had certainly put Maria off going in at all now. Furious as to what had taken place, she decided to find out what this woman was doing, and what on earth was going on once her friends were in that room alone with her.

Maria strode purposefully towards the curtain and pulled it aside without waiting for Madame Ortiz to appear through it to come and collect her.

***

The woman was still sitting at her table; she looked as shocked as Caroline had done when she'd returned to the waiting room, and her Tarot cards were still laid out on the table in front of her. It was as if she was trying to process what had just happened. Maria's arrival took her by surprise, and she looked up with surprise at her visitor. Clients didn't usually enter her chamber of their own accord; they seem to automatically know not to do so until called in.

'What did you tell my friend?' Maria demanded, banging her fists on the table so hard that the crystal ball shook on its stand, but Madame Ortiz quickly gathered up her cards and put them back into the pack. She too was shaking as she did so, her apparent air of tranquility having now left her. What could she have told Caroline that had got them both into such a state as this?

'I cannot reveal what the cards said to someone not destined to hear it.'

'That's bullshit and you know it.'

The psychic looked stunned by Maria's outburst. 'Like I said-'

'You've scared the crap out of her, and you don't look much better either. Now what did you say?' It was more of a demand than a question, but Ortiz wasn't going to give anything away that easily.

'Like I said, I cannot.' She was more composed now, and Maria could tell that she wasn't going to get anywhere with her questioning so she turned to leave.

'Don't you want your reading?'

Maria couldn't quite believe what she was hearing. 'You have to be kidding, surely?'

'No, not at all. You came for a reading so I am obliged to give you one.'

'After what's just happened?'

'Sometimes the cards show us difficult things ...'

'You know I don't believe in all this, right?'

Madame Ortiz nodded. 'But don't you want to know about your marriage?'

Maria stared at her in shock. 'What did you just say to me?'

'Your marriage. That's why you came here, wasn't it? You want to know about John's past history; the things he hasn't told you?'

'How ... how did you know my husband's name? Did Caroline tell you?'

'Nobody told me, I just know things.'

This was becoming far too much for Maria to cope with. The woman was a charlatan, a fraud, but how did she know about her husband and, more to the point, what did she know about his past history – something she knew very little about herself?

'All right then, I'll go along with your little game.' Maria sat down on the seat opposite Ortiz. 'Deal me the cards and tell me what you see in them. Then you're going to really tell me how you know what you say you know.'

CHAPTER THREE

Maria watched as the cards were shuffled then put into three separate piles. Madame Ortiz then collected up the piles into one larger one, shuffled again, then dealt five cards face up in a row on the table in front of her. Although still seething from the events of the past few minutes, Maria tried to keep her cool as she watched her do this. She had no idea what any of the cards meant; she did however know that Tarot cards were not like a regular pack of playing cards, but had odd old fashioned-looking pictures on them signifying goodness knows what. Gobbledygook, most likely; at least that's how the whole thing looked to her. But, after seeing Caroline's face after she'd left this room, and hearing what the fortune teller had said to her, she wanted to hear what the woman had to say.

Madame Ortiz frowned at the cards in such a way which disturbed Maria.

'What is it?' Maria demanded, but the only response was a shake of the head.

'Your marriage will not last. Seeds have already been sown that will cause it all to end quite soon.'

That was the final straw for Maria. She had now heard more than enough. She rose from her seat, sending the chair flying backwards behind her. 'My husband and I are very happy I'll have you know!' she declared with more than a tad of venom in her voice. 'You're sick, you know that? Sick.'

And with that outburst she turned her back on the woman and marched out of the room, returning to the one where her friends were.

'Come on, let's go,' she said to them, not even stopping as she passed by them, and completely ignoring their questioning expressions.

'Wait ... wait ...' Maria could hear Barbara calling after her, but by now she was half-way down the stairs with her sights on heading straight out of the front door. She didn't stop until she'd done just that and was standing on the pavement at the front of the building waiting for the others to follow. Fury rose inside of her. *How dare she say that to me*, she thought to herself, or had she said it out loud. She wasn't sure, such was her annoyance of the phony, money-grabbing woman and her pathetic little parlour tricks. The approaching sound of her girlfriends and their collective high heels clattering loudly on the stair treads made her turn around.

'What happened?' Caroline asked her, now apparently recovered from her Tarot card reading.

'What do you mean what happened; I went in there to sort her out after what she must have said to you.'

'No, no,' Caroline grabbed Maria's hand, 'I was just pretending she'd said something off to me just to see the look on all your faces!'

'What?' Maria couldn't believe it. That couldn't have been the case as Madame Ortiz herself was disturbed by what she must have told Caroline. 'But she must have said something to you to make you act in that way; she was in the same sort of state as you when I went barging in there.'

Now it was Caroline's turn to say 'what?'

'Oh look, let's just forget the whole thing and put it down to experience.' Selina was being her old practical self, as ever. If something wasn't as she'd expected, she'd just move on and forget about it. Knowing her, she could happily go home tonight and forget about the whole thing.

However, Maria would not let it go. 'So, you're saying that your little act when you came out was all put on just to fool us?' She shuddered when a sudden coldness flooded through her body. Was it with annoyance, or was it the fact they were now standing outside on the pavement despite it being a warm evening?

But Caroline was ruminating over what Maria had said before that. 'What do you mean she was in a state too?'

'Stop it Caroline!' Maria spat at her. 'You two have probably hatched this little trick together, knowing how I'd react to it-'

'Now wait a minute,' Caroline stopped her in mid-sentence, 'it cost a lot of money to book this appointment for us all tonight; do you think I arranged this just to get you riled up? You must think an awful lot of yourself to believe that!'

'Now come on you two,' Barbara intervened, 'this is not what you're like.'

16

'Let's all just call it a night, what do you say?' Selena, as ever, taking the peaceful route in order to pacify what was now turning into an overly heated conversation.

Barbara agreed while Maria and Caroline were still eye-locked with one another.

'Okay, I'll call us a cab then.'

***

All four were silent in the taxi; the night having been well and truly ruined for them. Maria now wondered why they'd even come out for the evening in the first place. She hadn't seen all three of her friends since the wedding, and had been looking forward to tonight as she'd really missed their old get-togethers, but this had put a strain on her friendship with Caroline in particular. The others had been fine, but she had been particularly venomous towards her for some unknown reason.

Selina arrived at her destination first, followed by Caroline, leaving Maria alone with Barbara. Maria hadn't said goodbye to any of them as they alighted, in fact, she hadn't spoken to anyone at all since getting in the cab.

'I'm sorry about all that,' Barbara began, worried that the evening was going to put a barrier between them all, 'I really don't know what's wrong with Caroline these days. I saw her the other week, and I swear she was a bit off with me as well.'

But she didn't get an answer from Maria, who was now sitting with her head resting on the side of the cab and looking away from her.

'Come on Maria, there's no need to take it out on me; I haven't done anything wrong to you.'

As she reached out and put a hand on Maria's shoulder to reassure her, Maria slumped forward then sideways, with her head ending up on Barbara's lap.

'Stop the cab, stop the cab,' she shrieked to the driver, who slammed his brakes on and came to an immediate halt at the side of the kerb, albeit at an odd angle.

'What's wrong?' he asked, turning around to look at the remaining two passengers behind him. It was then that he saw Maria's face, and he instantly knew from the expression on her face that she was dead.

CHAPTER FOUR

Sally Fielding had just fallen asleep when her phone rang on the bedside table, and it took a few seconds for her to fully wake up and get her bearings. Reaching out to answer it, she saw that the caller was her boss, DCI Ambleton. As it was her turn to be on-call for anything major happening overnight, Sally knew that it must be important if she was ringing her as well. A few more weeks and her boss would be free of all this, taking the early retirement she'd happily told them about at the beginning of the year.

'Yes boss,' she said, after sliding the green answer indicator to the right.

'Sorry to bother you so late, but a call came in from Pendlebury a while ago about the suspicious death of a young woman, and I attended as senior investigating officer. The on-duty medical examiner confirmed that it looked questionable, and for that reason he's agreed to do a post mortem in the morning. The deceased has been taken to the

Royal Oldham Hospital, so can I ask you to ring Joe and the pair of you go there for half eight and take over the case?'

'Yes, of course we will,' Fielding replied. 'Anyone in particular to report to?'

'Doctor Robert Mansfield; he was the duty medical examiner. I've told him you and Joe will be attending, so he'll be expecting you. I'll also email both you and Joe my report when it's finished.'

'Okay, we'll be there, thanks boss.' And with that she ended the call. It was then she sensed a stirring in the bed next to her.

'When did you come to bed?' she said looking at both her cats, Sooty and Sweep. Last time she'd seen them they were curled up in a ball at one end of the sofa in the living room, but they must have sneaked in after Joe had left. 'He's left it nice and warm for you, hasn't he?' she laughed, and they responded to the sound of her voice by stretching and snuggling in closer to her. As she stroked them both, she pressed 1 to make a call straight through to her partner, Joe Burton.

'Did I wake you?' Fielding asked apologetically when he answered the phone.

'No, I was still up. Doing a bit of late-night reading.'

'Oh, what are you reading; is it still that one from the other day?'

'Yes,' he laughed. 'More like from the other year, though! You know how long it takes me to get through something.'

'I'm the one who should be reading right now; I've got to prep for my inspector exam next month.'

'You'll be fine,' Joe assured her. 'You could pass that now without the need to do any studying.'

'I wish I had your faith!' she joked. In reality, she was dreading the whole thing. She'd even had a bad dream the other night about taking the exam. Having sat down and prepared herself for what lay ahead, she found a blank examination paper in front of her. She'd tried to get the invigilator's attention, but he completely ignored her. As she recalled, she'd woken up in a cold sweat.

Quickly shaking off the memory, she then told him about Ambleton's call.

'Okay. Do you want me to come and pick you up at 8?'

'Yes, that would be good, thanks.'

And with that they both bid one another good night.

***

It was a few minutes before half eight when they arrived at the Royal Oldham Hospital morgue. Normally they would have just walked in and asked at the reception desk, but with it being a Sunday the place lacked the usual weekday staff and they had to press a buzzer on the door of the main entrance to get someone to come and open up for them. Announcing themselves to a disembodied male voice, they were met at the door by a member of the mortuary staff, then taken to Robert Mansfield's downstairs office which adjoined the autopsy room.

Mansfield looked up from his desk as they were shown into the room. 'Detectives Burton and Fielding, how wonderful to see you both again,' he said, rising to greet them, 'although, it is always under such dire circumstances, isn't it!'

Burton shook his outstretched hand. 'Bob. Good to see you too.'

The doctor then shook Fielding's hand. She always found him to be warm and welcoming when they'd met in the past. Some of the medical examiners both she and Burton had encountered over the years weren't so friendly, and just proceeded in a cold and, in her opinion, too clinical way.

'I heard that you're both in line for a promotion soon.'

'Oh?' Burton seemed genuinely surprised. 'Word certainly travels fast around here.'

'Well, congratulations to you both then, and to DCI Ambleton for finally being able to escape from all of this!'

Formalities over, Mansfield directed them to the viewing area where they could watch while he performed the autopsy. Truth was, Burton needn't have been told, as he'd been there far more times than he cared to think about. He usually attended alone when he was required to oversee such things, fully aware of his partner's aversion to them.

'Now, I know that you are aware as to how this works,' Mansfield stated.

'Yes, I've been to far too many of them, I'm afraid,' Burton said to him.

'I know what you mean,' Mansfield nodded understandingly before heading off to the changing room to don his protective clothing and begin the autopsy.

'You okay with this?' Burton turned to his partner.

'Yes,' she said somewhat hesitantly. 'If I'm aiming to be a detective inspector then I'll have to get used to a whole lot more I imagine.'

'Sadly, that's true.'

For the next twenty minutes they watched in silence as Doctor Mansfield completed his investigation of the body. Fielding overcame her queasiness early on in the proceedings as a matter of necessity, forcing herself to think about the needs of her future role and how she'd be required to stand there looking at a dead body being cut up more frequently. It helped that at one point Burton grabbed her hand and gave it a gentle squeeze. She appreciated that; but then that was Joe Burton, always courteous to a fault.

Doctor Mansfield conducted his investigation professionally throughout, keeping them abreast of every single thing he was doing as he did it. Maria Turnbull would have appreciated his thoroughness too, no doubt.

'A very healthy woman, considering,' Mansfield said at his briefing afterwards. 'Of course, I need to see her medical records as well in case there are any underlying disorders.'

'So, what did she die of?' Fielding asked, wondering how someone so apparently fit and well could end up on the mortuary slab at such a young age.

'Beats me,' the pathologist said somewhat unexpectedly. The two detectives just looked at one another in surprise. 'I'll tell you better after the blood and toxicity results come back, and when I've seen her medical history of course.'

'Which should be when?' Burton asked him, hoping that it would be sooner rather than later.

'With it being a Sunday, the labs aren't running with a full staff, but I can take samples and send them off and mark them down as being urgent, but I wouldn't expect anything back until tomorrow afternoon at the earliest.'

'First guess as to her death?'

'Well, if I were to take an educated guess, I'd say she was poisoned at some point within the last few hours of her death. But that's just a guess you understand.'

'But an educated one?' Fielding reiterated his initial speculation.

'Yes, an educated one, based, primarily, on the colour of her skin in certain areas.' Seeing the detectives' frowned expressions Mansfield continued to explain further. 'Alcohol poisoning can cause the skin to turn a shade of blue on parts of the body. As you can see, there is a distinct hue around certain parts.'

'Alcohol poisoning, so this could have simply been a case of her drinking too much then?' Fielding asked, wondering why Mansfield considered her death to be suspicious if that were the case.

'Well ...' Mansfield's voice trailed off, evidently not wholly convinced of this.

'So, you don't think it was accidental?'

'The blue hue can be caused by extreme hypothermia, or a low body temperature. When I was called in last night to take a first look at the body in situ, I can definitely confirm that her body temperature was normal. For that reason, I'm thinking that it is a suspicious death, but let's wait until the results come back from the lab, shall we, when we'll know a bit more in-depth information. But I have to say, I'd be very surprised if poisoning wasn't the cause.'

Thanking Doctor Mansfield for coming in to do the autopsy on a Sunday morning for them, they decided to head to the station to go over DCI Ambleton's initial paperwork on the case.

CHAPTER FIVE

A s it was all now a waiting game until the test results were back, Burton and Fielding decided to go into the station to check out DCI Ambleton's scene of crime report, together with the accompanying photographs on the computer. Even though this was a Sunday morning, the SOC team would have already uploaded everything they'd taken from the previous evening. As crime never stops, neither does the all the behind the scenes forensic work. Burton couldn't praise the work they did enough, both them and the attending medical examiners and forensic experts. As Doctor Robert Mansfield said he suspected Maria Turnbull's death to be suspicious, then they would treat it as such. Medical examiners, although predominately dealing with facts, are rarely wrong in their suppositions either, so an opinion such as this was not one to be overlooked.

While Burton sat at his desk in his office and logged in, Fielding grabbed one of the chairs from the main room and wheeled it in to sit alongside him. True to her word, Ambleton's report was waiting in the inbox; they hadn't expected it not to be, such was her endless efficiency. She was still on the ball regardless of her only being a few weeks away from retirement.

The report itself outlined the circumstances in which the body of Maria Turnbull had been found, together with the movements of herself and her companions prior to her death. They read that he and her friends had been to see an clairvoyant/astrologer, and were returning home from that. Doctor on-call, Robert Mansfield declared Ms Turnbull dead at the scene, expressing concern that it did not look to him like natural causes. This statement was in lieu of the fact that the deceased was of a relatively young age, and he was concerned about the colour of her skin on certain parts of her body. The DCI had interviewed the driver of the cab and the other passenger who had been sitting on the back seat next to the deceased. The driver, Bob Beasley, was in a state of shock, as was the other person in the vehicle, Selena Douglas. Ambleton went on to say that both the girls had been out for the evening with two others, whom she'd contacted by telephone, and added all their details to the report. They'd all been told to expect visit from the investigating team in the morning; the investigating team being Burton and Fielding.

The photographs, sent separately from the SOC team, showed Maria Turnbull slumped down on the back seat of a vehicle. From subsequent pictures, the vehicle was revealed to be the taxi cab. Other than that, there was nothing relevant to her death or the manner in which she'd died. They could, however, see the blue colouration clearly in the photographs that Mansfield had described and shown them during the post mortem.

'Strange one,' Burton muttered after reading it and examining the pictures.

'What are we thinking about this?' Fielding always picked up on her partner's nuances, and she could tell something was already going around in his head.

'It's just that, if she was poisoned,' he speculated, 'it seems feasible to think that it was done last night, although I have to confess, I'm not all that keyed up about poisons.'

'There can be slow-acting ones, I believe.'

'Yes, and then there's this blueness about her; that's what's got me curious.'

'Well, the pathologist seemed to think it was down to hypothermia,' she reminded him.

'You see, that's the thing. Hypothermia isn't slow-acting, is it?'

'I'm not really sure, Joe. Perhaps we should get back on to Doctor Mansfield again for clarification?'

'Yes, we should,' he agreed with her, 'but if Mansfield's right and she was poisoned, then that's not by accident, is it? Then again, was she poisoned during the course of the evening, or has this been going on for some time and it just caught up with her last night?'

'Suspects then?' Fielding asked.

Burton sighed. 'Well, looking at it logically, if it was during the evening, then her companions have to be suspects. If she'd been poisoned long-term over time, then her husband I guess.'

'What about the fortune teller they visited?'

'I don't think that's likely somehow, do you?'

Fielding had to admit that it seemed an unlikely possibility. 'But you never know,' she added.

'No, you don't.'

'You know, I've just had another thought as well,' Fielding was surprised that they hadn't considered it earlier. 'We're right in treating this as suspicious, under the circumstances, but what it this was self-inflicted?'

'What, you mean that she could have poisoned herself?' Burton confessed that it hadn't occurred to him. 'But none of her friends even hinted at the fact she was depressed.'

'They did say that she was anxious about going to see the astrologer, perhaps she has an underlying health condition?'

'Good point. We'll have to get on to Doctor Mansfield about that one too. Didn't he say he was requesting her medical records from her GP?'

'Should we call in the team, or is this something we can leave until the morning?'

Burton reflected. 'I think we can leave it until Monday, and see what the test results bring back. I'm afraid that there's little we can do in the meantime.'

***

Even though they now had the rest of the day to themselves as nothing could be done until the next day, they had difficulty leaving the case at the office. Burton had taken note of the names and addresses of the friends who had accompanied Maria Turnbull on their evening out, and decided to contact them to arrange an interview with them for the following day. He also rang her husband to organise a meeting with him, but found that his telephone was turned off.

'Perhaps we should leave him until tomorrow,' Burton suggested, rightfully thinking that he'll still be taking stock of the situation. Fielding agreed with him.

Appointments made, they spent the rest of the day at Fielding's apartment, venturing out for lunch and then going for a walk around Heaton Park. Fielding had taken up running again, having bought a pair of trainers some time ago without having any real purpose for them, and found that she'd started to enjoy it. The current spell of fine weather helped, of course. So much so that the park was her favourite spot to go running when she had the time and energy after a long day's work.

Being a warm, sunny day, the place was filled with people out and about enjoying the June weather, and she enjoyed just strolling around taking it all in rather than going at her usual upbeat pace. It was, of course, made even better by the fact that she was accompanied by Joe Burton, who could not be described as a runner or even a jogger. Although he kept himself in good physical shape, it was certainly not through that kind of outdoor activity. His exercise of choice was a local gym, lifting weights and using the exercise equipment, where, like his partner, he ventured when time and energy permitted.

After their walk he'd stayed with Fielding until around eight, then went home to prepare for what was to come the next day. Somehow, and for no apparent reason, he felt that this case was going to be an unusual one – more so than most. After he left, she had a quick bath, then settled down with her cats for a couple of hours in front of the television before heading off to bed.

CHAPTER SIX

Monday morning arrived as it usually did, with all the team in early apart from one; Sam Wayman was into his second week of annual leave on the sundrenched Greek island of Corfu. As DCI Ambleton was currently out of the office too, and scheduled for a meeting with the Chief Commissioner at 11am, Burton and Fielding couldn't speak to her until she returned back in the afternoon. So, prior to going out to interview Maria's husband and the friends she'd been out with the previous evening, they gathered the rest of their team together and briefed them on the case. DC Jack Summers would be stepping in and partnering Sally Fielding when Burton was promoted to Ambleton's role following her retirement in a few weeks' time, so he was tasked with organising things within the incident room in their absence. Summers had proved himself well in the homeless man case, a fact which had not gone unnoticed by the powers-that-be, so Burton didn't have any qualms about leaving him in charge whilst he and Fielding were interviewing the deceased woman's friends and relatives. In fact, he didn't have any qualms about leaving him in charge of anything. He would make a good partner for Sally Fielding when he himself could no longer be there for her in his role as her DI.

'Right then,' Burton instructed, 'if you set everything up, we'll add to it after we've spoken to all these people.'

'Right boss.' Summers felt proud to be given the responsibility. Like Fielding, he too was studying for the next level exams, in his case the sergeant's. Hopefully, he'd be a fully qualified detective sergeant in the months to come when he was permanently teamed up with Fielding. It was going to be unusual at first. All of the team, and not just him, had been used to the Burton/Fielding team-heading dynamic of the past few years, so having a switch would be initially strange. Burton deserved his promotion. His leadership was second-to-none, and Fielding would step into his shoes perfectly in the same way that he would step into the retiring DCI Ambleton's ones. Summers had enjoyed working closely with Sally Fielding whilst they were undercover, and had recognised her unfailing dedication to the job. She and Burton were very much alike in their attitude towards their work, which was most probably why they were together now on a more personal level ... thankfully. He and the team had seen that coming for a long time, even when the pair had perhaps not seen it themselves. Everyone had wanted it to happen and were now delighted that it had. Despite keeping it very professional and not unnecessarily displaying their new-found relationship, the look in their eyes when they spoke to one another said it all, and revealed a new and exciting side to them.

***

Having tried John Turnbull's phone again, it was now turned on but callers were met with a recorded message from his mother. It gave her name and number for anyone to call her rather than speak to him, which Burton did. She sounded overwhelmed when he spoke to her, but gave him her address and agreed to let him come over, but stressed that her son was 'not very well, as you will appreciate'.

Maria Turnbull's husband John was understandably still in shock when the two detectives went to see him at his parents' home in Didsbury village. After hearing the news the previous evening, Tim and Marion Turnbull had immediately got in the car and driven over his house. They found him more than a little worse for wear and highly intoxicated, having downed half a bottle of whisky before their arrival. Seeing the worrying condition he was in, they decided it best to take him immediately back home with them, for his own safety if for nothing else. While his mother had gone upstairs to the bedroom and packed a few things in a bag for his stay, his father tried his best to console him downstairs in the living room. However, all his best attempts were to no avail, which led to them both having to struggle to get him into the back seat of the vehicle once Marion was back downstairs. Friends were all well and good, they decided, but at a time like this, parents were the ones who needed to come in and take over. As soon as they got him to theirs they'd called their doctor, who attended and administered a sedative to help their grief-stricken son.

'He's not doing well, as you can imagine,' Mrs Turnbull said to the two detectives with red-rimmed eyes. She looked as if she'd been up all night. Her husband, who sat quietly in a wing-backed chair staring down at a space on the floor just past his shoes, didn't look that well either.

'If we can, may we see him?' Fielding asked, taking a kindly approach. It was never easy talking to relatives following the death of a family member, and this was going to be as difficult as any other time.

'Yes, of course,' Mrs Turnbull attempted a smile, but it only resulted in producing more tears. 'I'll take you up to see him.' She said in a broken voice.

While Fielding was talking, Burton took the opportunity to glance around the room and saw a lot of photographs on display. He noted a few of their son with their late daughter-in-law taken on their wedding day, but the vast majority were of them as a family, taken over the years at various holiday destinations around the world. Judging by the exotic and far-away locations he recognised, Burton presumed that the family was not short of a bob or two. There was also one of John, possibly a teenager, appearing in what seemed to be a school or college play. A Shakespearean one, by Burton's reckoning, as the costumes worn by those in the photograph would suggest that to be the case. Fielding would have been able to tell him better about it, and probably been able to name the play, being the Shakespearean buff that she was; but the only reason that it particularly caught his attention was that it stood out so much from the others. He figured that it must have had an extra special meaning to both him and them.

'Are you coming?' Fielding asked gently, drawing his attention away from the photos and back to the matter in hand, and together they followed Marion Turnbull up the stairs into a room at the back of the house. Her son, John, was sitting upright on the far side of the bed with his back to them. He was looking out of the window and completely oblivious to their arrival.

'John, darling,' Mrs Turnbull began, somewhat tentatively, 'there are two police officers here to see you.'

John Turnbull turned his head around in their direction. His face was the colour of clay, drained of all its normal pigment. He pushed himself up with both hands and moved slowly around the bottom of the divan to the other side before stumbling back down onto the bed again. His mother moved to help him, but he held up a hand to stop her.

'It's all right, it's all right,' he managed to say to her. His voice sounded hoarse through lack of sleep, and quite possibly dehydration from all the alcohol he'd consumed the previous evening. He looked a mess; whiskey stains covered his shirt, and his hair was wild and untamed. His parents must have brought him up the stairs as best as they could and simply left him on the bed where he'd fallen.

'Do you feel up to this?' Burton asked him, feeling the man's pain. He contemplated that if he ever lost Fielding then this was probably the kind of state he'd be in.

Turnbull nodded unconvincingly, especially as he looked as if he'd throw up at any second.

'We'll be quick,' the detective assured him. 'Tell us if you can about last night.'

The husband cleared his throat and began to relate the events leading up to his wife leaving with her friends to go out for the evening.

'She hadn't been happy when she was told where they were going, as I recall.'

'Oh, why's that?' Fielding asked. She saw her partner take his notebook from his inside jacket pocket and scroll through to find a blank page, earmarking it with the elastic closure. His 'trusty book', as she called it as he and it seemed inseparable. He'd had it, or one just like it, for as long as she could remember.

Turnbull sighed. 'One of her friends, Caroline, said that she'd booked a session with some kind of fortune teller. She knows that Maria ...' He paused at the mention of her name, gulping hard, before composing himself again and carrying on. 'She hated anything mystical like that. Caroline knew that, so I don't know why ...'

'It's okay, you're doing very well, Mr Turnbull,' Fielding reassured him.

'Anyway,' he cleared his throat again, 'she agreed to it in the end. They left to go, and I gave her a kiss, and that was the last I saw of her.'

'And what about Maria's parents?' Burton asked.

'They both live in Spain,' Mrs Turnbull offered. 'We contacted them as soon as we heard, and they're coming over as soon as they can arrange a flight. They should be over in the next day or two.'

'What do they do?'

'They both took early retirement a few years ago, detective inspector. Maria's father ran a highly successful investment business, but then sold the company so that he and his wife could spend more time together. They already had a villa out there, so went to live there permanently. They were so looking forward to the possibility of grandchildren, as were we ...' Her voice trailed off.

At that point John Turnbull broke down, and his mother rushed forward to sit next to him. He didn't stop her this time.

'Do you need to ask him anything else, detectives?' she pleaded with them, to which Burton replied that they did not.

As Mrs Turnbull cradled her son in her arms, Burton and Fielding decided to leave them alone. Stopping by the living room door to tell the father that they were now leaving, they found him sitting in the same position that they'd seen him last. He looked up at them and nodded slowly, before continuing to stare hopelessly at the spot which fascinated him so much on the carpet. The two detectives let themselves out the front door, closing it behind them and leaving the family to support themselves as best as they could in their shared sorrow.

CHAPTER SEVEN

Burton had decided that it was best to meet Maria's friends all together to interview them. That way, he could get their reactions simultaneously. In his job, anyone connected to a dead person had to be considered a person of interest until proven otherwise. As the three women had been with the victim in the hours shortly before her death, it would be amiss not to consider them as suspects. Also, if she had been poisoned, as Doctor Mansfield had speculated, then it would be necessary to determine exactly when that had taken place and with what. Had she been poisoned quickly with one large dose, or had it been done over time? That was something that needed to be determined. If it was the former, then her three friends had to be considered as suspects; if the latter was true, then that would shift their interest on to her grieving husband.

Maria Turnbull's best friend Caroline Watkins had kindly offered her home as a meeting place, so that was where Burton and Fielding headed as soon as they left John Turnbull's parents' home.

'Everyone's here,' she said to them after answering the front door. 'We're all in the living room.'

Backing up a few steps in order to let them enter, Caroline indicated with a wave of her hand the first door on their right. As it was already ajar, Burton pushed his way through first, followed by Fielding. The detective sergeant took note of her surroundings. The room, like the house's exterior, was modern and bright, and filled with expensive-looking furnishings. Her interior designer sister would have most likely categorised this style as Contemporary due to its clean, slick lines and unadorned appearance. Burton, she thought, probably hadn't even noticed. But then again, he might have; he could still surprise her even after the seven years they'd known one another. It kept things fresh between them, not that they were in any way stale, especially now that they had taken their relationship from a professional one to something more personal.

The other two women were sitting on the sofa and stood up as soon as the detectives entered. Taking it upon herself to be the natural spokesperson for the group, Caroline introduced each in turn, both of whom still looked in a state of shock by what had happened the previous evening. Only Caroline herself appeared to be holding it all together, but Fielding detected fear behind the put-on smile. Her primed and perfected exterior was far too primed and perfected, and was most likely for appearances only. The detective assumed it to be her way of supporting her grieving friends in the detectives' presence. She was probably falling apart on the inside as much as the other two visibly were. When Burton and Fielding were asked if they would like something to drink they declined, and sat on the two chairs opposite the sofa. Caroline sat down beside her two friends.

'Can each of you tell me in your own words exactly what you did yesterday evening prior to meeting up, and then how everything played out after that?' Burton's notebook was already out of his pocket to record their answers.

Caroline again took the lead. 'Well, I was here getting ready, then Selena and Barbara arrived in a taxi at about 7 … wasn't it?' She looked at the other two for confirmation. They both remained silent but nodded. 'Then we all went over to Maria's house. John was there, of course; he let us in and we waited until she came downstairs from getting herself ready. I'd booked something special for the evening …' Caroline's voice trailed off as she realised the connotations of that. It had proved to be far from the 'special' evening she'd intended for them all, even before Maria's untimely death.

'Sorry,' she continued, composing herself again before speaking. 'I'd booked an appointment for all of us to go and see a clairvoyant I'd read about. Thought it would be a good night out for us, a good laugh. I wish I hadn't now, under the circumstances.'

'You weren't to know, Caroline,' Selena comforted her, 'who would have?'

'She wasn't too keen on going, I know and I'm sorry now for pushing her, but I didn't think it would upset her so much that she'd have a heart attack though.'

'A heart attack?' Fielding intervened. 'Why would you say that; did Mrs Turnbull have a heart condition that you know of?'

Caroline appeared to be confused, looking towards the other two women. 'Why, yes, she did. 'But I thought that you must already know that, with it being the cause of her death?'

'We didn't say that she died of a heart attack,' Burton raised his eyes from his note-taking to tell her.

There was a gasp from Barbara. 'What do you mean?' she asked, as the realisation of what he'd said sank in. 'Are you saying that she didn't? But we thought-'

'It's too early to say,' he admitted, stopping her mid-sentence, 'but what I can tell you is that we are treating her death as suspicious.'

All three women fell silent at that revelation, and for once Caroline appeared to be lost for words.

Fielding waited until they'd taken that piece of news in before asking them to elaborate on Maria Turnbull's health condition.

Selena Douglas responded this time. 'She has … had … a problem with her heart pumping correctly-'

'Bundle branch block,' Barbara offered. 'I was a medical secretary before my current job,' she continued as an explanation, 'and I recognised the symptoms she was having and suggested that she see her doctor about them. This was a few years ago now, but she was being treated for it.'

'So, what is it, exactly?' Burton asked, still jotting down notes.

'It's a condition in which there's a delay or a blockage along the pathway that electrical impulses travel to make the heart beat, causing it to sometimes beat irregularly and making it harder for the heart to pump blood efficiently.'

'Dangerous?'

'Not necessarily. In Maria's case it was easily treatable with medication and regular check-ups.'

'I see.' Burton made a note to look it up as he was unaware of it, and to mention it to the medical examiner, although by then Mansfield should have received her GP information and that fact would be included.

'So, why was Maria not keen to go on this night out?' Fielding asked, looking to each of the women in turn but settling on Caroline as she'd been the one to mention that the deceased had not been too happy with them going there.

It was Selena who replied first. 'Maria didn't like anything like that. I remember her telling me that a couple of her friends had experienced something odd following them using a Ouija board at a party. They seemed to lose all sense of time and space on their way home. Scared her witless, as I recall, and she was never quite the same with anything paranormal after that.'

'I didn't know that.' Caroline commented.

'No, you really don't know anything, do you!' Barbara suddenly snapped. 'You forced her to go along last night when she didn't really want to. I wouldn't be surprised if you already knew that she hated that sort of thing and just did it for spite! That little trick you pulled after you'd been in was well out of order too.'

'Barbara ... no ... no, I didn't. I never would. How could you?'

Selena put a hand on Barbara's shoulder, and pleaded with her to stop. It was like they'd all forgotten they had two police officers in the room with them.

'What little trick?' Burton certainly hadn't missed that comment, and his question stopped their bickering.

'It was nothing-' Caroline began.

'Yes, it was,' Selena contradicted her. 'You deliberately came out of your consultation and pretended that what Madame Ortiz said had upset you. A pretty stupid thing to do really.'

'I only did it for a laugh-'

'Well, we're not laughing now, are we?' Barbara's voice was trembling and her hands were shaking on her lap.

'Ladies, please!' Joe Burton intervened, putting himself in the middle of what was becoming a heated debate between the three of them. 'The best thing you can do for your friend now is to tell me exactly what happened as it happened.'

'I'm so sorry,' Caroline spoke first. 'That was unforgiveable, of all of us.'

'So, Caroline,' he continued, 'you came out from seeing the astrologer and put on an act to make believe that what she'd told you scared you somehow?'

'Well, put that way it does now sound stupid-'

'And petty!' Selena retorted, still annoyed by what she'd done.

'All right, all right, it was out of order, I know that now. Yes, I did, I'm not proud of doing it, but I did it and I can't really go back on that now can I?'

Barbara continued with the story after Caroline had, yet again, tried to defend herself and her choices.

'Maria went storming in to give Madame Ortiz a piece of her mind. Caroline by this time had told us that she'd just been joking, but when Maria came out, she was very upset; marched straight past us and down the stairs. We all followed her down to the pavement; she and Caroline had a little set-to again and then we called a cab. Quite frankly, I'd had enough by then too. The evening had turned into a disaster.'

'So why did you have another "set-to" as it's been described?' Fielding asked.

'She knew my reaction when I came out had been a pretense, but she also looked a bit disturbed by what must have taken place with Madame Ortiz.'

'Okay then, we'll have to have a word with this Madam Ortiz person,' Burton nodded towards his partner.

After then asking for and taking down the details of their movements between leaving Maria's house to arriving at the astrologer, he closed his notebook and put it back in his pocket.

'Thank you for your co-operation,' he said to them. 'We may need to get back in touch with you again; we have your numbers so we'll give you a call if we do.'

After ending with 'I'm very sorry for your loss', both detectives took their leave.

***

'What did you make of all that then?' Burton asked his partner when they were back in the car.

'Well,' Fielding began, 'Caroline Watkins appears to think of herself as the main player there, the one in charge ... or wants to be. Thinks she's the group's leader, but I'd say she's not as well-liked as she imagines herself to be going by the reaction to that silly trick that she played on Maria. Selena comes across as being very quiet and doesn't like anything confrontational, and it seems that

Barbara's patience for Caroline is wearing a bit thin. But, of course, they've just lost their friend and probably all feeling guilty about insisting she go out with them last night.'

Burton started the car. 'Yes, I agree with your observations. But I think that what we saw was well-rehearsed, don't you?'

'Not sure about that, but there did seem to be something a little off, something absent.'

'Like the fact that not one of them asked how Maria Turnbull's husband was you mean? Isn't that something anyone would do, isn't it, bearing in mind he's just lost his wife?'

'Now that you mention it. Unless, of course, they're so wound up about losing their friend and are having to deal with their own grief.'

'You're probably right,' Burton agreed, 'but I have to say I wasn't too keen on that Caroline.'

'I know what you mean. That was quite a cruel trick she played on her friend. The others seem to be a bit sick of her as too judging by Barbara's outburst. I wonder what she does for a living, as she has an air of authority about her, although I did think she was putting on a bit of an act for our benefit.'

'In what way do you mean?'

'Oh, you know, just her overall demeanor, and trying to put on a brave face. I thought she seemed a bit frightened underneath it all.'

There was silence for a moment while Burton took that all in.

'Okay, where to now?' Fielding finally asked.

'I'd like to meet this Madame Ortiz, and get her take on what happened the previous evening.

CHAPTER EIGHT

The door to Madame Ortiz's business premises was locked when Burton tried it. He looked the place up and down trying to find a contact number somewhere. There was nothing on the etched glass panel on the door other than her name and the by appointment only message, or on either of the two upstairs windows. He was surprised by this as business premises usually had their number on display somewhere.

'Didn't the women say that she has a website?' He asked his partner in frustration.

Fielding nodded.

'Have a look will you, and see if there's a contact number for her on there.'

While Fielding did an internet search on her phone, Burton went into the business next door to see if they could give him any information about the woman. When nothing was forthcoming, he tried the premises on the other side. Fielding was still scrolling as he quickly walked past her.

'She's been there about a year and a half I'd say,' a girl on the reception desk of the hairdressers informed him. 'Only works in the evening though, I think, as it doesn't appear to be open during the day.'

'I think it does open sometimes, Janet.' One of the two clients sitting in the waiting area spoke up. 'I know someone who's been in to see her,' she then said to Burton, 'and most of the appointments are in the evening, but there must be some at certain times during the day too.'

Thanking them both, he returned to his partner.

'There isn't anything on the website apart from an online booking form. No contact number, nothing; and the only business address mentioned is the one right here. Might be a good idea to have our Tech team take a look at the site and see what they can glean from it?'

'If that's the only way then, yes. I'll get Peter Westerby on it, he's the best in the business. If anyone can find his way around this he can.'

***

'Yes, that should be easy enough,' Westerby said when they went to see him in the tech department.

'So how would you actually go about doing that?' asked a curious Fielding. She was far keener than her partner when it came to wanting to know how things worked. Burton was far happier not knowing; as long as whatever tech he had worked then that was fine for him. It set him apart from most men she knew, but then he *was* totally different to any man she'd ever known – in a very good way.

Westerby seemed delighted that he was being asked to elaborate.

'Well,' he began, smiling, 'in simple terms, what I'd usually do in order to determine the source is find the web server. All domains are registered with domain name registrars, but in this case, you know who the website belongs to so it should be a lot easier. What happens then is I find out where the site was created and then go in and find the details of the person who created it.'

'That's simple terms?' Burton joked.

'I know how your non-tech mind works, so, yes, that's as simplistic as I could make it for you!'

Burton laughed. He knew that Peter Westerby was well aware of his knowledge shortfall when it came to up-to-date technology.

'So, it's more complicated than that?' Fielding found all this very interesting.

'Just a bit, but leave it to me and I'll get you what you need from it.'

'I knew you'd be able to do it,' Burton said to him. 'We need to get in touch with this woman as soon as possible, so I'd be grateful if you could treat this as a priority, Peter.'

'No problem,' he smiled as he started on his search. 'I'll ring you with the information you need as soon as I find it which, hopefully, shouldn't be long.'

True to his word, Westerby contacted them within twenty minutes.

'Well, that's quick, even for you Peter,' Burton commended him on his speed.

'Told you this one wasn't too difficult.'

After the detective jotted down Madame Ortiz's telephone number Westerby added, 'Oh, and by the way, the lady's name isn't Ortiz; that's just her professional name. She's not even Spanish if it comes to that. Goes by Marilyn Parkinson when she's not working, and she's a local lass too.'

'Thanks Peter, much appreciated.'

'Anytime Joe. You know where I am when you need me.'

'Right,' Burton announced to Fielding, 'let's get in touch with this woman and then go and see her.'

***

Madame Ortiz aka Marilyn Parkinson lived in a detached house in Ashton-under-Lyne.

'Must be well-paid, this astrology business,' Fielding noted as they drew up at the curb outside.

As they opened the gate, they heard a dog barking from inside the property.

'Not another dog!' Burton declared, remembering the last time they'd come across a canine when interviewing a witness. It was what he had called the Baskerville hound simply because of its sheer size. It was a Great Dane as Fielding recalled, and had taken a chunk out of the fabric of one of his trouser legs. The owner had assured him that his beloved pet was a pussy cat and was simply playing, but he hadn't seen it that way despite being offered a replacement pair as compensation. He'd refused, of course, but hadn't forgotten the incident. It was probably why he enjoyed the company of Fielding's two cats so much; they only purred and swished around his legs, and certainly hadn't wanted to devour his pants any time.

'Don't worry, I'll protect you!' Fielding offered, remembering the incident with humour, but was met with a wan expression from her partner which made her laugh out loud. By the time they reached the front door, and Burton rang the doorbell, she'd managed to compose herself. However, despite wanting to laugh again when she saw the size of the tiny dog being held in Ms Parkinson's hands, she successfully held it in check. The Pomeranian didn't look like it would have managed to nibble at his shoe let alone anything else.

'Detective Inspector Joe Burton and Detective Sergeant Sally Fielding,' Burton introduced themselves. 'We spoke on the phone.'

'Ah yes, of course. Do come in.'

Fielding knew what Madame Ortiz looked like from the photographs on her website, but the domestic version was far less dramatic that her professional appearance. In its place she wore a pair of cream chinos, flat ballet pumps in a matching colour and an oversized pink shirt with several of the top buttons left open, dipping it far lower to the cleavage than perhaps necessary. The almost Egyptian-style eye make-up used on her alter ego was gone, to reveal a fresh, unadorned complexion. She was undoubtedly a very attractive woman, a fact which she must have been fully aware of.

Madame Ortiz/Marilyn Parkinson led them into a room at the back of the house, its big picture window revealing a spacious and well-tended garden beyond. Inviting them to sit down on the light grey fabric sofa, she did likewise on the oversized chair opposite. As she put the dog onto the floor Burton braced himself for the worst, but it just scuttled off into the bed set aside for it by the French door leading out into the garden.

'Her bark's worse than her bite,' Marilyn laughed, and Fielding tried hard not to look at Burton.

'You're hard to track down,' he told her, happy in the knowledge that the pooch was out of the picture for the time being.

'It's a privacy thing, detective inspector. As you can imagine, I do get all sorts of strange people trying to find out things about me that they've really no right to – things like telephone number and where I live – my personal life is a far cry from my public one.'

Burton couldn't imagine, but nodded, nevertheless. 'So, are you saying it's all an act, the whole astrology/clairvoyance thing?'

'No, not at all. But I would never claim to be a clairvoyant as such in the way many people would interpret it. I read and convey the meaning of Tarot cards, which is quite different from the more generalised term of fortune teller. My mother and grandmother before her had the gift, and I appear to have inherited it as well.'

'And what about the astrology?' Fielding asked her. She'd never believed in that kind of thing. How on earth could the position of the stars at our birth determine anything about us, with the same thing applying to the daily and monthly astrological forecasts you'd find in magazines? In her mind it was playing on the superstitions of those who were vulnerable to that kind of suggestion, despite the fact that it appeared to be a popular belief.

'I do birth charts for people based upon the astrological position of stars at the time they were born.'

'And people believe all that?'

Marilyn smiled. 'I can see that you are an unbeliever, detective sergeant.'

'You could say that.'

'And you DI Burton, how do you feel about it?'

'It's of no consequence what I think,' he said somewhat abruptly. He was there to ask the questions, not her. Like Fielding, he had grave doubts about the whole thing. He and his partner dealt in facts, not in airy fairy predictions. In any case, he'd once read that there was a knack to Tarot card reading, and most of it came from how the client reacted to certain questions during the consultation.

'Tell me about what happened last night, with the group of women who came to see you,' he continued.

'It was a normal appointment from what I could see. I often get groups coming in as well as individuals. Everyone books through the website, which I think from a safety point of view is the best way to do it. As you will no doubt have seen, I don't work from home for this very reason, especially as I have had some crank calls and some very odd mail in the past.'

'You've reported all these, haven't you?' Burton asked her.

'What's the point, detective?' she admitted. 'I've had so much over the years that I really don't want to keep coming back and forth to you every week or so. How would that have made me look in the long run?'

'Well, that's a fair point I suppose. But you know that we would have investigated as we're obliged to do that.'

'I know, and thank you; but, like I said, there's been so much, which is why I've tried to keep my personal details as far away from my business as I possibly can. Just out of curiosity, may I ask how you managed to find me?'

'We have our ways,' Burton explained, adding, in order not to make his reply so cold, 'and a very good tech team.'

Marilyn smiled, 'Yes, of course.'

Fielding suspected that she was flirting with Burton. Her purring voice and alluring eye-contact made it pretty obvious, to her, anyway. Her partner, however, appeared to be oblivious to the woman's attempt to charm the pants off him. Time to put an end to it, she thought.

'So, talk us through the events of yesterday evening,' Fielding abruptly said, taking Marilyn Parkinson by complete surprise. She knew that her partner would not be taken in by the woman's performance, had he noticed that is, and she certainly wasn't going to take her in either.

'Right, okay,' Marilyn's eyes were now on Fielding, whose expression could have frozen the hottest flame, 'but I'm still a little confused. This person who died-'

'Maria,' Burton interjected, 'her name was Maria.'

'Maria,' Marilyn repeated, taking note of Burton's stress for respect. 'How does this have anything to do with me?'

'We're treating her death as suspicious.' A simple sentence, but Burton delivered it succinctly. It served its purpose, effectively stopping her in her tracks.

'You didn't say on the phone that this was in any way suspicious, I just thought-'

'I didn't mention it for a reason; we just wanted to know the outline of the events of last night without you initially knowing it.'

'Yes, yes, of course, of course.' The revelation had visibly affected her, which didn't go unnoticed by either of the detectives. It was the reaction they'd expected, under the circumstances.

'Well, each of the women came in in turn. I read the Tarot cards for the first two, all straightforward enough, no great chit-chat or anything like that, but when the third came in she did ask me quite a few unexpected questions.'

'Like what?' Fielding asked.

'Questions about me, really. I got the impression that she was a bit of a fan so, like with other fans, you know, the kind I told you about before, I kept my answers to a minimum for privacy's sake.'

'Then the last woman, Maria, came in. How was she?'

'Well, there's the funny thing. I normally go out into the waiting area to invite whoever's out there into my private room for the consultation, but she came barging in demanding to know what I'd just said to her friend.'

'And what was it that you had you just said to her friend?'

'Nothing untoward, if that's what you're thinking. I read her cards, and she seemed content with the results, so I didn't understand what she was going on about. Still, she said that I could do a read for her, but she wasn't happy with what the cards revealed.'

'And what did they reveal to her?' Fielding asked.

'That her marriage wouldn't last.'

'Well, that came true.' A surprising off-the-cuff quip from Burton. 'Nevertheless, continue.'

'As you can imagine she wasn't very pleased with what I told her, and she stormed out of the room. I followed at a distance and overheard a row breaking out between her and the friend who had been in prior. I don't know what they were arguing about as Maria left the room and was followed by the others. It was a very odd thing all round.'

'Were they your last appointment of the evening?'

'No. A couple came in about half-an-hour afterwards and left at around ten.'

'So, when the four women were there, did you notice anything unusual?'

'Like what?' Ms Parkinson frowned, unsure what he wanted from her.

'Anything that caught your attention, apart from the one asking you fan questions?'

'As I said detective, I only saw them individually. I did see them as a group when they entered, but then I asked for the first client to go through with me into my consultation room. Each seemed fine, whether or not they were happy with what I'd told them is another matter. However, having said that, the woman before Maria, the one asking me the personal questions, seemed to have played a trick on her back in the waiting room as she came storming in demanding to know what I'd said to upset her friend. I had said nothing to upset her; in fact, in some ways she upset me with her questioning, but I'm a professional and very much keep my consultations that way.'

'And Maria herself when she came in to see you, did she seem unwell or unsteady on her feet?'

'She was annoyed, I can tell you that, as at that point she was unaware that her friend had misled her.'

Burton wrapped the elastic marker around the page he was on and closed his notebook, putting it safely back into his pocket.

'Okay, thank you Ms Parkinson, you've been very helpful.'

'Just doing my duty, detective inspector,' she purred. Fielding gritted her teeth. Did women still do that in this day and age, she pondered? 'If you need to ask me anything further, please don't hesitate to get in touch.'

'I will,' Burton responded. 'And remember, if you do get any further mail from strangers please let us know.'

He rose from his seat, followed by Fielding and then Marilyn last.

'I'll be sure to do so,' she informed him as she walked with them to the front door and then showed them out.

'She was coming on to you big time!' Fielding said to her partner outright once they were both seated in the car.

'No, surely not!' Burton exclaimed, eyes wide and proclaiming ignorance.

Was he joking, Fielding wondered, or was he indeed completely oblivious to what the woman was doing right in front of his eyes, and hers come to that? Obviously, she didn't know that apart from them being police partners they were also partners in real life too, how could she? But it was way out of order in her eyes, as blatantly flirting was something she would never herself do under any circumstances.

'Not my cup of tea anyway,' he said with a wink as he turned the key in the ignition and pulled away.

CHAPTER NINE

'So, what's the next move?' Fielding asked as they drove away.

Burton quickly glanced at his watch. 'The DCI should be back from her meeting, so I think we should update her with what we have so far. After all, it was initially her case wasn't it, and she'll want to know.'

'Yes, I agree. Plus, if we get the toxicity screen back before the end of the day that will be a big help. I think it's feasible to act upon Doctor Mansfield's suspicion, but it would be good to have it confirmed.'

'Interesting case,' DCI Ambleton said to them once they were in her office. 'At first glance I would have said natural causes despite her young age but, as we now know, Doctor Mansfield suspects otherwise.'

'And he's usually not wrong.' Burton had known him for a number of years now, since he was first partnered with Ambleton as sergeant to her inspector. Mansfield had been the on call medical examiner for more times than they could count, and if he had a hunch about something, or doubted the credibility of the manner of someone's death, then he wouldn't hesitate to cast doubt on initial speculation, no matter how natural it may have looked. He was a consummate professional, and highly respected by both members of his own profession and police officers alike. And, besides, he was a highly likeable man, mixing both humour and seriousness in equal measures.

'No, he's not usually wrong,' Ambleton agreed with Burton's observation.

'So, what is it that's giving you cause for concern amongst the witnesses?'

'Nothing specific that we can put our fingers on,' Burton said, 'but I think that we're both agreed that there's something they're omitting to tell us.'

'A hunch, then?'

'More than a hunch I think, boss.'

Ambleton was well aware of her former partner's hunches, and had always trusted him to go with them when they occurred. They'd served them well in the past, so there was no reason to think that his occasion was any different from that.

'The friend of Maria, Caroline, I don't think she's much liked by the others we interviewed,' Burton continued.

'I got that impression as well,' Fielding agreed with him. 'I was carefully watching all their reactions to the news, and we had a mixed bag in there.'

'Didn't you say that she was the one who had misled the group into thinking that she was upset after her consultation with the medium,' Ambleton asked.

'Yes. But as Madame Ortiz took great pains to tell us, she's doesn't claim to be a medium, but just an interpreter of the Tarot cards.' Burton repeated Marilyn Parkinson's own statement.

'With a bit of astrological prediction thrown in for good measure,' Fielding said scornfully.

'You didn't like her then?' Ambleton asked, noticing the disdain in the sergeant's voice.

'First impressions? No, not really. She seemed to have a high opinion of herself.'

'And you Joe, what did you make of her?'

'Not really sure. Certainly, she was confident, I'll give her that, but she did seem genuinely surprised by the fact that we were treating Maria Turnbull's death as suspicious.'

'I do agree with the shock element,' Fielding nodded, 'but there's still something there that's bothering me.'

'Okay then,' Ambleton sat back in her chair and deliberated. 'Let's see what Doctor Mansfield comes back with regarding toxicity and take it from there, should we? In the meantime, let's do some digging into all of them, including the husband, and see what turns up. Also, while we're on, we might as well speak to people at Maria Turnbull's work too. Do we know where she worked?'

'No, we don't,' Fielding confessed. That was the last thing they'd considered under the circumstances. 'But I'll get in touch with the husband's mother, as she seemed to be handling the situation fractionally better than either her son or her husband.'

'Good. Okay, let me know how things go then.'

***

Following the meeting with Ambleton, Burton and Fielding returned to the incident room to bring the team up to speed. Jack Summers had already put quite a bit of information up on the board, including photographs from Madame Ortiz's website, as well as images of the deceased. While Fielding was on the phone to John Turnbull's mother, Burton gave everyone their instructions. DS Jack Summers was to find out what he could about the victim's husband, and the others were to look into the backgrounds of each of her friends. As for Madame Ortiz, he and Fielding would be handling the investigation into her themselves.

Doctor Mansfield contacted them later in the afternoon after he'd received the results from toxicology. As he'd initially suspected, Maria Turnbull's death was not down to natural causes and had, in fact, been brought about by a large dose of digitalis some time prior to her death. However, it was impossible to determine the precise time it had been given to her or in what form. Apart from tablets, digitalis can also be found in the Foxglove plant which, to anyone in the know, is highly poisonous, with all parts of it considered toxic to humans.

'I think it's a pity that such an attractive-looking plant as the Foxglove is so dangerous,' Mansfield had added, saying that he had many in his own garden at home. 'I looked it up, and did you know that ingesting 0.5 of a gram of dried or 2 grams of fresh leaf is enough to kill a person? I didn't, but it goes to show how effective it is as a poison.'

'Is it flavourless though Bob, because if not wouldn't Maria Turnbull have tasted it when she was given it?' Burton speculated.

'I suppose it depends on how it was given to her. Research also says that it tastes spicy hot or bitter and smells slightly bad, so if it was disguised in something else she probably wouldn't have noticed. I know that it's been posited that poison is a woman's murder weapon of choice, but I don't feel that's entirely true. If it's that easy, anyone of either gender could successfully use it.'

'Is the Foxglove only dangerous to humans?' Burton asked him, to which he'd replied that it was not.

'No, the plants are also dangerous to cats and dogs. Thankfully, I'm not a pet-owner, so no worries on that score.'

Mansfield also went on to say that he'd now seen Maria's patient record, and it indicated that she was prescribed the medication in the pharmaceutical form of Digoxin for atrial arrhythmia. But, even so, the amount found in her body was way beyond the expected norm. Mansfield had no other option but to record official cause of death as 'suspicious', pending an enquiry. Burton thanked him for getting back to him so quickly. Now they knew for sure that they were investigating a murder they could proceed accordingly.

'It's a pity that the time she ingested it couldn't be pinned down for you; I suspect it would have made things a lot easier?'

'Yes, it would have, but if it can't be done then it can't be done,' Burton said.

'So, nobody noticed her behaving differently, like feeling queasy, being dizzy or having stomach pains even?'

'They didn't seem to, otherwise I'm sure they would have mentioned it.'

'Strange,' Mansfield pondered to himself rather than to Burton. 'I've never heard of death by digitalis poisoning being so sudden and without displaying symptoms. What I've read up on the subject, people who have inadvertently been poisoned from the plant display all, or some, of the signs I've just mentioned before seeking medical attention.'

'So, it's unusual then?'

'Very.'

Burton considered the timeline again. 'If you can't tell when she ingested this – and it was definitely ingestion, was it?'

Mansfield confirmed it.

'Then we really can't say when she was given it.'

'That's true. It could have been last night, or it could have been a day or so ago. So, if you have any suspects, the I'd say any one of them could have done it.'

Great, thought Burton. *That's four suspects, at least.*

'So, is it possible that it may not have had immediate effect because she was already taking the medication?'

'No, I don't think so. Like I say, the amount we found in her was more than enough to kill her. The Digoxin tablets she was taking were only 125 micrograms; enough to help her condition, but not enough to do lasting damage.'

'So, could someone have crushed up her tablets and given them to her that way, in a drink or food, say?'

'There was nothing in her stomach to show that. And if she'd been given them earlier in time and they'd already been digested, that quantity would have had an impact on other bodily tissue as well, and I saw nothing to indicate that. I feel confident in saying that was not the way she was given it. But I'm still puzzled as to how she appeared so normal right up to the time she died and didn't display any symptoms whatsoever.'

'Okay, thanks, for your help with this, Bob.'

CHAPTER TEN

'**F**antastic!' Fielding declared somewhat sarcastically after hearing about the conversation with Doctor Mansfield. 'Any one of them could have done it then.'

'Or someone we don't even know about yet!'

'Go on, just make it worse than it is!' They now had four possible suspects, more perhaps that they didn't know about, so the sooner they started to look into all of their backgrounds the better.

'Well, the rest of the team are looking into the girlfriends and the husband, so let's start on Madame Ortiz. We need to know every little thing about her, where she's from, who she knows, absolutely everything.' Burton was going all out on this one. He was relentless when he was on the job, like a dog with a tasty bone, gnawing at it until there was nothing left to glean from it. It was one of the things Fielding loved about him, his dedication and passion for the police force. She'd miss the professional work partnership with him when he was promoted to DCI following Elizabeth Ambleton's upcoming retirement, but she still had the personal side of him. They were even starting to talk about buying a house together; things had progressed that much.

The alter ego of Madame Ortiz, Marilyn Parkinson, was born in Leeds in 1979. She'd told the detectives that both her mother and grandmother had 'the gift', something now confirmed by their research. Both women were well-known names in the astrological world. Marilyn's mother had worked on one of the national newspapers, and her weekly horoscope column gave those who believed in such things an idea of what to expect for the next seven days. Her grandmother had Romany ancestry, and had worked as a fortune teller with one of the largest travelling carnivals in the United States. But on one of their stop offs an Englishman on holiday had swept her off her feet and brought her back to his native country to start life afresh. Whether any of them truly had the gift was anyone's guess, but they all seemed to have made quite a name, and an income, for themselves over the years. As Burton himself knew, Tarot reading was an art and not just a mysterious supernatural bestowment, meaning that it was a skill rather than something other-worldly. Fielding was of the same opinion as him. She'd never experienced anything mysterious herself, so until the time she did (if ever) then she'd continue to be a sceptic like her partner. Proof was everything to both of them, especially in their line of work.

'She seems to have a large public following,' Burton declared after viewing both her Facebook and Twitter accounts. 'I'm not surprised she likes to keep her privacy to herself though.' He'd just read a particularly derisive comment on a post, calling her out as a 'fraud and a charlatan', as they'd put it. That was the thing about social media, anybody could hide behind a keyboard and say whatever they liked, especially hurtful and ill-informed things. Cyber bullying was prevalent, especially where those in the public eye were concerned, and Burton found that to be a heinous and malevolent crime in itself – not that he was that fond of those who purported to be celebrities, but even so, crime was crime no matter where and how it reared its ugly head. Marilyn was now at the peak of her career, and well-known in social circles, not only in Manchester but also in London as well. Her 'talents' were sought after by the rich and famous as well as everyday folk so, as they say, business was booming. So why, if that were the case, did she stay in a house on the outskirts of Manchester when she could be lording it up anywhere she chose? That question was answered in a magazine article that Burton also found in his web-wide search. Her mother had been born in a village nearby, and still lived there. Despite writing for a big London newspaper, and living down there for quite some time during her own career as an astrologer, her roots were and always would be in the Midlands place of her birth. In that case, Burton considered it to be an understandable reason to stay put. So that question had been easily answered to his satisfaction. Also in his research, Burton tried hard to find any named romantic partners but found none which, to him, seemed very unusual. The woman was attractive, there was no disputing that, with or without her elaborate professional make-up, so not to be linked to anyone who moved in the same kind of circles as she did appeared odd. Unless, as she said, she wished to retain her privacy. But if she was seeing someone, privacy to that extent had to be difficult to maintain.

'I hope the rest of the team are having more luck than we are!' Fielding exclaimed as she sat back in her seat. They'd been scrolling through pages and pages for hours and her eyes were becoming tired. 'I don't know about you, but I need a coffee.'

At the mention of his favourite beverage, Burton was up out of his seat and grabbing his coat before Fielding had even moved an inch.

'Come on then!' He teased, 'I thought you said that you were thirsty?'

Fielding threw a notebook at him, which he successfully managed to dodge. It landed with a thud on the floor a few feet away from him.

***

After their short impromptu break, when they arrived back at the station it was an unexpected hubbub of activity.

'We've just had a call about a murder,' DC Jack Summers said to them at the same time as DCI Ambleton walked into the room.

'I think you should go and attend this one,' Ambleton said, already up to speed with what was going on.

'Why, what's happened?' A stunned Fielding asked her.

'A body of a man has just been found in the city centre, and there was an astrological sign left on the body.'

'But we can't speculate that this is connected in any way, surely?' Burton rightly observed.

'Maybe not,' Ambleton agreed with him, 'but in light of things it seems to be an odd coincidence, doesn't it? Worth checking out, I think. Send Fielding and Summers out on this one as I'd like to have a word with you in my office if you don't mind, Joe.'

CHAPTER ELEVEN

The SOCO team and Doctor Frank Collinson were already on the scene when Fielding and Summers arrived at the rear of the city centre building. Fielding had only met the medical officer once before, and was very surprised that he remembered her.

'Nice to see you again,' he said to her as he handed them both a pair of nitrile gloves.

'I didn't think you'd remember me,' Fielding responded.

'Never forget a good detective,' he laughed, pulling down his face mask so that he could talk better 'Not your usual partner I see?'

'No, this is DC Jack Summers, soon to be my full-time partner when DI Burton is promoted to DCI.'

'Ah, yes, I heard that he was taking over from Elizabeth Ambleton. Give him my best, won't you?'

'I certainly will. So, what have we got?' She looked down at the body on the ground. There had been no attempt by the perpetrator to hide him, as he was lying out in the open behind one of the high street stores.

'Well, as you can see, he's been shot in the heart with an arrow. Good shot, by the look of it; however not so good for the poor soul it penetrated. I would say, from the angle of entry, that whoever took aim and fired was left-handed.'

'Why do you think that then?' DC Summers asked him, scrutinising the entry point a little closer.

Doctor Collinson replaced his mask over his nose and crouched down beside the body. 'If you look at the angle of the entry here,' he pointed to where the shaft could be seen coming out of the body, 'it's angled slightly towards the right, meaning that whoever did this was aiming from the left.'

'And if the person had been right-handed then it would have been the opposite,' Summers concluded.

'Precisely.' The medical examiner stood up and pulled down his mask again.

'First reports say that there was a card on the body, with some kind of astrological significance?' Fielding took over the conversation.

'Yes, although I wouldn't call it a card as it was more a slip of paper. But I did recognise what was on it as an astrological symbol, although I have to say I'm not exactly sure which one it is. The SOCO team have bagged it up; do you want to take a look at it?'

'No, that's all right,' she said, 'I'll see it when they've sent everything through to us. To be honest,

I wouldn't know what it would be either. Would you, Jack?'

'No, that's not my kind of thing I'm afraid,' Summers admitted. 'I only know that I'm a Leo, but that's the end of it.'

'About the same here!' Fielding agreed with him. 'Do we know who he is, doctor?'

Rather surprisingly, Collinson said that he did. 'And it wasn't through any kind of astrological intervention,' he smiled. 'The gentleman's name is Harry York, and this is the rear of his office.'

'Who found him?' Fielding asked looking around her. This wasn't the place to hide a body, therefore whoever did it wanted it to be found, and quickly.

'One of his co-workers, coming back from a lunch break. As you can imagine, she's pretty shook up about it.'

'We'll need to have a word with her,' Fielding said to Summers, to which he nodded.

'Okay, thank you doctor,' she said to Collinson. 'Do we need attend the autopsy for this one, or is it fairly cut and dry do you think?'

'I think I can say that he very likely died from the arrow but, as you know, things are often not quite as they seem. He could have been dead already when the arrow entered his body, but by the look of the blood loss around the wound I don't think that's likely as he's bled out quite a lot. However, he may have been drugged or poisoned beforehand, so I think it's prudent to go ahead and still do the autopsy to see what shows up. If you're wanting to leave this part of it entirely to me, I can let you know what the results are when I'm done.'

Fielding was happy for that to happen so she agreed to his kind offer. She smiled to herself, as she could almost hear Burton tut-tutting at her for dodging an autopsy already, followed by: *Just wait until you're an inspector, you'll have to go to them all then!*

***

While the SOCO team were finishing at the scene, Fielding and Summers paid a visit to the person who had discovered Harry York's body in the back alley.

The atmosphere inside the estate agent's office was one of shock and sombre disbelief. Announcing themselves as they entered, the detectives were then directed upstairs to the staff room and found a distraught Angela Patterson being consoled by two people, a man and a woman. The two introduced themselves as the branch manager and his assistant office manager. Angela, they explained, was one of the company's two secretaries.

Sitting down beside Angela, Fielding introduced herself and asked if she felt she could speak to her. The woman looked at her and slowly nodded. Fielding didn't wish to upset her any more than she already was, but it was necessary to question her.

'Can you tell me if you saw anyone, or anyone passed by you as you were coming back into work?' Fielding asked as caringly as she possibly could.

'No ... nothing,' Angela stumbled with her words. 'Just Harry ... lying there ... with that arrow ...'

'It's okay; you're doing all right,' Fielding reassured her, although she didn't think that the woman would see it that way. 'And what time was this?'

'About five to one. It must have been that as I was due back in on the hour.'

'Okay, that's fine, that's fine. Thank you, and I'm so very sorry for your loss. All of you,' she added, looking at the other two people in the room as well.

Rising from her seat she asked the branch manager if she could have a word with him outside the room.

'I know it's a difficult time,' she said to him when they were in the corridor, 'but I have to ask, did Mr York have any enemies that you know of?'

'No, not at all!' The manager spluttered. 'He was just the nicest man you could hope to meet.'

'And what exactly was his role here?'

'He deals with housing contracts, and also setting up tenancy agreements for landlords.'

'Was there any friction at all between him and the clients, any disagreements or anything like that?'

Again, the manager replied in the negative. 'He's always good with everyone, a real people person, who will go the extra mile to help. Everybody thought the world of him, staff and customers alike. I just can't imagine why anyone would want to do something like this to him; he'd never harm a soul.'

'And his home life, was everything okay there?'

'Yes, yes, of course. They couldn't be happier ...' Then he stopped at the mention of the man's family. 'Has anybody told his wife; should I ring her and tell her?'

'We'll take care of that, sir, you won't have to do it.'

As there didn't appear to be any work-related reason why Harry York had been targeted at his place of employment, it would mean looking into his background outside of it. Perhaps his home life was fine, as the manager had stressed, but perhaps it wasn't, and she would task one of the team with looking into that.

CHAPTER
TWELVE

The evidence board was almost filled up by the time they returned. The team had worked well and quickly in their absence. Much of the information had been taken from social media sites, which was an easily available place to obtain such information. For once, Fielding considered that such a public display of personal information was welcome. She never liked the whole social media thing, believing that, as Burton also did, that it was open house for anyone wishing to obtain another person's identity. Or, in extreme cases, to post false information, often to scam others for financial gain. She hadn't specifically come across it herself in her daily work as her team was predominantly involved in murder cases, but knew that other teams, particularly the fraud and cyber-crime ones, concentrated on such obnoxious and vile behaviour.

'You've all been busy!' Fielding said to DC Jane Francis, who was still positioned at the board and adding one more item.

'Yes,' she chirped, pleased with all their efforts, 'we've all been lucky with what we've found so far.'

'I can see,' Fielding complemented her as she looked around for Joe Burton.

'Where's the DI?' she asked.

'Still with DCI Ambleton. They both went upstairs to her office as soon as you two left.'

'Wonder what they're talking about?' Fielding pondered, mainly to herself and not expecting an answer.

'No idea. The DI told us just to carry on until either he or you returned first.'

'Okay, thanks Jane.'

'No problem.'

While she was waiting for Burton to return, Fielding examined the board. As well as the dead woman herself, on it were the photographs of Maria Turnbull's husband, her three friends, and the astrologer. Underneath each was details of their present occupation and place of work. As she scanned over it, she wasn't really surprised to discover that the outspoken Caroline Watkins was a solicitor, which could explain her way with words and her apparent love of using them. The other two friends worked in the Civil Service, both holding positions as Administration Officers in the Ministry of Justice in Salford. John Turnbull, the inconsolably distressed husband, was employed as an architect in a prestigious company in Portland Street. It was noted that the company was recognised as one of the finest in Manchester, having received a plethora of awards and local contracts over the years. So, on first glance, none of whom would have any special scientific knowledge to know about the poison digitalis. Then again, the internet was a wonderful source of information, sometimes *too* wonderful, and anyone could find out about absolutely anything they wanted to if they were so inclined to do so. For that reason, finding out where they were employed was relatively useless to their enquiries. The next big question was, who held a grudge against Maria Turnbull, and why? And now, apart from this, there was another death that could very well be connected to the puzzle: Harry York. If it was the case, how did he fit into this? She needed to speak to Burton to get his take on it all.

'So, what about Harry York?' DC Jack Summers asked, 'Should I start looking into his background?'

'Yes, if you can,' she instructed him. 'From all accounts it sounds as if he was well-liked, but somebody evidently didn't think that way.'

Fielding then turned back to Jane Francis. 'Keep working on what we have so far,' she said to her, 'I need to have a word with Burton, but I think he'll probably tell us to go and speak to the people all the suspects work with, except Marilyn Parkinson.'

'But she might have a silent partner?' DC Francis posed a pertinent question, and one Fielding hadn't considered.

'Good point; I'll mention that to Burton when he gets back. Oh, by the way, we now have a new face to add to the list.'

'The murder victim this morning; how is he connected to this?'

'I've got a feeling that he's strongly linked to our enquiry in some way. Maria Turnbull dies after visiting someone who practices astrology, then a man is murdered and the killer leaves an astrological symbol on the body That's too much of a coincidence to ignore for my liking.'

***

'Take a seat, Joe.' DCI Ambleton instructed Burton when they were in her office. He was curious as to why she'd asked him in for a 'quick chat', as she'd put it.

'As you know,' she continued when he was seated, 'I haven't got long to go now before I retire. The new death this morning, and the possibility of it being connected to Maria Turnbull's death, begs the question do we have a serial killer on our hands? And if we do, there's a possibility that the investigation may continue over the space of a few weeks, so I'd like you to hand the reins over to Fielding for this one. You'll need to be able to step straight into my shoes when I'm gone, so giving her the lead at this point seems to be the right way to go. Besides, I have to have you shadow me for at least a week before I leave.'

Burton was stunned. He knew that he'd have to step in at some point, but this was quicker than he'd expected. It wasn't so much the new responsibility that worried him, but the fact that his seven-year work partnership with the woman he now considered to be his soulmate, was coming to an end. Of course, they'd still see one another during the day, plus there was now the prospect of them buying a house together too, but, nevertheless, it was the end of an era for them in their professional capacity.

'I know what you're thinking,' Ambleton read his mind, 'and I know it's going to be hard, but Fielding is more than able to take up the role, don't you think?'

'Yes, of course she is, but it's not that ...'

'It's the fact that you can't spend time with her as a partner, I get it. I know it's completely different, and that's how I felt when I was promoted to this position. I lost you as a partner and I was devastated, so I know how hard it's going to be for you too. But it's not like you're moving to a different city; that would be much worse for the pair of you. You'll be sitting here in my office and she'll be coming in to report to you on a regular basis. And, if you feel so inclined, you can step in at any time and take over a case.'

Although what she said made perfect sense, Burton still felt heartbroken.

'You two are strong,' Ambleton continued, 'strong and devoted to one another enough to get through this. I know you can do it.'

Burton just nodded in acknowledgment.

'Well, while you're here, and while the team are working on the case, we might as well begin with the introduction right now. It'll only take thirty minutes initially, and I'll take you through a few things to see how you get on, although I'm sure you'll breeze right through it. Like I said, you need to shadow me for a week, but that doesn't mean that the days have to be consecutive ones.'

***

Fielding was at her desk when Burton returned from his briefing with DCI Ambleton. He quickly stopped to look at the board to see how far things had progressed before sitting down at the desk next to hers.

'Oh, hello,' she said looking across to him. She'd been so absorbed researching Marilyn Parkinson's background that she hadn't even noticed him come into the room. 'The team are progressing well, and gathering a good deal of background information. I wasn't sure how long you'd be so I suggested that they carry on by questioning the people the suspects worked with.'

'Good idea,' he said. 'About that …' he began, not really sure how to tell her Ambleton's news.

Fielding stopped what she was doing and looked at him. She knew him far too well to know that something was troubling him.

'What is it?' she asked, apprehensively.

'Well, it's Ambleton, she's asked me to shadow her before her last day, which means that as I'll be up in her office for a considerable part of the next few weeks I'm going to have to put you in charge of the team. I'm sorry, I didn't expect this to be happening so soon.'

Although delighted by the prospect of the increased responsibility, Fielding felt terribly disappointed.

'It's okay,' she said looking across to the other members of the team. As they were all crouched over their monitors she reached over and took hold of his hand. 'This is fine. Perhaps we weren't expecting it to happen so soon but we were expecting it, right?'

Burton nodded. Like Ambleton had said, if the need arose, he could involve himself in a case at any time like she sometimes did. It wouldn't be the same, but at least they were still in the same building as one another.

Changing the subject, he asked, 'So what happened with the body you went out to see earlier?'

'Quite a lot. Frank Collinson sends his best, by the way.'

'Ah, Frank! I haven't seen him in a while. I thought he might have been retired by now.'

'No, he's still going,' Fielding laughed. 'He recognised me from a few months back, and that was the first time I'd ever met him.'

'Well, you must have made an impression on him.'

'He did say that he always remembers good detectives!'

Now it was Burton's turn to laugh. 'Yes, that sounds like something he'd come out with!'

'Anyway,' Fielding continued, 'about the body. The doctor said that he would do a post mortem as soon as he got the man back to the mortuary.'

'Was the death questionable then?'

'No, he thinks it's straightforward, if you can say being shot with an arrow through the heart is straightforward that is-'

'With a what?' Burton thought he'd misheard her at first.

'Yes, and he'd been alive when it happened judging by the blood loss. However, Doctor Collinson suggested doing an autopsy to check to see if he was drugged or poisoned prior to that. I mean, how many people would stand and let anyone fire an arrow at them?'

'Shock, maybe? So, did he not ask you to attend the autopsy?'

Fielding knew it; he just had to ask. 'He suggested that he do it himself and then let me know the outcome.'

'And, of course, you took him up on that!' Burton laughed.

'Of course I did!'

'You're so predictable,' he teased.

'Just like you,' she retaliated.

'So, an arrow?' he asked in a more serious mode. 'That's an unusual way to kill somebody. And there was an astrological symbol on the body too?'

'Yes, Collinson said that it was sticking out of his shirt pocket. I've been looking at the SOCO photos online, and it looks like what I've discovered to be the one for Sagittarius, the archer.'

'I really can't see how this is linked to our enquiry, though, can you?'

'I'm keeping an open mind on this, Joe,' Fielding said to him. 'I'm wondering if indeed he *was* poisoned prior to his death. It would have made it a lot easier for whoever killed him, unless they're a skilled archer, that is.'

'I once tried that you know, a very long time ago, and it was extremely hard on the upper arm and shoulder as I recall, and I was black and blue from it afterwards. Hats off to anyone who can pull that off. However, not to the extent that they kill somebody in that manner.'

Fielding looked at him in surprise. 'You're the last person I would have imagined to pick up a bow and arrow.'

'Well, I did,' he laughed. 'Mind you, I was in my teens when I did it, and it was when I was away on a school outward bound trip. What sort of person would you have imagined to have done it then?'

'Oh, well, you know, Hawkeye, perhaps!' Fielding laughed.

Burton knew of her particular fondness for the Avenger character from the Marvel movies.

'I should have known!' he declared with a smile.

'And there's another thing,' she added, 'Collinson believes the archer to be left-handed, judging by the angle of entry.'

'That's good to know.' Burton then adopted a more serious mood. 'So, until the good doctor gets back to you, we keep digging deeper into our current suspects. Go through CCTV for the area as well. I imagine someone carrying a bow would have been spotted.'

'Unless they were hiding it in some way. Plus, remember York was killed behind the building he worked in, so perhaps whoever it was kept low and avoided any cameras.'

'Still, where can you hide one of those as they're not exactly small? Maybe the killer was parked up nearby and didn't need to carry it through the streets then. Actually, I'd better have a word with the others regarding what Ambleton said to me, and promote both you and Jack to acting DI and DS while I'm busy shadowing her.'

CHAPTER
THIRTEEN

Doctor Collinson called Fielding first thing the next morning, and what he said to her was, to say the least, unexpected.

'It's a good thing I did an autopsy,' he began, 'as it wasn't just a simple case of him just being shot with an arrow.'

'Oh, why's that?' she asked, eagerly awaiting what he had to say to her.

'The toxicity results revealed a strong concentrate of poison around the site of the wound.'

The hairs on the back of Fielding's neck stood up as she heard this.

'Was the poison digitalis by any chance?'

'Why, yes,' Collinson sounded surprised, 'how did you know that?'

'From another case we're working on; that particular poison was found to be in the bloodstream of the deceased.'

'Pretty coincidental, don't you think?'

'That's the thing, doctor, I really don't believe in coincidences. So, were you able to tell the source of the poison? I mean, was it in a pure form, or was it plant-based?'

'You mean was it taken directly from its plant form and used raw? I'm not sure of the source as the tests only reveal the properties which, in this case, specifies digitalis.'

'I see. Okay, thank you for getting back to me Doctor Collinson. It's much appreciated.'

'You're welcome, detective. Take care now.'

Joe Burton was again upstairs with DCI Ambleton, so she texted him a message to reveal the new findings before announcing the news to the team. Two deaths in two days, each being poisoned with digitalis, was not a normal occurrence; and for that reason, Fielding had no other option than to officially make Mr York the second victim. But what was the connection other than the poison and astrology? Did Maria Turnbull and Harry York know one another? It was a question Fielding needed the answer to.

Harry York worked for an estate agency firm, and his body had been found by a work colleague at the back of his offices on Whitworth Street West. A hard-working and seemingly enemy-free man his mid-forties, he left behind a widow and two teenage children. As Burton had suggested CCTV, Fielding had set DC Simon Banks on the job of going through everything near the premises around the time of death, which doctor Collinson had determined as between 1 and 2pm the previous day.

'Phillipa?' Fielding called over to DC Preston, 'can you go and interview the estate agency staff and see if they recall who came into their offices around that time? Did someone have an appointment with Harry York perhaps? Also see if they have cameras inside. I'm thinking perhaps not, but maybe they do. Burton has suggested that perhaps the killer had a car nearby, as I'm sure the sight of someone carrying a bow around the streets would have raised a few eyebrows. I think we also need to look at Harry York's phone. Did someone contact him and lure him out the back, or was he also returning from a lunch break?'

'Yes boss,' she said, before grabbing her coat and bag.

Boss? Fielding thought, *I'm going to have to get used to that in future.*

DC Jane Francis had printed off a photograph of their latest victim from the internet and was adding it to the board.

'See what else you can find on him Jane, will you?' Fielding asked her. 'Concentrating on if he knew Maria Turnbull or any of our suspects.'

'Will do.'

As Fielding was looking over towards the photographs and the accompanying information, she noticed that Simon Banks had added to Maria Turnbull's profile. When he saw her move towards it and start reading, he called over to her.

'You were busy when I put it up, so I couldn't let you know at the time.'

'That's fine,' she assured him, reading the notes below her photograph. 'She was a teacher then?'

'Yes,' Banks confirmed. 'Secondary. I'm waiting for the Head to get back to me; she was in a Governors' meeting when I rang but should be free in an hour or so.'

'When she rings back will you also find out what subject Maria taught? Also, find out if she's upset anyone – staff or pupils. Oh, and,' Fielding added as an afterthought, 'It's a long shot, but ask her if the name Harry York means anything to her.'

When Maria Turnbull's Head rang back, Simon Banks spoke with her for a while before putting the call on hold and dialing Fielding's extension.

'I've got Mrs Sinclair from Thornton School on the line, and I think you're going to want to hear this,' he said before forwarding the call on to her.

Fielding's interest was immediately sparked. Simon Banks was often a man of mystery when it came to forwarding telephone calls, preferring the caller to reveal their own piece of information rather than doing it for them. But one thing she knew, whenever he did this, the information conveyed played a crucial part of any investigation … hence the heightened interest.

'Hello, this is acting Detective Inspector Sally Fielding,' she began. Announcing herself that way seemed so out of place and, in many ways, she felt as though she was usurping Joe Burton's long-held and revered position.

'Hello detective inspector,' the deep, husky voice said down the line, 'your detective constable wanted me to speak to you personally regarding what we were talking about.'

Fielding pictured her as an older version of the actress who often appeared in the 'Carry on' series of films, Fenella Fielding – ironically, sharing her own surname. Perhaps that's why she remembered her so well. She often portrayed sultry sex symbols, but it was her voice that was the most memorable thing about her, deep and almost purring.

'I see. Thank you for calling back so quickly.'

'Maria was such a lovely girl, and I can't imagine why anyone would want to kill her. She only just got married last year too. Such a shame. I can't imagine what her poor husband is going through at this moment.'

'He's not doing very well, as you can imagine.'

'No, I didn't think he would be. We're currently organising a collection for him. As for her having any enemies at school, well, I can say most definitely not. Her students all loved her; she had this happy knack of being able to relate to them and to talk to them on their own level. I can't imagine what we're going to do without her.'

'And what did she teach?' Fielding asked.

'She taught Biology.'

At the mention of the subject, a memory surfaced in Fielding's brain. She didn't like Biology at school, and didn't take it at exam level, opting for Physics instead. Something she later came to regret as she failed it dismally. However, she did recall that, although a separate subject, Botany was a branch of Biology.

'Did Maria also teach Botany, Mrs Sinclair?'

'Why, yes, she did, to a lesser degree though. Botany is, of course, part of the curriculum, but only a small part. The main core is essentially human biology rather than plants and their biological structure.'

'Of course. So, in your opinion, did she know a great deal about plants and their properties?'

'Well, she studied Botany along with Biology at degree level, so I believe she had a very good knowledge of it. What are you thinking, detective inspector?'

Fielding paused for a moment. To go ahead now and ask about whether or not Maria was aware of poisonous plants would almost certainly pose a question in Mrs Sinclair's mind. However, as the manner of death would soon be common knowledge in the press, Fielding felt it was a question worth asking.

'So, she would know all about poisonous plants?'

'I should think so ...' The penny then seemed to drop with the head teacher. 'Are you saying that she was poisoned?'

'I'm afraid that I am.'

'But I thought that with her heart condition, perhaps it was that?'

'No, we're treating her death as highly suspicious at the moment.'

The line went quiet while Mrs Sinclair was taking it all in.

'I'm sorry to have to be the bearer of such bad news.'

'No, no, it's okay. It's just that we've also had some more bad news today as well. One of our governors died suddenly too, so that's two deaths in two days.'

'Oh?'

'Yes, I was telling your detective constable, which is why, I think, he put me on to speak to you.'

Again, Fielding's interest peaked. It couldn't be, surely?

'Another lovely person. Again, I can't imagine why anyone would want to do harm to him either.'

'And what was his name?' Fielding's heart was in her mouth.

'It was Harry York; when he wasn't one of our governors he worked for a local estate agency firm.'

CHAPTER
FOURTEEN

A chill went down Fielding's spine when she heard the name. After thanking Mrs Sinclair for her assistance, and her confirmation that Harry York and Maria Turnbull knew one another, she put down the receiver and sat back in her chair, mulling it all over in her mind. So, the two deaths must be linked. Two people, with a distinct connection to Thornton School, had died, both having traces of the poison digitalis in their system. That was a fact, not just a coincidence. But the question uppermost in Fielding's mind now was, why had they died? Why were they killed? Was the reason for their death linked to the school somehow, or was that merely a common denominator between them? She picked up her phone and dialed Simon Banks's number.

'That was a good shout,' she said.

'I knew you'd find it interesting,' he replied.

She wondered how long Burton would be upstairs in DCI Ambleton's office. She desperately needed his take, and his nose, on this one. He had an uncanny knack of figuring things out but, in this case, she suspected that it would be a puzzler even for him. Her head was spinning with all of this, and pulled open the top drawer of her desk and took out the box of Paracetamol which was always in there, shaking it to make sure there was something inside it. Were all her future cases deemed to be headache-inducing like this? What she needed right now was a coffee, and not just one from the machine outside or from the station canteen. She needed a proper one, froth and all, and she could only get that from the café down the road, the one she and Burton regularly frequented.

Grabbing her coat and bag, and telling the team that she'd only be a short while, she went in search of her caffeine fix, hoping that perhaps the fresh air outside would clear the fog that was forming inside her head. Apart from the coffee, what she needed was her old partner back. Even going for a beverage during the day would never be the same again without him. She'd known that this day was coming soon, but now it was really happening and it just seemed to have come far too quickly for her to fully take it in. It wasn't that she was concerned about the responsibility, as she knew she could handle that well enough, it was just … well, she must stop thinking that way now. What was done was done, and that was all there was to it.

When she returned back to the station, she was more than a little surprised to find Burton standing talking to the team.

'Where's mine then?' he asked, looking at the carry out cup in her hand.

'But ... I ...' Fielding spluttered.

'Just joking!' he said laughing, adding, 'I'm here for the rest of the afternoon if you want me.'

As everyone was gathered together, she decided to update the team with what they knew so far. It's what Burton would have done, so it seemed only fitting that she continue his legacy. As Fielding ran through everything, Burton listened with interest, admiring her for handling it so well. Even though he'd only been away from the team for a few short hours, he felt like he'd missed a lot, which caused him to have doubts regarding his forthcoming promotion. They were more than ready for their own respective ones, and agreed that it was a great chance for both of them, but the sad truth was they'd been together as a team for a very long time and any change to that would undoubtedly have an impact on them.

'So, Harry York and Maria Turnbull knew one another then' Burton asked after the briefing. He rubbed his forehead, a habit of his when troubled by something. 'In that case, we know there's a connection there, but what? What could they both have in common, or what did they know that got them both killed?'

'Something about the school maybe?' Acting DS Jack Summers suggested.

'That's a distinct possibility,' Burton agreed. 'One worth looking into.' Rather than asking Summers to get onto that himself, he turned to Fielding and raised an eyebrow. It was her case now, so it was up to her to call the shots.

Fielding took the hint. 'Yes, if you get onto that Jack, that would be great. Perhaps have a word with his wife too if she's up to it.'

'What about the school finances?' Summers suggested. 'Governors can oversee budgets, can't they? Perhaps he found something amiss there and, if he knew Maria Turnbull particularly well, he may have spoken to her about it.'

'That's a very good point,' Fielding noted. 'Yes, by all means, take a closer look at the school's finances and see if anything untoward turns up.'

'How's things going with Maria's friends? Burton asked.

'Jane and Phillipa are each going to their places of work this afternoon to get some background information on them. I've asked Simon to visit the husband's offices too in order to ask similar questions. You never know, they might turn up something, but I think this new connection to the school has potential. If it is something to do with money, then that's always an established basis for murder.'

'I agree. So, if we're free, what are we going to do?' Burton seemed keen to get involved.

'Well, we've still got Madame Ortiz's past and background to look into. I can't believe a woman like that hasn't left a trail of man friends behind her.'

'Maybe she has, and is being cautious about it. Okay, let's see what we can find on her.'

CHAPTER
FIFTEEN

Despite their diligent investigation into the background of Madame Ortiz, or to use her proper name of Marilyn Parkinson for the purposes of the search, they could find very little about her other than what they already knew. No boyfriend, no partner, no husband – or wife, come to that – absolutely nothing. She was an enigmatic non-entity despite her claim to fame in social circles.

'Surely nobody can leave no trace at all, can they?' Burton was confounded.

'Unless Marilyn Parkinson isn't her real name at all,' Fielding offered.

'But all the initial research we did pointed to that; her mother, and her grandmother before her.'

'But what if that was just what she wanted the public to know, with a convincing back story to go with it?'

'That's possible I suppose,' Burton saw that as the only option, unless she was squeaky clean to a degree he'd never heard of before. 'But it's only serving to warn me that she has something to hide.'

'It does seem unusual in this day and age with digital footprints being the way they are. So, do we go and see her again?'

'I think we should, don't you?'

Fielding couldn't find any reason to disagree with him. The woman had sparked an anomaly that needed to be looked into further to find out the truth.

***

Marilyn Parkinson was surprised that the two detectives wanted to see her again. She couldn't understand the need for further questioning as in her opinion she'd told them all they needed to know the first time around.

'You see, as you're indirectly involved in a murder enquiry, we did a search on you. And to be honest, we couldn't come up with anything,' Burton confessed. He hadn't wanted to show his hand so early on, but felt that under the circumstances that he had no other option but to do so.

'Are you saying that you are doubting what I've told you? If you're looking for validation, I can refer you to many people that I know and who I've helped over the years. You only need to look at my website to see all the wonderful testimonials from my clients all around the world.'

Burton could tell by the tone of her voice that she was not happy with his line of questioning. She was starting to become defensive, which may or may not be down to her trying to hide something from him. He couldn't tell at this point.

'I don't doubt that for a minute, Ms Parkinson. It's just that the website appears to be the only place where there *is* any information about you, which is odd bearing in mind your social status.'

'Like I told you the last time,' she responded, beginning to sound like a parent reprimanding their child, 'I prefer my privacy. I let the world see what I want it to see, nothing more. There are no skeletons in my cupboards, I can assure you, but, of course, I will co-operate with you however you want me to. I am not trying to block you in any way, detective inspector.'

Burton felt like he had met his match in this person. She seemed genuine enough in her response, and appropriately upset at his questioning. So much so that he turned to Fielding and raised an eyebrow. She would know what that meant, she always knew what his gentle signals were for.

'We didn't mean to upset you, Ms Parkinson,' Fielding began, taking the hint from her partner, 'and I apologise for making you think that we doubted you. It's just, you see, we now have another murder case, and it appears to be linked to this one.'

Good old Fielding, Burton thought, *searching for a reaction.*

'Oh?' The astrologer was curious, her eyes glancing from one detective to the other. Burton held his ground, but Fielding continued. 'It wasn't one of the other women who came to see me, was it?'

'No it wasn't, but there is a distinct similarity, so you see, we are anxious to follow up any lead possible and as quickly as possible. We are just doing background checks on everyone Maria

Turnbull saw in her last few hours and, like we say, there's very little on you.'

'No, I understand, and I know you can't say anything about the other murder either. But I'm afraid that there's really nothing more I can tell you. I'm a private person, always have been, always will be, I guess. Best to keep private and public personas separate, don't you think?'

'I can understand your reasons.' Burton was now a little gentler on her after hearing her explanation. Just because he hadn't come across someone with very little information about themselves in the public domain didn't make them guilty of anything. In his mind, all the woman was guilty of was wanting to keep herself to herself. Her astrology and Tarot cards may all be an act, but that was the way of life she'd chosen for herself; and if she wanted to keep her private life out of things, then good luck to her for being able to do it in this social media-orientated world. However, all that aside, the astrological symbol found on the body of Harry York still bothered him. It had been confirmed by the team as being the sign for Sagittarius the Archer. Appropriate enough, bearing in mind the manner in which he died. But the link here was astrology, and that was something that Madame Ortiz specialised in, fake or not. However, he didn't want to make her aware of the link at this juncture.

As she was showing them to the door, Burton asked one last question of her.

'If you don't mind me asking, is there anyone special in your life right now?'

He noticed a slight, barely noticeable hesitancy before she answered.

'No, detective, there isn't. Why, are you asking me out on a date?' she laughed.

Burton felt his cheeks start to burn at the question, especially as he could see Fielding out of the corner of his eye looking over in his direction.

'Of course not,' he said adamantly.

'Ah,' Marilyn laughed, 'I can see that perhaps you two are a little more than just colleagues judging by the look your lady has just given you!'

'You're very observant,' Fielding cut in to save Burton having to explain, 'but I can assure you that Detective Inspector Burton was asking a question relevant to our enquiries.'

'Okay,' Marilyn smiled. 'If you need to speak to me again you know where I am.'

Thanking her, they walked back to the car.

'I got the impression that there *is* somebody special in her life, judging by that slight pause before she answered the question,' Burton said as he put the key in the ignition and turned it.

'Maybe he's high-profile, or married even,' Fielding suggested. 'So, you're lucky; she'll not be wanting to go out on a date with you then!'

'Stop it!' Burton rebuffed as he drove away.

'So, do we think that she's off the hook then?' Fielding asked him.

'You know, I'm still not sure. It's this whole astrological sign thing that's bugging me. It's too much of a coincidence, but I can't figure it out right now.'

'It's like somebody is directing our attention onto her, isn't it?'

'I know what you mean,' Burton agreed. 'I'm thinking the same thing, too. Somebody with a grudge, perhaps. Maybe that's why she likes to keep herself to herself, and doesn't let anyone get too close. It sounds to me like she's had a bad experience in the past?'

'And all the odd correspondence she told us about.'

'Yes, and there's that.'

CHAPTER
SIXTEEN

'I've arranged for forensic accounting to take a look at Thornton School's finances,' Jack Summers announced when Burton and Fielding returned to the station.

'And was the Head happy with that?' Burton asked, amazed that the request hadn't been met with opposition.

'Yes, she was more than happy to let us look into their accounts.'

'Did she say who was the Board of Governor's financial treasurer?'

'One of the parents,' Summers referred to his notebook, 'by the name of Sandra McMillan. She's a bank manager, apparently.'

Burton thought for a moment, throwing ideas around in his head. 'Okay, so I know this is reaching, but if she manages a bank she could know ways to hide money, if that's what's been happening. Perhaps Maria and Harry York found out about it?'

'Well, if there is anything untoward to be found, then forensic accounting will be able to root it out,' Summers informed them.

'Yes, I'm sure they will. Did they say how long it would take?' Burton asked.

'I did ask, but they said that they couldn't specify a timeframe as such as it depends upon a lot of factors.'

'I understand,' Burton nodded. However, there again, there was this nagging doubt within him. Could it be as simple as fraud? He'd known people murder for far less than that, so yes, it could be that simple, he reminded himself.

Summers had been the first one of the team to arrive back after they'd each been given their instructions. Despite the 'fraud' aspect being a very plausible one, he wanted to know what the others had found out about the women's and Maria's husband's backgrounds.

'Have you heard from any of the others?' he asked Summers, although not knowing if they'd even arranged to call one another once they'd ended their interviews.

'No,' Summers confirmed. 'We didn't agree to that, only reporting in on what we'd found when we got back.'

'Okay.'

As the DC went back to his desk, Burton strolled over to the evidence board. Fielding joined him. It was growing bigger by the second, with six people now featured on there.

'I tell you what's bothering me,' he said to his partner after scanning the information. 'If this *is* something to do with fraud, where does the poison come into this?'

'The only connection I can see is the fact that Maria Turnbull was a biology teacher.'

Burton frowned. 'Mmmm, perhaps. But it doesn't really make sense, does it? Whoever it is who's doing the killing, they're highlighting the poison aspect of it. I mean, surely, it would have been enough to have shot Harry York through the heart with an arrow without using the poison, wouldn't it?'

'I agree,' Fielding nodded. 'Even if it was to subdue him, why that particular one? And of course, there's the astrological symbol; that's pointing us directly to Madame Ortiz.'

'Ah,' Burton sat back on the desk while still staring at the board, 'this one is a bit of a puzzler.'

'That's a bit of an understatement!' Fielding laughed.

'I think there's more to this than we're actually seeing, and I don't think it's a simple case of fraud either.'

While Burton was still engrossed in the evidence board, Fielding went back to her desk. She wanted to draw up a chart of who was who, and what linked each one of the suspects and the victims to one another. Deciding that the best way would be to put it all on a spreadsheet, she opened up a programme and started to add the information. By the time she'd finished she had a complete list which was starting to look like the main premise of a game of Cluedo. All she needed was Professor Plum in the library with a candlestick as one of the suspects and the comparison would be complete. Pleased with her work, she printed it off and studied it in great detail.

The main points were this:

Point one - Maria Turnbull and her three friends visit Madame Ortiz. Maria dies in the taxi on the way home. Cause of death – poison.

Point two - Harry York is found dead behind his business premises with an arrow through his heart. Poison was found around the entry point of the arrow.

Point three - Maria Turnbull and Harry York knew one another, the extent of which was unknown, but they are linked by Thornton School – Maria was a biology teacher there, and Harry was on the board of governors. The big question was, what connected Maria and Harry other than that fact? Was it to do with the school's finances, or were they both having an affair and their tryst was discovered by one of, or both, their respective partners? So, if that was the case, then there was another suspect to add to the list – Harry York's wife.

One thing Fielding realised as she was reading through the facts was that there were endless possibilities – and one or none of them may be true. She now considered the possibility of Harry York's wife and Maria Turnbull's husband being in cahoots with one another to murder their cheating spouses, as unexpected or as unlikely as that seemed. That was how confusing the whole thing was, and which gave rise to questions like this one. If that were the case, then why implicate the astrologer? A diversion, maybe? She felt the throbbing in her head start up again. Burton's 'puzzler' was just that, a proper brain teasing conundrum.

She needed a break from all the information that was spinning frantically around in her brain.

Fortunately, the other members of the team returned while she was still trying to desperately figure it out. Although not distracting from the case, and hopefully shedding a degree of light on it, a group discussion would stop the brain fog that was accumulating. Burton stood back while she took the briefing.

DC Phillipa Preston started first, describing how she'd visited the Ministry of Justice and spoken to Barbara and Selena's bosses. They'd both been shocked by the death of one of their colleagues' friends and had taken some time off, but couldn't praise the two girls' employment with the business highly enough. They were both hard workers with exemplary records, with no worrying red flags at all.

Likewise, DC Jane Francis reported the same of Caroline Watkins. She was a dedicated solicitor, who never shirked from hard work. The partner Francis spoke to did agree that she occasionally 'took over', as he put it, but stressed that was down to her enthusiasm to do a good job for both her and the firm. 'A natural born leader', he added.

Following in the same pattern, DC Simon Banks confirmed that John Turnbull's architectural firm saw him as an asset to the company in that he provided them with good, structured business plans and great conceptual work. In their opinion, he was heading for a partnership in the new few years.

'None of their employers or line managers reported any worries or concerns about any of them then?' Fielding asked each of them.

They all shook their heads.

'They're squeaky clean, it seems,' Banks stated.

'I don't like squeaky clean,' Burton interjected. 'Sorry Fielding,' he apologised for cutting in.

'I still think that there's something here they're not telling us, any of them. It's like everything is "rehearsed" somehow.'

'I'm not sure what else we can do in that respect, save from keeping an eye on them?' she responded, even though she doubted the resources they had to keep a constant watch on all four of them at the same time.

'We'll leave them up there on the board,' he nodded his head over towards it. 'Call it a hunch, but I don't think they're out of the woods just yet.'

Fielding always trusted his hunches. It was then that she mentioned what she'd been thinking about Harry York's wife and John Turnbull.

'Well, it's a possibility, I suppose,' he pondered, not really wanting to add any more suspects to the already expanding list. But if that was the case then it had to be explored. 'It's probably worth looking into. Good work, Fielding, and good work team,' he added, extending his praise to the other members. 'I think this might be the point where we call it a night. Tomorrow we can sort through all the facts that we now have and try to apply logic to it.'

Everyone was glad of the break.

CHAPTER
SEVENTEEN

'**D**o you want to come over for a takeaway?' Fielding asked Burton as they exited the office last.

'Do I ever!' he exclaimed, glad of a semblance of normality in this confusing and baffling case. A takeaway was always welcome to him, despite, or maybe because of, the recent removal of his gallbladder. Having a treat now and again made them all the more enjoyable.

'Your choice,' Fielding said to him, leaving it up to him what he fancied to eat.

'Well now, let me think about that!' He parodied deep thought by bringing a hand to his face and extending his index finger along his chin.

Despite his mock-deliberation, Fielding knew what the choice would be, it was what it always was, either Chinese or Indian. The only question was, what was he going to go for tonight?

'Would you like me to stay over as well?'

'If you're going to have a drink then I think it might be for the best, don't you' she said, not that he needed any excuse for stopping over.

'Then I'll need to stop by mine to pick up a few things for the morning.'

'No problem,' she said to him. The day had been heavy-going, so having him there would take her mind off all of that until the next day when they'd have to go through the whole process again. It was the distraction she so desperately needed. They'd already talked about getting a place together at some point in the future, which would put an end for the need of either of them to pack an overnight bag when they stayed with each other. It would be a great start for both of them, and she knew that her cats would love the option of a cat flap and the ability to go out and prowl around a garden of their own instead of being stuck indoors all the time. Truth be told, she couldn't wait to go ahead and do it. But after the events of the past few days the one thing she would not be buying for her future garden were Foxglove plants, for the cats' sake.

Perhaps somewhat expectedly, and despite all attempts to avoid it, when the meal ended the conversation turned to the case.

'I had planned to leave this until the morning,' Fielding began, 'but the whole thing is constantly running through my mind; it's driving me nuts!'

'So, I can't even distract you for the evening!' Burton laughed, pulling her closer to him.

'Well, you *can* distract me,' she smiled, 'but you have to admit that this is one hell of a strange case.'

'We have solved some corkers over the years, so I have every confidence that we'll get to the bottom of this one too.'

He was always the confident one, always certain that a criminal will make one big mistake that will get them caught in the end. It was his whole philosophy, and one which had served him well over the years.

'Unless the average criminal is a MENSA genius, then they all make the same mistakes in the end,' he reassured her. 'And that's how we catch them, by being one step ahead all the way and recognising where they've gone wrong.'

'But here's a thought, what if they *were* a genius? I mean, just think of it, a criminal with a higher-than-usual IQ plans the perfect crime, and considers all the possible variants and outcomes. What do we do in a case like that?'

It was a fair question, and one which Burton had thought of on many occasions in the past. Fortunately for them, they hadn't come across one yet, but he always speculated that some day they might. What if this was that day?

'Then I'd say we would do exactly what we do now, try to beat them at their own game.'

***

The next morning, the cats just couldn't believe their luck that there was still an extra human in the apartment with them. They did their figure of eight dance around Burton's legs again, much to his amusement.

'Are they always like this?' he laughed, trying to avoid falling over them as he made his way to the kitchen.

'Well, I don't know,' Fielding responded, 'I don't have any other men coming in apart from you!'

'Touché.'

Fielding wasn't one for eating much at breakfast time, preferring just a cup of tea, but Burton liked an early morning meal and demolished two slices of toast and scrambled eggs. Even though she loved her cappuccinos during the day, she found coffee far too harsh first thing in the morning, hence her regular habit of one cup of tea, with perhaps a small bowl of cereal. She dispensed with the cereal this morning, however.

'Mmmm, I must come her more often,' Burton said, putting the last morsel into his mouth.

'Great service, too.'

'As long as you leave a tip on the table you *can* come again,' she joked.

Whilst getting dressed a call came in on Fielding's phone from DC Summers.

'Sorry to bother you, boss,' he said to her, 'but there's been another murder.'

Fielding felt a chill run through her.

'Similar circumstances?' she asked, although neither of the two previous murders had any similarity apart from the poison.

'Well, this one's a bit different to the others; I'll text you the address.'

'What was that?' Burton asked coming out of the bathroom.

'Summers. There's been another death,' she told him, glancing at the address Summers had just sent her.

'Where this time?'

'The Quays.'

'I've got to be in Ambleton's office first thing; are you okay to go there yourself?'

'Of course. I'm a very capable detective, I'll have you know, and I can go out and about on my own now and again!' It was said jokily, but Fielding was anything but laughing on the inside. Another day, another death, and, by the sound of it, linked to the other two. The bodies were piling up, as were the suspects. She wondered just who the new victim was and how, if at all, they were related to the other two.

CHAPTER EIGHTEEN

Acting Detective Inspector Sally Fielding pulled up on Broadway behind the two police cars stationed there, their blue lights flashing out of sync with one another. A visual warning for people to keep away, although despite this, or perhaps because of it, there were still a few people gathered further along the road curious as to what had happened. As she walked past, she saw a man sitting in the backseat of the first car. He must have been the one who found the body, a jogger out on an early morning run judging by his clothing. One of the officers in the front seat was holding a clip board, and was making notes on an incident form. It was never easy for anyone who came across a dead body, and the man in the back looked drawn and haggard from his experience with it.

The constable standing in front of the police tape stretched across the width of the road made a move to walk towards her as she drew nearer. As she produced her warrant card for him his whole body language changed, and he lifted up the tape for her to walk under.

'There's a path over there leading down to the bank,' he said, indicating a gap in the fencing. 'The others are already there.'

Fielding assumed that the 'others' he was referring to was the SOCO team, but she knew for a fact that Jack Summers was also down there amongst them. Following the police constable's instructions, she went through the gap and along a canal side path to where she could see the white tent erected. Several people were working on the area around it, including DC Jack Summers, who stopped what he was doing when he saw her and sprinted across to join her.

'Who's the medical examiner?' she asked after bidding him a good morning.

'Robert Mansfield,' Summers said. 'He seems to get his fair share of them, doesn't he?'

'He seems to get a fair share of ours, that's for sure.'

Pulling the tent flap to one side, both detectives entered.

'Good morning, Sally,' Doctor Mansfield said when he saw her, rising as he did so.

Fielding returned his greeting. 'What have we got?' she asked looking down at the body on the ground.

'For all intent and purpose, it looks like a straightforward drowning,' he said to her, 'but in light of the recent events I'll refrain from diagnosing that until I get him back to the morgue for an autopsy.'

'So why do you think this might be connected to the others?'

Mansfield bent down and picked up an evidence pouch, then handed it to her. There was a blank slip of paper inside but, fearing the worst, she turned it over. This time she recognised what was on it; it was the astrological symbol for the birth sign for Pisces. She knew it as it was her mother's. *Somewhat appropriate*, she thought as he had been found in water.

'Was there any identification on the body?' Fielding asked, still staring at the symbol.

'That's the funny thing,' the medic replied, 'nothing at all, not even a wallet or phone.'

'Could they have ended up in the water?' DC Summers speculated.

'Yes, I suppose they could have,' Mansfield could see the logic in that, but it seemed to him to be too obvious an answer. 'But if I could hazard a guess, I'd say that they were removed from the body prior to, or even after death, in order to put you at a disadvantage.'

'So, you're definitely thinking deliberate?' Fielding asked him.

'I'm thinking that it's possible but, as I say, let's see what the autopsy turns up. We're just about done here. I'll perform it at 10, so if you'd like to come over then we can see what's going on with him.'

Fielding hadn't expected to be attending another autopsy so soon, but said that she'd be sure to be there on time.

On the way back to her vehicle, she stopped by the police car and asked if she could speak to the witness. As she slipped into the back seat alongside him, she could see that he was still shaking. She also noticed that, from the look of his clothes he had not been in the water. There was no more than normal joggers' sweat on his top.

'What's his name?' Fielding asked the police constable with the clipboard.

'Frank Wilson,' came the reply.

'Frank,' she said his name but there was no reaction. On the second time he answered.

'Was he lying on the path by the canal when you found him, or did you have to get him out of the water?' Even though she suspected the latter not to be the case she still felt obliged to ask him. After all, the victim could have been half in and half out, making it relatively easy to put him out by placing both arms under his.

'Yes,' the young man replied weakly. 'He was just lying there. I did bend down to check if he was okay, but then I saw his face and I knew that ...' his voice trailed off, and his eyes took on a vacant look again.

'That's okay, Frank,' she said gently, placing a hand on his arm. It surprised him and made him jump.

'You've taken a statement?' Fielding asked the constable, and he confirmed it.

'In that case it might be wise to take Mr Wilson home.'

She turned back to Frank. 'If we need to ask you any more questions we'll be in touch.'

The man nodded, but she wasn't entirely sure that he'd heard what she'd said.

***

As soon as Fielding and Summers returned to base, she asked her new partner to print off the photographs he'd taken of the body and the symbol in order to pin them both up on the board alongside the others.

'Not another one!' DC Phillipa Preston exclaimed what she saw what he was doing. 'Who is it this time?'

'That's the one thing we don't know about him; there was no identification on him.'

'I guess we'll have to wait until his fingerprints have been tracked then.'

'If he's in the system, that is.' Fielding had the feeling that they may very well not be, given the lengths the killer had gone to remove anything which may have identified him straight away. 'It's a bit of a long shot I know, but I think it might be an idea to quickly check through the social media friends of everyone up there on the board, see if he pops up anywhere.'

That done, she asked Summers if he'd accompany her to the autopsy. He was a bit like Fielding when it came to viewing a post mortem. Although knowing that they were vital, they both disliked being there when it actually happened, preferring to leave that entirely to the medical examiner with them getting the results when it was over and done with. But there were rules surrounding that, so go they must. And on this occasion, it was a good thing that they did.

It was not usual for any medical examiner to provide more than a verbal commentary of what they find to those in the viewing area, but on this occasion Doctor Mansfield felt obliged to add some of his own personal observations.

'I know that you're both the detectives here,' he announced, giving Fielding and Summers a quick glance on the viewing platform whilst he continued with the examination, 'but I often wonder how some cases come to arrive on my dissection table. It gets me thinking sometimes. In this poor soul's case, I wonder how he came to be at that particular spot on the canal. I can already confirm that he did drown, judging by the water content of his lungs, but that being the case, why was his body hauled up onto the side of it? If I was the killer, I'd have left him in there, let him either sink or drift down to one of the locks. Which raises the question, did he actually drown at that spot or somewhere else?'

'You'd have made a good detective, doctor,' Fielding said to him.

'Over the years I have read quite a number of crime fiction books where the main character does both.'

'So they do,' she laughed gently, having read a few of them herself.

'We did take a sample of the water from the canal at that point, so I'm going to go ahead and compare that with the lung content.'

'So, you're thinking that he might have been killed elsewhere?' Summers asked him.

'It has been known to happen. Best to check, I think.'

'Good idea.' Whichever way this went, Fielding wouldn't be surprised in the slightest, and it was good that Doctor Mansfield was being as thorough as he possibly could be. They were very lucky to have two very good medical examiners in the area, with Frank Collinson being the other. But if it did happen that the victim had been killed elsewhere, why then dump him beside the canal? Did the murderer think that the water would not be checked? Perhaps not, as Fielding herself wouldn't have initially considered it. Maybe it was just to link it to the astrological sign that was found on the body?

'I look forward to the results,' she said, although she suspected that wouldn't make the case any easier.

CHAPTER
NINETEEN

'The latest victim's name is Norman Bishop,' DC Phillipa Preston announced, writing his name on the board under his picture.

'Who is he and how did you find him?' Fielding asked, rising from her seat and walking over to it.

'I did as you asked and went through all the suspects' public information. He's on Caroline Watkins's list of social media friends.'

'Interesting. Do a quick check for me, will you? It's just a thought, but see if Norman Bishop by any remote chance knows Harry York.'

'Will do.'

'What are you thinking?' Summers asked. Fielding smiled to herself as that was what she normally asked Burton.

'I'm just wondering if he's on the school's Board of Governors as well. If he is, then there's a clear link to all three victims and the school.'

'So, it could all be to do with the school finances?'

'It could be.'

'But what about the astrological symbols left on two of the bodies?'

'That's something I don't yet understand,' Fielding admitted, 'other than trying to shift our attention onto Madame Ortiz.'

'Does *she* have a connection to the school?'

Summers raised a good point. 'We'll also have to look into that.'

'I can do that if you like,' he volunteered. 'I can ring the Head back and ask her.'

Fielding thought that it had to be the quickest way, so gave him the go ahead. About fifteen minutes later she had the answer to both questions. Sadly, it wasn't the ones she'd hoped for. Norman Bishop didn't know Harry York, a fact confirmed by the latter's widow, and Marilyn Parkinson had no connection whatsoever to the school.

'Well, there's that theory gone,' Fielding sighed after hearing the news. 'We'll have to approach it from another angle.' Although she had no idea what that angle was.

'We're still waiting to hear from forensic accounting regarding the school's financial records,' Summer reminded her.

'That we are. I'm hoping that's the answer, but I'm not holding my breath.'

'Why is that then?' Summers asked, thinking that it seemed the most likely theory.

'I can't really put my finger on it, but I think I've somehow inherited Burton's penchant for hunches. Something just doesn't sit right with me about this; I can't say what simply because I don't know. But I'm of the mind that somebody wants us to think that Madame Ortiz is involved in this, at least that's the way I'm seeing it, but the question is, why?'

***

I think it's going well the text message read.
The plan seems to be working came the reply.
We've just got to keep our cool and make sure we have our wits about us.
We can do that.
Can't wait for this to be all over.
Me too!

***

Fielding's fears were realised when Summers received a call back from forensic accounting. Everything was in order, with nothing hidden or misplaced; the records were clean. *Squeaky clean*, Fielding thought, to use both Banks's and Burton's term. Why was everybody coming across as such unless, of course, that was what they were? Could all the suspects be pawns in someone else's game, and was this now an option to consider moving forward? However, this was not the only flattener, it was soon compounded by the fact that the water in the lungs of Normal Bishop wasn't from the canal, or any other external body of water. In Robert Mansfield's professional opinion, the water came from a regular household tap. From this he concluded that Mr Bishop had met his demise in a domestic setting, which was as far away from the canal as it could be.

'So, you're saying that somebody drowned him in a tub of water then moved his body to the canal to be found there?' Fielding asked the medical examiner.

'Or in a kitchen or bathroom sink – perhaps even a toilet bowl. I would consider that to be the only explanation. As you know, the water in the canal comes in from the Mersey Estuary near Liverpool, so is saline. Easily discernable from your tap water.'

'Wouldn't the murder know that, though?'

'They might, but possibly not. Some people consider water to be water in a case of drowning, but it's not when you consider the differences.'

'Burton and I were just considering the IQ of criminals the other day. If there was a murderer with a high IQ, wouldn't he have considered this?'

'It might depend upon the moment, perhaps? Maybe an intelligent criminal will be able to plan the perfect murder but then be unable to execute it with the same precision. I don't know, Sally, I'm a simple doctor who cuts dead people up and not a trained psychologist; it might be best to ask one of them.'

Fielding thanked him. He'd made an interesting observation about calling in a psychologist, though, and she knew exactly where to find one. Phillipa Preston's partner was highly revered in the profession, and had been helpful when called in before. Perhaps this was the time to engage her services again. She'd have to get the clearance from DCI Ambleton, but as Louise Simmons had been an asset to the team in the past, she didn't think that there'd be any objection to bringing her in once again.

Following on from that bombshell, Fielding thought it only pertinent to pay a visit to their latest victim's home. Even if Normal Bishop's wife wasn't at home at the time, surely, she would have noticed something out of place in the bathroom no matter how hard the killer would have tried to tidy it up? Bishop wasn't a slender man, so he must have put up a fight unless, of course, Fielding mused, he had been rendered unable to fight back. And, knowing what they knew so far about the murders, perhaps he, too, had been disabled by some artificial means. Could there also be traces of digitalis in his body too? She quickly rang back Mansfield and posed the question.

'I'm still waiting for the tox results to come back, but that's a possibility.'

'Do you think that if he was disabled in such a way that one person, say a woman, could have drowned him?'

'Well, Mr Bishop was quite well-built as you know, so I'd say she'd have to be strong. A tranquilized, or poisoned body, would be dead weight so additionally difficult in that respect.'

'But one man, or two people even, would be able to do it?'

'I'd say a strong man would, yes. As for two people, that would make it a lot easier. Two men, or a man and a woman together, would be able to manage it.'

Fielding thanked him for a second time. However, the answer posed a new question: was the murder acting on their own, or did they have an accomplice? It just added to the complexities of the case.

CHAPTER TWENTY

Mrs Bishop's sister had temporarily moved in with her. As everybody else was working hard by trying to find some kind of common denominator apart from the poison, Fielding went on her own.

'Is this really necessary right now?' the sister asked. Fielding had faced objection before, but appreciated how the family must be feeling right now. She'd experienced it herself in the past, so had first-hand knowledge of what it was like to be informed that a loved one had died. All anybody wanted at that time was to be left alone. This, however, wasn't a natural death, and in order to find out who had committed the crime, it was necessary to ask questions as early as possible in the investigation.

'I'm afraid it is,' Fielding said to her.

'Do you know what it's like to lose somebody?' It was a question asked in the heat of the moment, she knew that, but one which she felt required a firm answer.

'Yes, as a matter of fact, I do.'

The sister appeared stunned by that, then seemed to realise what she'd asked.

'Look ... I'm ...' she began, her tone more subdued than before, but Fielding held up a hand to stop her.

'We're treating this as a murder enquiry ... Mrs?'

'My name is Andrea Fuller,' the woman offered her name, now having composed herself a bit more, 'but it's Miss, not Mrs.'

'We need to act quickly, under the circumstances. I just have one question to ask your sister then I'll be on my way. May I see her?'

'Yes, yes, of course. She's upstairs in her bedroom. I'll go and fetch her.'

'No, that's all right, please don't bring her down. I can easily go up to her.'

As Miss Fuller led the way up the stairs, Fielding glanced around her. Although she hadn't seen the man at his best, Mr Bishop looked to be a man in his late forties, but that was just a guess on her behalf. However, the décor seemed to fit in with that estimation. It wasn't what she would call a younger person's home, with trendy sofas and matching furnishings, but a more middle-aged look and feel about it, without that sounding too discriminating against that particular age group. It looked eclectic and lived in, scattered with photographs and treasured memorabilia of the couple's life together.

'Does Mrs Bishop have any children?' Fielding asked.

'No, it's just ... well, it was just the two of them. I don't know how she's going to get through this.'

Fielding felt like saying that she would in time, but refrained from doing so. It wouldn't have helped, even though she knew it to be the case.

Mrs Bishop was trying to sit up in bed as they entered the room, having heard the doorbell and the voices coming up from downstairs. Her sister hurried to her side and told her who Fielding was.

'I'm sorry to have to do this, Mrs Bishop, but it's imperative that I ask you something.'

The lady nodded as her sister put her arm around her shoulders.

'When did you last see your husband?'

There was a long pause, as if she was trying to organise her thoughts before speaking. And when she spoke it was slow and lumbering, as if she was having difficulty forming the right words.

'It ... was ... yesterday ... morning,' she replied.

'You didn't see him last night?'

'No ... no ... he was away on business ... and wasn't due back until ... this evening.' At that point she broke down and her sister looked towards Fielding for compassion.

'Okay, that's all. Thank you. I'm sorry for having to come to see you like this. Before I go, though, it may seem like an odd question but please bear with me on this, do you think I might take a look at your bathroom?'

Both women gave her a strange look, but Mrs Bishop said that was okay, asking her sister to show Fielding where it was.

As bathrooms go it was a little larger than average; quite modern with the sink set into a vanity unit and the toilet set into the wall, and the bath was one of those freestanding ones with the taps fitted centrally. The whole room looked in stark contrast to the decoration in the rest of the house. Perhaps they'd been revamping, starting with this room. Lifting the mat, she carefully examined the floor underneath it and around the base of the tub for any traces of displaced water. None was evident. She did the same around the wash basin but, again, the floor was dry, likewise with the base of the toilet. If Norman Burton had been away on business, then chances were that was where he might have been killed. She needed to find out where he'd been. If they were quick enough, and lucky enough, then the killer may have left some evidence behind. Satisfied that he had not died there, she went back to the bedroom.

'Can you tell me where your husband worked please, Mrs Bishop?'

'He was a planning officer with the local council.'

'And what was the meeting about that he went to yesterday?'

'Detective Inspector!' The sister again pleaded, seeing that this was causing more stress.

'Yes,' Fielding said, looking at her, 'this is the last thing, I assure you.'

'He said it was a seminar on planning, but you'll have to ask them down at the Town Hall for the details regarding it.'

'I will. Again, thank you for your time.'

The sister moved to rise from the bed, but Fielding stopped her.

'No, I'll show myself out, you stay here with your sister.'

CHAPTER
TWENTY-ONE

Norman Bishop's boss, Sam Younger, sat behind a well-stocked desk in his office on the second floor of the council building. Behind him, a row of alphabetically-labelled metal filing cabinets filled the entire width of the room. The only personal touch appeared to be the plant sitting on top of them. It looked healthy enough, but seemed out of place somehow. As he didn't appear to be the green-fingered type, perhaps his secretary had put it there to inject a sense of homeliness for any visitors. It didn't really work. He hadn't attended the seminar with his employee, but several others from the department had and he'd already informed them of the tragic news. The meeting had been cut short due to this and the five men and women were returning back to the office, due in some time after lunch.

'I may need to speak to them when they return,' Fielding said to him.

'Yes, of course.' The man appeared visibly upset by the loss of his employee.

'Can I ask you where the seminar was?'

'In Blackburn, at the Premier Hotel.'

In order to get the room checked, Fielding briefly excused herself while she rang Summers and instructed him to travel there as soon as possible.

'Get somebody from SOCO to accompany you and have his room thoroughly checked over, can you, especially the bathroom?'

'Sure thing, boss.'

She then turned her attention back to Mr Younger. 'Can I ask you if you know someone called Caroline Watkins? I believe she knew Norman.'

'Caroline? Yes, I know her, and so did Norman. She's one of our local government legal advisers. Why? What does she have to do with this?'

'It's not exactly clear at this point, but one of Caroline's close friends has just died and there's a similarity in the way they died.'

Younger frowned at that remark.

'We're trying to find out if there's a connection. Had Caroline and Norman been working on anything legal recently?'

'Well, yes, they had actually. About a week ago she came in to draw up a couple of documents for us, to do with public tenancies.'

'Would it be possible to see them?'

'Of course. I'll get my assistant to bring them in for you.'

Younger leaned forward and picked up his phone. Punching in a few numbers, he waited until it was answered then asked for the Northern Quarter file.

Fielding's ears immediately pricked up on hearing that. It could just be pure coincidence, but the Northern Quarter was where Madame Ortiz had her business premises. Younger's secretary knocked on the door and he called her in. She smiled at Fielding as she handed the file over to her boss, then promptly left again. He opened the manila folder and took out the top document.

'This is what they were working on, detective,' he said as he gave her three sheets of paper stapled together.

As Fielding read it over, she saw that it was a tenancy renewal statement for several business properties. But the one thing that interested her the most was the fact that Madame Ortiz's address was one of them. Seeing that, she skipped to the last page. The document had been signed by both Caroline Watkins and Norman Bishop.

'And would Caroline and Norman have had to visit each of the premises to see the owners?' She asked.

'Yes, they would, and they did. We have the individual tenancies if you'd like to look at a specific one?'

'Yes please,' Fielding replied, still trying to take it in, 'it's the one registered to a Ms Marilyn Parkinson.'

There must have been around ten separate documents in there judging by the bulldog clips on each of them, and Younger stopped when he came to the one he needed.

'Here you are,' he said as he handed it over.

Fielding scanned through it, hoping that something of relevance would pop out at her, but the flowery legal jargon was simply a confirmation of a five-year extension to the tenancy. It didn't reveal anything of interest other than the fact that Caroline Watkins and Norman Bishop knew one another, and they'd both had dealings with Marilyn Parkinson. So, the question was, had Caroline picked the Tarot card reading as a night out for the girls on the basis of the work connection, and had the cost of it been in lieu of their legal dealings? It was a question she would have to ask her. But even if it did, what did that have to do with Maria Turnbull's death, or Norman Bishop's for that matter?

'I see that the tenancy for this person started eighteen months ago.'

He nodded.

'Why wasn't it a longer tenancy then?'

Younger explained that eighteen months is the initial tenancy agreement for any new businesses. After that time, five years ones were the norm. 'You see, it's really a safeguard for both parties. If the business is successful, then it works for both them and us and we're happy to extend the contract, but if it fails within that time, we don't extend it and then they're not tied into a five-year contract with all the associated fees and legal obligations.'

Fielding found that logical. 'So, this particular person's business was successful then?'

'More than, I would say. She regularly pays her dues on time, which is always a good sign, plus we do check in now and again just to make sure everything is going okay with all our tenants.'

It was then that another thought came to Fielding's mind. Harry York was an estate agent. Could *he* be involved in this in any way, apart from the connection to Maria Turnbull via the school.

'Just one last thing,' she said to Younger. 'When commencing a tenancy, would a tenant be required to initially go through an estate agent?'

'Why, yes, that's the normal way, then the business licenses are renewed via the council.'

'Is there any way I can find out which agency Ms Parkinson had initial dealings with?'

'It will be on record.' Saying that, he picked up the phone again and asked his secretary for Marilyn's separate file from the records stack.

'It may take a while,' Younger said. 'As you can imagine, we have a great deal of businesses in Manchester, and hold a lot of records.' Fielding decided that he was being practical rather than trying to put her off, as he'd been more than helpful so far.

'That's okay, I've got all day,' Fielding forced a wan smile, although she did have all the time in the world to wait. They were getting nowhere with the investigation, other than accumulating more bodies by the day. Even if she did find out what she now suspected, it wouldn't help the investigation one bit, and would only add to the questions already unanswered.

Despite Sam Younger thinking it would take some time for his secretary to return with the records, there was a knock on the door after only ten minutes. Again, she had a polite smile for Fielding as she handed the information over.

The file wasn't too large, so she found what she was looking for relatively quickly. Marilyn Parkinson first viewed the property eighteen months ago, and a rental agreement was signed the following month. The estate agency firm handling the transaction was, as suspected, the one Harry York worked at.

After thanking Mr Younger for his invaluable help, Fielding headed back to the station. She needed Burton's insight into all this, hoping that by the time she got back he'd be free of his duties with the DCI for the day and would be available to work with the team again.

CHAPTER
TWENTY-TWO

It was as if the powers-that-be had heard her, for when she returned to the office Burton was sitting next to Simon Banks and looking at his computer screen.

'I've got an hour free,' he said on seeing her. 'Thought I'd come in and see how you're all doing.'

'Thank goodness!' she declared with an urgency in her voice, which caused him to raise an eyebrow.

'What's happened?' he asked, concerned by a response which was most unlike her.

'Let's go into your office and I'll bring you up to date.'

While Fielding filled him in, Burton sat back in his chair and listened with interest.

'You just couldn't make this stuff up!' he said after hearing her out. 'So, what are you thinking about it all?'

'I'm really not sure, which is why I need your take on it.'

'Okay then, let's go through it all at the board.'

By the time they'd gone over it all, they both had to admit that it didn't make much sense. The one real lead they looked like having, believing that Maria Turnbull's and Harry York's death might be somehow related to the school's finances, had now been disproven by the forensic accounting team, so they were back to square one again. The new information from Fielding, regarding the tenancy lease on Madam Ortiz's premises, now linked the astrologer to not only Caroline Watkins and Norman Bishop, but also to Harry York. Both York and Bishop had been found with an astrological symbol on the body. So, what was the killer, or killers, trying to say, and exactly why had there now been three deaths? There seemed no logical answer, apart from everything pointing towards Madam Ortiz. The odd one out was Maria Turnbull, who did not have a symbol on her body but, there again, she was not alone at the time of her death. This begged the question; might she have had one if she hadn't been? Also, there was the matter of the digitalis poison. They were yet to find out if it was in Bishop's system when he died, but Fielding suspected that it might be, the same as the others. Hopefully, the results would come through soon to either confirm or deny. The only one of the three victims with a confirmed link to digitalis was Maria Turnbull, being a Biology teacher who had also studied Botany, plus the fact that she took the medication for a mild heart condition.

So, what did Maria Turnbull, Harry York and Normal Bishop know, or what had they done, or indeed seen, that got all three of them killed?

Forget Cluedo, it was reading like a who's who in an Agatha Christie novel.

***

Burton felt nervous about telling Fielding that DCI Ambleton had instructed him to organise a press conference for 4pm, mainly because as acting senior investigative officer she'd be the one having to head it up.

'Oh, I can't!' she declared when he finally plucked up the courage to tell her. 'I've never even been to one before. They'll catch me out and I'll let something slip that I shouldn't.'

'You can't let anything you don't know slip out,' he reassured her with a smile.

He was right, of course, she knew that, and the truth of the matter was they did know nothing, nothing that pointed to motive, that is.

'Okay then, can you prep me on what they'll ask and how to respond to them?'

'Because I'm an old hand you mean?' he laughed.

'If you want to phrase it that way, then yes!'

'I'll miss you when I'm upstairs,' Burton said softly after a short pause. 'I'll miss this, our working together and sharing ideas, and trying to solve all the complex puzzles.'

'But didn't Ambleton say that you could always have the option of coming down and getting involved in cases now and then?'

'Yes, she did. But now and then isn't the same as every day now is it?'

'I know what you mean.'

'I'm beginning to think,' Burton ruminated, 'that maybe it's not such a good idea me taking on the DCI job.'

'What?' Fielding asked incredulously. 'Don't be stupid. It's a great honour to be offered such a prestigious position, and you're surely not going to pull out and let somebody else take it. Tell me you're not thinking that?'

'Well, I was consider-'

'No!' she cut in, 'you can't let that happen. It's a great career move and Ambleton *wants* you to have the position, to take over the role from her. Tell me you're not going to let her or yourself down. You just can't Joe!'

Burton sighed deeply. Being away from his long-term partner had affected him more than he realised over the past few days, more so now that they had finally started a relationship.

'Oh, forgive me Sally,' he said at last, 'it's just that it's all so new and different upstairs. You'd think the work would be the same, but it's not really; it's more administration than actual physical police work. Plus, I'm really missing you being there being with me during the day, that and our coffee trips. The ones from the machine just aren't the same.'

'I could put my arms around you just now,' Fielding smiled. 'But I won't, bearing in mind your blinds are all open!'

Burton laughed. At last, she'd managed to get him into a better frame of mind than he was a few moments beforehand.

'I don't think anyone would mind,' he joked. 'I know I certainly wouldn't!'

'On a more serious note,' Fielding continued, trying not to go ahead and do it. 'What about this press conference then; what exactly do I need to tell them and what do I not?'

CHAPTER
TWENTY-THREE

Although Burton's briefing was thorough, explaining what and what not to give away to the esteemed members of the press, Fielding still didn't feel confident going into the meeting. Not wanting to go it alone, she took Jack Summers along to the press conference with her as back-up. He seemed far more happier with the prospect than she did, and willingly went along without any objection whatsoever. She remembered that he'd once told her that he'd been into acting back in his youth, even having an audition with the prestigious London acting school, RADA, so perhaps he looked upon it as simply an on-stage appearance. Although she'd always loved English Literature and the theatre, she'd never wanted to get involved in productions, preferring to study and write about literary works rather than perform them. That option would have taken her way too far out of her comfort zone. Maybe that's why the thought of being on the public stage frightened her so much.

Even though Burton had told her exactly what to expect, Fielding felt completely overwhelmed by what she was confronted with as soon as she opened the door. She'd never been in the press room before, and certainly hadn't expected it to hold as many people as it did. All the memories of taking her sergeant's exam came flooding back to her again. Although passing it with higher-than-average marks, more than even she had hoped for or expected, the experience hadn't been a particularly pleasant one and the memory of it had lived with her for a long time. However, she was more than happy to see an unexpected presence in the room in the person of DCI Ambleton, who was already seated at the table. Burton hadn't mentioned she was coming in on this, but perhaps he didn't know she'd be in attendance. Was she going to lead, or would that all be left up to her, she wondered? As if sensing what she was feeling, and perhaps seeing her flinch as they entered, Summers whispered 'you'll be all right' in her ear as they moved towards their seats beside the DCI. If only she felt that positive. All she could do was to keep telling herself that it would be over soon, and to keep her wits about her when asked questions.

Once seated, the onslaught began. DCI Ambleton, in her own inimitable way, quickly quietened them then introduced Fielding to the throng. Burton had said that Ambleton could silence a room with a single stare, which Fielding could well believe to be the case, only this time, it was the firm verbal request of 'silence please'.

The first question had no bearing on the case whatsoever, as Fielding was asked why she was 'acting' Detective Inspector. After giving the DCI a sideways glance, and seeing that she nodded, she explained it in a brief sentence, hoping that the remainder of the reporters would ask specifically about the ongoing investigation. As all hands seemed to go in the air at once, Fielding picked out one from the third row.

'What leads, if any, do you have?' the young bearded man asked her.

'We are following a few at the moment, but I'm afraid that I cannot comment on them at this time.' Fielding felt a little better for having answer the first question, although she knew that her ordeal was far from being over.

The next person didn't wait to be selected and just went straight into it. 'And what about the notes found on the bodies; they're astrological symbols, aren't they?'

Fielding followed the voice and settled on a bespectacled middle-aged man with rosy cheeks. She was temporarily taken aback. Burton had always wondered how members of the press received their inside information. This one troubled her, as the symbols had not been released to the public.

Acting cautiously, she asked him where he'd obtained that information from.

'From a reliable source,' came the reply, 'and one I can't comment on.'

Touché, she thought, but it was worrying. Perhaps the jogger witness she'd seen by the canal had overcome his shock and contacted one of the local newspapers for financial reward, or maybe there'd been another witness who hadn't waited for the police to come and find the body? It had to be either one or the other, as how else would they have known about the symbols on the paper? What would Burton do in a situation like this, would he go along with it or would he just ask for the next question? Again, she looked to Ambleton, and again she nodded. Thank goodness she was there for her, to help her on the right way to proceed.

'I can confirm,' Fielding began, 'that there is a connection between the deaths and we are now asking for anyone with any information regarding the deaths of Harry York and Norman Bishop to come forward. Anyone who was near Mr York's place of business two days ago and might remember seeing something which looked out of place. Likewise, with the area around the Quays last night or this morning. If you've seen anybody looking suspicious, either standing, driving or running from the area quickly, we'd like you to come forward or contact your local police station.'

A woman from the front row was the next to speak up. 'The astrological symbols that you've mentioned, are they in any way related to how the victims died?'

Fielding felt like she was being grilled, and could feel herself begin to come out in a sweat. It was bad enough being the centre of attention and sitting in front of a large audience, but then it was made worse by having to answer questions from them as well She looked down at her clasped hands resting on the table; there were moisture beads on each of her fingers and thumbs. Ambleton must have also noticed her looking at them as she came to the rescue.

'I think that my team have said all that they can at this juncture. A statement will be released for you all this afternoon,' the DCI said beginning to rise from her seat. Taking her lead, Fielding and Summers did the same. When they were all upright and just about to turn to leave, one of the reporters shouted out a final question.

'And what about the poison?'

All three turned as one to face the voice. The other reporters in the room also swivelled around to face the person who had asked the question. A young girl, no more than twenty if Fielding's judgment was anything to go by, stood looking at them with a determined and resolute expression. She even stunned Ambleton, the die-hard veteran of the press conferences who could usually handle the most difficult of grillings. Poison had most definitely not been disclosed to anyone outside of either the mortuary or the police force, so how was it that this young girl who stood before them knew all about it?

'Can I ask you which newspaper you are from?' the DCI asked her, to which she replied that she was working freelance. This concerned Ambleton as it was usually only registered press officials who were invited to such conferences, and only allowed into the building on production of a press pass.

'And do you have a pass?' she continued.

'Yes, I do,' came the reply, to which she held something up in the air.

'May I see it please?'

All eyes were on the young girl as she approached the table, and there were a couple of camera flashes. Taking the card handed to her, Ambleton scrutinised it and found it to be a university student card with the girl's name and course on it.

'How did you get in with this?' a confounded DCI asked her, presuming that she'd quickly shown it as she followed the rest of the crowd into the room. She'd be sure to take this up with the person on duty who was supposed to be checking all the reporters' passes coming into the building. This was outrageous. The girl, Amanda Pearson, was a third year Journalism student and hardly a freelance reporter as she claimed. However, Ambleton was far more concerned as to how she specifically knew about the poison.

'I just showed it,' Pearson said with a smirk, instantly getting the DCI's back up.

'I think we need to have a further word with you about this. Summers,' Ambleton said turning to the DC, 'can you please escort Ms Pearson to one of our interview rooms.'

'Yes boss,' he said, taking hold of one of her arms and leading her away. Surprisingly, she went willingly.

However, her question had raised increased interest amongst the other members of the media, which prompted an onslaught of new and more invasive questioning. Ambleton instructed Fielding and Summers to remove the girl from the room while she stayed behind to inform them that reporting on this revelation was strictly forbidden. She even mentioned police action if any of them violated her strict order, which gave rise to shouts of 'what about freedom of the press' and 'you can't do that'. They were still calling out to her as she turned her back on them and headed for the door, but she'd said her piece and that was final. After the interview with the young Ms Pearson she'd also be having strong words with the police officer who was supposed to be checking the credentials of the press cavalcade when they arrived.

CHAPTER
TWENTY-FOUR

'You don't have the right to hold me here,' Amanda Pearson had been silent whilst being escorted from the press conference, but found her voice again when she was sitting across the table in the interview room.

'I believe I do,' Ambleton said firmly. 'Why did you say you were freelance?'

'I *am* freelance.'

'Hardly. You're a student, it says so on your university card,' Fielding reminded her.

'But I'm almost a fully qualified journalist.'

'Almost is not the same as actually being one, Amanda,' Ambleton reminded her. 'In fact, I'd call what you did fraud.'

'Okay, okay,' the girl said, finally dropping the façade. 'I did it as a credit towards my finals, all right? I thought that if I got a scoop then it could only be of benefit to my future career.'

'Be that as it may, but you shouldn't have been allowed into the conference room.'

Ambleton thought that for such a young girl she had guts, along with confidence and intuition. She'd make a good journalist with those attributes and the drive to succeed on her side. But she needed to refine her approach, and it didn't excuse her from the fact that she knew about the poison when nobody else had knowledge of it, apart from those who should know of course. She was keen to hear exactly how she was aware of it.

'Well, that's a funny thing,' Pearson began, 'I didn't hear about it; I was told by my mother's friend. She knew I was training to be a journalist, and thought it would be a good chance for me to get a foot up on the ladder, you know, get myself recognised.'

'Well you certainly did that,' Fielding said sarcastically, still annoyed by the way the whole press conference had gone. Although she'd had some difficult questions which she thought she'd managed to handle adequately under the circumstances, they were nothing by comparison to this girl's bombshell at the end. She'd timed it to have the most impact, and it worked. She wasn't sure what Ambleton had stayed behind to say, but she hoped that it was to remind the journalists that what they'd just heard was not to be printed under any circumstances.

'We'll need the name of your mother's friend,' Ambleton said.

'I'm not sure I can release my source-'

'Oh, do stop this, you're not a fully-fledged journalist yet you know!' Fielding flared out at the girl; her usual unflinching patience replaced by something akin to raw anger. 'And if you keep up this act, we can make sure you never will be.'

Ambleton looked towards her colleague with admiration, along with one raised eyebrow. Of course, the police didn't have the power to stop anyone pursuing their choice of career, but the threat to do so might make her stop and think. Unbeknown to Fielding, her own presence at the press conference was double-edged. Firstly, as it was her officer's first time before the press, she was there to support her; and secondly, and perhaps more importantly, she was there to assess her as part of the Inspector's practical exam. Burton had known but had been asked by Ambleton not to say anything, as she, and Burton too, believed it would distract her. He had felt bad not giving her the heads-up about it, as they didn't have any secrets from one another, but Ambleton had stressed the necessity to keep that to themselves – for Fielding's sake. The first time in front of the press was bad enough for her, but to also know that she was being marked for her performance wouldn't have been beneficial. In any case, the actual practical assessments were supposed to be unknown to the participant anyway.

Fielding wasn't sure where the outburst had come from, but it served its purpose as the girl's posture stiffened at the rebuff. She was probably not used to being told what to do; she looked to be that sort of person. Whereas Ambleton saw her having the potential to be an adequate journalist at some point in the future, Fielding just saw her as an arrogant spoilt brat who thought she knew everything about everything and deemed herself invincible. She remembered the type from her school days, the ones who believed themselves to be better than anybody else, always attention-seeking, always making those less confident feel inadequate. Truth was, had chips on their shoulders, and they'd take their anger out on others at school who were less able to stand up for themselves and were, in fact, out and out bullies.

When Amanda Pearson answered, she was less confident that before, and almost cowering. It appeared that Fielding's temporary aggression had paid off.

'My mother is on the Board of Governors at Thornton School, and it was the Head Teacher, Mrs Sinclair, who told her. One of the teachers there died, and another of the governors and-'

'All right, that's enough,' Fielding interjected. Not another connection. Everybody in this, the victims and the suspects, all seemed to be linked to one another. She'd never had another case quite like it. But the one common denominator in all this appeared to be Madame Ortiz, even the astrological signs on two of the bodies pointed towards her. But if she was being framed, what on earth was she being framed for, and why did someone think she deserved it?

***

Amanda Pearson was let off with a warning.

'You did very well back there,' Ambleton said to her smiling, as they walked to the lift after leaving the interview room. 'I sensed a new take on things?'

As Fielding took that to mean that she wasn't her normal self during the interview, she had to agree with her. The question was, should she apologise for that, or should she take it as a compliment? She decided to keep quiet about it.

But that didn't stop her launching into a rant about the young pretender.

'The girl got my back up, coming into the meeting like that. She blatantly gatecrashed, the attention-seeking bi-'

Ambleton cut her off before she could fully vent her anger on the girl. 'I wholeheartedly agree with you. Could it be that heading up the investigation has given you a whole different outlook?'

'It's different, I'll give you that.'

'Perhaps that's why you did it in a new way.'

Fielding knew that when she sat in with Burton when he was doing interviews she was more of an observer than overseer. She would, of course, ask questions when she had something to ask the interviewee, but she'd always leave it to him to lead the way. As acting DI on this case, and now senior investigating officer, it seemed that she'd naturally adapted to take over his role; although his outbursts were very few and far between, as his approach was one of calm, and perhaps more subtle, interrogation. Her explosion at the faux journalist was unexpected, even to her, although DCI Ambleton seemed to have liked the way she'd handled the situation.

'Do you mind if I come into the incident room to take a look at how things are going?' the DCI asked as they reached the lift doors, to which Fielding replied that she didn't mind in the slightest. In fact, she welcomed a new pair of eyes looking the board over.

'Joe tells me you've got more suspects than a whodunit crime novel.'

'He's not wrong there. I'll tell you what's odd, as well. It seems that everybody, both victims and suspects, are somehow linked to one another.'

Ambleton's brows furrowed; it was an unusual scenario, with not many cases having all the main players intersecting like that. Burton had already told her as much, but she wanted to see it for herself. She knew how much he missed being partnered with Fielding on this case, it was obvious from the way he'd discussed it. But, as far as she was concerned, both he and Fielding were managing very well with their new challenges.

Ambleton stood and carefully looked over the photos and information beneath them. Whoever had been working on it had now gone all-out and threaded red string to and from each link. There was more criss-crossing than she ever seen before on an incident board. Both Burton and Fielding were right; at least five people were connected in some way to one another. That in itself was unusual, with the odds stacked highly against it.

'And you say the common denominator seems to be this Madame Ortiz,' the DCI said to Fielding as she pointed to the promotional photograph of the astrologer taken from her website.

'She seems to be. Firstly, because Maria Turnbull had just visited her prior to her death. Secondly, there's the fact that Maria's friend Caroline Watkins is a solicitor who, along with Norman Bishop, Harry York, and possibly Maria Turnbull's husband, had a connection to her in the form of a tenancy agreement for the premises she operates out of.'

'Why John Turnbull?' Ambleton asked after quickly reading his notes.

'It's just a tentative thought, and we haven't checked it out yet, but he is an architect with a firm in the city, and we were wondering if he had anything to do with the building itself.'

'You mean like some kind of bribery, or corruption in high places even?'

'Still not sure, but maybe. Perhaps it involved one or two of them, and another found out.'

'Enough to get them all killed?' Ambleton pondered, sitting back on the edge of the desk behind her and crossing her arms while still staring at the array of victims and suspects in front of her.

'That's something we're busy working on.'

'So, what about forensic accounting; did they turn anything up?'

Fielding shook her head. 'Unfortunately not, so that idea fizzled out.'

'So, what's next?'

'Well, after I speak to the head teacher at Thornton School we'll see if John Turnbull's firm can either confirm or deny any link to Madame Ortiz or the building she's in.'

'Okay,' Ambleton said, rising from the desk. 'But let me ring the head teacher. I'd like to remind her of confidentiality breaches. It's all very well trying to help the daughter of a friend, but not when we're in the middle of murder enquiries and trying to keep what information we give to the press to a minimum.'

'Do you think we've done enough to deter young Amanda Pearson then?' Fielding was still concerned by the girl's cockiness and over self-confidence.

'I think *you* have,' Ambleton smiled. 'But, seriously, I hope this teaches her a very important lesson.'

'Which is?'

'That members of the press, or those intending to join them, don't have the freedom they think they have, at least not when it comes to murder enquiries.'

'Let's hope so.

CHAPTER
TWENTY-FIVE

L eaving her DCI to deal with Thornton School's head teacher by giving her a verbal castigation which, by the sound of it, she was going to enjoy, Fielding concentrated on making enquiries into John Turnbull's background. If she discovered that his firm was in some way connected to the building which was home to Madame Ortiz's business in the Northern Quarter, then it proved that he, too, was a credible suspect. But suspect to what? Could it simply be a case of back-handers between him, Caroline Watkins's firm of solicitors, local planner Norman Bishop, Harry York's estate agency and Madame Ortiz? It didn't appear to be too credible, killing three people for something like that, but Fielding knew that in her line of work people had killed for far less. So, as the survivors, the only real suspects in her mind were John Turnbull, Caroline Watkins and Madame Ortiz. But then again, why use a concentrated poison which Maria Turnbull took in a small dose tablet form, to kill the victims?

This was all going through her mind as she drove to John Turnbull's firm. Parking up in one of the visitor bays, once she was inside the building she was asked to sign in and given a badge to wear. She was then told that the office she wished to attend was on the fourth floor. Martin Scott had been informed of her arrival and would meet her from the lift. Fielding had no idea who Martin Scott was, or his designation, but got the impression that he may very well know why she was visiting.

The gentleman in question was already waiting by the lift doors on level four and welcomed her as she exited it. She took his outstretched hand; he had a firm, if slightly clammy grip, and Fielding took that to be down to the fact he was dressed in a three-piece suit and tie when the temperature outside must have been higher than the seasonal norm. Fielding disliked buildings such as these, the ones where you couldn't open a window, and the temperature control was artificially regulated by machines. They seemed to be hit and miss at the best of times. At least in the office where she and her team now worked, anyone could open a window when they wanted to, and the men would have their ties off and shirts rolled up to the elbows under conditions such as these.

Scott was a middle-aged man with thinning hair, which he appeared to be very conscious of. He had styled it into a neat comb over, but his valiant attempts to keep it there were proving unsuccessful, as strands of it were fighting for freedom from their placement. She fought back the temptation to suggest a hair spray to help him, or maybe just a barber to have the elongated strands cut off. As he led her into his office, she realised why he was feeling the heat so much. The corner office had two large picture windows on two sides of it, with a desk directly in front of one of them. And despite the fitted vertical blinds on both, they didn't prevent the glorious June sunshine still pouring in through the partly-opened slats. They would defeat anyone in this heat, herself included if she had to stay in the room for any length of time.

'Please sit down,' he said, sitting himself and indicating Fielding take the chair in front of his desk.

She felt like saying take your jacket off, but it remained firmly on his back. Chances were it was stuck onto him like a piece of discarded chewing gum on the sole of a shoe.

'I imagine this is about poor John Turnbull?' he asked astutely, clenching his chubby fingers together on the desk. 'Dreadful news about his wife, dreadful. They'd only been married a short time too.'

'Yes, it is,' Fielding confirmed his assumption. 'Just how long had they been married?'

'Oh, let me think,' he began, leaning back in his chair, 'it must be, what, seven, eight months now. No time at all, really.'

'No, it isn't,' she agreed. 'And what is John's position in the firm exactly?'

'John's one of our best architects; he actually helped us win one of our finest awards last year.'

'My sister is an interior designer, and I know that she does work with architects, but talk me through, if you could, what an average day for him would be.'

'Ah! Does your sister work here in Manchester?'

'No, she's from the North East, although she does quite a bit of work around the country, London and the South in particular.'

'I see, I see. What's a typical day for John? Well, apart from drawing up designs and plans, he also goes out to potential and existing sites to see how we can either develop or improve upon them. He works very closely with surveyors from both the council and private building companies.'

'And would he have worked upon any buildings in the Northern Quarter?'

Scott laughed. 'I think every architectural practice in the city has! It's been such a huge development, and good for the business as a whole. Yes, he will have been involved with a few, most certainly. I can get someone in to help with this, you know, get records and the like, if there's something in particular you're looking for?'

'That might be a good idea, yes.'

Scott leaned forward again. 'If you don't mind, can you tell me why you're asking about this; I thought that you'd perhaps just come to ask about John as the person and not the work he's doing?'

'I'm just interested in one particular property on Portland Street, so if he's had anything to do with that area then I'd be grateful for any information on it.'

'Of course,' he said, picking up his telephone and dialling. 'I'll get one of the admin assistants to come in to help out.'

From the information provided Fielding discovered that John Turnbull had been instrumental in developing most of the Portland Street offices and, much to her delight, had also worked on the block Madam Ortiz's business premises was situated.

'This one here,' Fielding said, pointing to the astrologer's number on the schedule. 'Do you hold any further information on it like, say, who moved into it and who handled the legal work? Or perhaps your firm is only involved with the design and doesn't hold that kind of information?'

Scott leaned in to take a look before picking up the receiver again and instructed the person on the other end to retrieve the required documentation.

'Yes, we do hold that, simply as an extension of the work we do. If we didn't, the company feels that it's like leaving the job half-finished.'

'I understand.' Fielding was grateful; she hadn't expected the company to be this efficient. But, as Scott said, you can't leave a job half-done; it was something she wholeheartedly agreed with.

When a further document arrived, she scrutinised it carefully, looking for any suggestion that John Turnbull had met or had dealings with Madame Ortiz, either in person or on paper. As she now knew that Caroline Watkins, Harry York and Norman Bishop had, so to find out that John also had a connection would put him on the list of suspects. And found it she did, clearly there in black and white. John Turnbull had met with Madame Ortiz prior to her taking the tenancy to discuss the actual function of the business.

CHAPTER
TWENTY-SIX

Thanking Martin Scott for all his help, Fielding left the offices of Durning and Tate happy in the knowledge that she had fulfilled her purpose of going there. However, she now had to contend with another name to add to the list of possible suspects. It was, though, still unclear how the three people *were* linked, other than the fact that they were all connected to the victims via work and in John Turnbull's case, through marriage. That one didn't really need an explanation. The work itself all seemed above board, but there must be something under the surface that she and the rest of the team were missing. She would have to ask them to delve even more deeply into their backgrounds.

On arriving back at the station, Fielding found that profiler Louise Simmons was the and looking at the board. It was a great relief, as what she needed now was someone with her credentials to take a good long look at this from a psychologist's point of view. After giving the team instructions as to how to proceed next, she took Louise into Burton's office to discuss the case with her.

'I hope you don't mind both DCI Ambleton and Phillipa filling me in on this,' Louise said on sitting down and opening up her briefcase.

'No, of course not, I'm glad that they did. So, now that you've had a chance to look at it, what's your initial take on it all?'

Simmons put a notebook on the desk and opened it up. Fielding saw the first page filled with comments and additional asides.

'Well, I have to confess it's an odd one.'

'Tell me about it,' Fielding laughed, having already come to the same conclusion.

'For one thing, there are far too many suspects.'

'We now have that whittled down to three: John Turnbull, Caroline Watkins and Madame Ortiz.'

'Even so,' Simmons continued, that's still too many for my liking. And the victims, they are all oddly connected.'

'So, what would someone's motive be; what would the killer get out of this?'

'This is something that's bothering me. As you yourself have concluded, everything is being directed to Madame Ortiz – for example, the astrological symbols left beside the body, apart from the first victim that is. I concur that there wasn't one left because she wasn't alone when she died, by the way.'

'But then there's the poison.'

'Ah, yes, the poison. It was found on all three victims, isn't that right?'

'Yes.'

'But each were killed in a different manner, so that again appears to be a misdirection.'

Fielding admitted that it had her confounded. 'You know, this is my first senior investigating officer case, and I don't feel it's going at all well.'

'I really wouldn't worry about that,' Simmons comforted her, 'this one's got me puzzled too, and I'm a trained psychologist. It's usually quite easy to see motives and intentions in the way people behave, and in the way they kill, but this one is a lot more difficult to work out than most. As you know, because we have discussed this before in a previous case, people kill for a variety of reasons. Mental illness has often been touted as the primary cause, but I, like most psychologists, dismiss it in all but a handful of cases. It's only really been proven to be the case when someone has been receiving psychiatric treatment. The more common motives to kill are for gratification, for personal revenge, monetary gain, or simply to silence someone who is going to reveal a hidden secret – such as committing fraud or adultery. Basic, yes, but they are the most prominent motives. The reasons behind the motives are the ones which need to be discovered though. A killer may lack morals and a sense of conscience, thereby having no compunction about taking a life in order to get what they want. Often how they kill explains why they kill. In most cases there is a thought-out plan; multiple murderers rarely kill without reason. What we need to find here is the reason for the deaths and, as I say, this is harder to work out than usual.'

'I was thinking on the lines of something underhanded going on regarding Madame Ortiz's business premises, as two of the victims had clear links to that.'

Louise shook her head. 'I can see that being a clear possibility, but I'd say you're looking for something other than that. Just put my reasoning down to experience, if you like, rather than evidence direction. If it was that, then it would make the poisoning illogical. No, this is something more personal to the killer than a dodgy business deal.'

The last statement made Fielding sit back and think. Perhaps that was why she was thinking something was off with her reasoning. She was looking at it being linked to the business, but could it be something as simple as what Louise was suggesting? Sometimes the simplest possibility was the correct one.

'Occam's razor?' Fielding suggested, which made Louise look at her in something akin to respect. That wasn't a term she usually came across outside of her profession.

'Ah, I'm impressed; a student of philosophy, I see.'

'No, not really, it's just that I know what the principle of it is. Say there are two possible explanations for an occurrence. The one that requires the smallest number of assumptions is usually the correct one. So, in layman's terms, the simplest answer is most likely the correct one.'

'Very true. In that case, you need to look for the simplest thing that links all these people, the suspects and the victims. Just look at what the signs are telling you.'

As Fielding thanked her for her input, the psychologist then said something to make her reconsider what she knew so far.

'Of course, there is always another option you could bear in mind,' she added.

'Which is?'

'Sometimes multiple murders take place to mask the killer's real intention.'

'Meaning what?'

'That only one person was the real target here, and the others were simply collateral damage.'

Burton and Fielding had experienced a couple of cases over the years when this had indeed been the case, but then, as she reminded Louise, none of the victims in those ones had known one another and had been randomly chosen.

'Then I'd say that the killer is someone who is clever enough to realise this and include victims who *do* know one another, and then, very importantly, have the control and calmness to carry it out. This is, of course, all conjecture, you realise, as I'm just throwing out possibilities here.'

'But it is interesting, and something to bear in mind. So, do you think that if it were the case, the killer would need to be highly intelligent then?'

'It's possible, but then, what drives a person to kill? It could be for the simplest of reasons but they themselves make it more convoluted.'

'One of our suspects could be putting on a very clever act then?'

'It is possible.'

At the end of their meeting, Louise had to go back to the university, but told Fielding not to hesitate to get in touch as and when she needed her. After her departure, Sally began to again go over all the facts they knew so far. Hopefully, when the members of the team returned from their assignments, she'd have more to add to them. But for the time being, she left Burton's office and sat down at her desk and looked over her own personal sheet before finally going over to examine the board.

She was still studying it when the phone rang on the desk next to her. Picking it up, she announced herself and then listened to what the person had to say. At first, she thought she'd misheard what was being said, but then realised that she hadn't. She was deep in thought as she put the phone down, and almost missed Joe Burton's arrival into the office.

'You look like you've just had some bad news,' he said, which startled her to the point that she physically jumped in her seat. 'Oh, Sally I'm sorry, what is it?' he continued seeing her unexpected reaction.

'There's been another death.'

'Same as the others?' He pulled out a seat from the neighbouring desk and slid it over towards her then sat on it.

'Yes, and no.'

'Very cryptic. How yes, and how no?'

There was a symbol left on the body, but I hear it's a bit different.'

'In what way different?'

'I don't know yet. I've just had a call from Robert Mansfield who's at the scene, that's why he just called me. He says it's similar, but not quite the same as the others. He wants me to go down there.'

'And the victim, is it someone we know?' Burton asked, getting up from the seat he'd just sat on, fully intending to go with her now that he was free for the rest of the day.

'Again, yes and no.'

Burton frowned; she wasn't making any sense. 'You've got me confused,' he said to her. Although he'd been away from the team for a day or two now, he had an idea of how things were going thanks to DCI Ambleton's now regular briefings. She'd also said that Fielding was handling things well which, for a complicated first case such as this, was high praise indeed. And it was a complicated case, that was for sure. It had been on his mind all the while he'd been learning the DCI ropes away from the team, and he was very torn between wanting to take over the role, which was his dream, and wanting to remain with them as their DI.

'Are you free for the rest of the day?' Fielding asked him, also arising from her seat and grabbing her bag.

Burton nodded.

'Then I'll tell you on the way.

CHAPTER
TWENTY-SEVEN

'You have got to be kidding!' Joe Burton looked at Fielding while she was driving.

'I'm afraid I'm not,' she replied, keeping her eyes on the road ahead but casting him a quick glance as she said it.

'So where does she fit into all this?'

'That's a very good question, Joe, and all I can think is that she saw something that she shouldn't have. In fact, this has only made things more complicated as far as I'm concerned. By the way, Louise Simmons came into the office earlier.'

'Oh, and what did she have to say; was she helpful at all?'

'I think she's as puzzled as we are, but she did conclude that we look at what the signs are telling us.'

'Meaning?'

'That perhaps the simplest answer is the correct one.'

'You brought up Occam's razor, didn't you?' He asked, grinning.

Fielding laughed. Joe knew her so well. The whole concept had caught her attention a long time ago after hearing about it and not knowing what it meant, and since that time she had found it helpful on more than one occasion. It was deduction at its most basic, but had proved correct time and time again despite murderers' attempts at distraction to throw them off the scent.

'I'll tell you what else she said,' Fielding added. 'She raised a very valid point in that all the killings could be hiding the fact that only one was the true victim and the rest were merely collateral damage.'

'Now that's interesting, and something we should probably bear in mind.'

Fielding stopped the car in the side street outside the latest victim's house, right behind the SOCO unit's van. A few people had started to accumulate, speculating what was going on but perhaps already suspecting the worst if the large police presence was anything to go by. Death always gathered an inquisitive crowd of people around it.

'But I thought that one of the DCs had and interviewed all the staff following Harry York's death?'

'Yes, Phillipa had, but she also said that there was somebody off that day for a week's holiday. As this lady's name wasn't on the list of the interviewees, I'm assuming that it's her.'

'So, who found her?'

'I don't know yet. All Robert Mansfield said about it was that there was a sign left on the body but it was different, and the address where I should meet him.'

Burton laughed. 'Mansfield enjoys his little mysteries; I think he secretly fancies himself as a detective!'

'Apparently, he's very fond of reading crime fiction novels.'

'Is he, and how do you know that little gem?' Although having known the man for many years, that fact was something he hadn't known about him.

'It was when Summers and I attended the autopsy the other day. He was speculating about how bodies ended up on his table and he confessed as much to us. So, you see, you're right, I'm sure he'd be happy tagging along as a DS!'

Getting out of the car, Burton and Fielding walked towards the terraced house which had been the home of Valerie Wilton. A uniformed officer stood at the gate with a clipboard, and as the two detectives approached, he asked for their names then wrote them down before allowing them to enter the premises. The front door was open, and as Burton entered, he looked on the inside of it and noticed that the security chain had been broken with only a few links remaining on the retainer. A forced entry then, most likely indicating that Ms Wilton did not know the person who had broken in. Once inside, the ground floor was a hubbub of activity, with white Tyvek-clad SOC officers collecting whatever evidence they deemed was of importance to the investigation. From the look of it there'd been a scuffle, with a canvas wall print lying on the floor sporting a long tear diagonally across it, and there were traces of blood on the living room door frame and on the stair banister. Burton stopped one of the people working and asked where Doctor Mansfield was, and was told that he was upstairs in the bedroom with the victim. Thanking him, they made their way to the scene of the crime.

'Ah, Joe, we meet again. I would say that it's nice to see you so soon after the last time, but we always meet in such dire circumstances, don't we?' Mansfield said in his own inimitable way when he saw them enter.

'Indeed. Death doesn't get any better, I'm sorry to say.'

The doctor then turned towards Fielding and bowed ever so slightly in a gentlemanly way. 'Always a pleasure detective.'

Mansfield stood back from the body to let them take a look. A colourful long scarf was crudely tied around Valerie Wilton's eyes, with the loose knot dangling to one side of her face.

'Strangulation?' Burton asked, noting the red mark around the woman's neck. 'Manual or with a ligature do you think?' He seemed to have taken the lead with the questioning, forgetting that Fielding was now actually in charge of the case. However, she didn't mind in the slightest, and was actually pleased that he'd slipped into his familiar role once again. So, she let him carry on regardless.

'Yes to the strangulation,' Mansfield nodded, 'the mark left on her neck would be enough to indicate that as cause of death, and she also has broken blood vessels in the eyes which make it a certainty. Unsure as yet as to whether the killer did it with their hands or they used the scarf, but it can be tested to see if there are any of her cells on it. I left it on for you to see, but I did check her eyes by lifting it up prior to your arrival.'

Now able to remove the scarf, Mansfield did so and opened it out fully in order to examine it before adding it to one of his bags. Fielding glanced at the victim's face and the two glazed red eyes which stared back at her. At first glance, she'd not have thought this to be connected in any way to the other deaths, but there again the doctor had mentioned the sign on the body, so she brought it up.

'You mentioned that another sign had been found?' she began, still staring at the lifeless features of the victim, at which point Mansfield reached across to retrieve a transparent pouch from his medical case and handed it to her.

'You see,' he said, 'it's similar, but not the same.'

She took it from him and Burton leaned in to take a look. The doctor was correct. The other two symbols were definitely astrological ones as they subsequently found out by printing off a list of them, and looked like they'd been made by the same hand. There was a definite similarity in the way they'd been drawn. This one, however, was different in that it wasn't a specific sign but a representation of one in the form of a pair of scales. Fielding immediately knew what it represented: Libra.

'The scales of justice,' she muttered to herself, and Burton picked up on it.

'You mean as in the legal system or a court?'

'Yes, just like that.'

'So, what's the killer trying to say here? If it's not the same could it be a copycat killer perhaps?'

'Mmmm,' Fielding murmured without answering Burton's question, still looking at the slip of paper in her hand. 'You know, I think that this deliberately drawing our attention to Caroline Watkins. She's a solicitor, isn't she?'

'Putting the attention on her you mean by making her a key suspect? But why do that, it doesn't make sense?'

'None of this makes sense, Joe.' Fielding handed the polybag back to Mansfield. 'And what about the blood downstairs, doctor? Is it the victim's or could it be the killer's?'

'The victim has some blood under her nails here,' he lifted up her right hand, which had been carefully encased in another polybag, 'so I'll check it when I get her back to the morgue. Apart from that, she has some bruising but no visible cuts, so chances are this could very well be the blood of whoever attacked her.'

'That's good,' Fielding thanked him. 'And another thing, can you check for any digitalis either on her or in her system. I can't see that there will be as judging by downstairs the killer must have broken in while she was answering the door, so there wouldn't be either opportunity or need to administer it before strangling her.'

'So, whoever's done this has led us directly to Caroline Watkins.' Burton's remark held true. The astrological sign, albeit different to the ones left of the other victims, clearly linked it to the other cases. Apart from that, the murder could have easily been carried out by a completely different killer.

Fielding nodded before asking Mansfield a final question. 'Do you think this was done by a man or a woman doctor?'

'In my professional opinion, detective, I'd say a man. I think it would take some force to strangle someone, whether that be with the bare hands or with an aid such as a scarf. The same applies to the front door. It looks like it's been kicked in, and with a force hard enough to break the chain. If it had been a woman, then I think you're looking for someone with extraordinary strength, and I'm not trying to cast aspersions on the female gender you understand.'

'No, I get it,' Fielding assured him, 'and I completely agree with you on that assumption. I would have thought the same.'

'Although,' Burton added thoughtfully, 'if she had been subdued by poisoning it would have made it easier for a woman to kill her, wouldn't it?'

'But the scuffle downstairs; it implies initial force,' the doctor reminded him.

'I know, but we did consider that Norman Bishop may have been killed by two people.'

Fielding looked towards Burton. He'd been away from the case but, thanks to Ambleton, he seemed to be well up-to-date on it.

'Ambleton's prepped you well,' she said with a smile.

'Just wanted to keep up with what was happening with my team. She volunteered, so I listened to what she had to say.'

'You know, we won't be your team when she retires,' she reminded him.

'You'll always be my team!'

As their eyes lingered on each other for longer than they perhaps should have, Doctor Mansfield intervened and said that he'd arrange for the body to be removed and taken to the morgue for an autopsy, primarily to check for the poison. He was fully aware of their new dynamic as a couple and decided to hurry things along so as to not embarrass them when they saw he was watching.

'We also found this,' Masefield said, cutting short the moment the detectives were evidently having. He held up another polybag, this time containing what looked like a piece of torn fabric.

'Where was this?' Burton asked, holding it up and examining it.

'It was lying on the floor inside the front door. I'm thinking that it maybe got caught on the handle and was torn off when the door was forced open.'

Fielding looked at the bag's contents too. It looked like a piece of green material, polyester perhaps. 'Is that not a piece of the scarf?' she asked the doctor.

'No. I was thinking the same, but I checked it for any tears when I just took it off her; it's undamaged.'

'You'll both be attending the autopsy then?' Masefield asked when Burton handed him back the bag and he slipped it into his case. It was more of a statement than a question, but Fielding was more than delighted when Burton said that they both would be. Even though she thoroughly detested them, the fact that she'd attended several over the past few days seemed to somehow ease it a bit.

'I'll see you both in an hour's time then.'

CHAPTER
TWENTY-EIGHT

While Fielding and Burton were visiting the scene of crime for the latest victim, DCs Francis, Preston, Simmons and Banks were fulfilling their own instructions. Banks was still reviewing the CCTV, but Fielding had asked the others to re-visit the suspects and interview them further, specifically regarding their whereabouts at the time of the murders. After visiting the scene of their latest victim, Valerie Wilton, she had telephoned Phillipa Preston and asked her if she could have a word with her psychologist girlfriend Louise that evening regarding crimes committed by two people. Fielding knew from her own forensic profiling courses that serial killer double-acts were not as marked as sole murderers, but they did exist, notably in the form of the American duo, Bianchi and Buono, and of course the UK's Fred and

Rosemary West. She was very interested in knowing the reasons why two people would jointly kill, as the concept was now fixed in her head following Norman Bishop's death.

DC Jane Francis was the first to report back in. Assigned to look into Caroline Watkins's background a bit deeper, she'd spoken to her friends about her in order to get a more objective view.

'I spoke to both separately, as I know you interviewed them together in a group,' the DC said to Burton and Fielding. 'I went to see Selina Douglas first. She told me what we already knew, in that the night out was Caroline's idea; nobody knew anything about it until she'd announced it when they were all together at Maria's house.'

'How do all of them know one other?' asked Fielding. 'I know that Selina and Barbara work together, but did you find out where they all initially met?'

'It seems they know one another from school. They kept in touch when they all went off to different universities, and connected again in person when they all returned back to work in Manchester.'

'What about husbands or partners?' Burton joined in with the conversation. 'Did you ask about them?'

'Selina is single, and I got the impression that she isn't really looking for anyone at the moment. But she did tell me that Madame Ortiz read the Tarot cards for her and told her she'd be married within the year. At first, she was a bit excited by the prediction, but then after talking about it with the others realised that it was very unlikely bearing in mind that she isn't actually going out with anybody.

When I asked her about Caroline, she says that, although they've known one another a very long time she's often reluctant to share the way girlfriends often do. She might have a boyfriend, but she might not. She wasn't really sure as Caroline doesn't talk much about her private life. She'll talk about work, and everyday things, but when it comes to things she doesn't want to tell about herself, she simply won't. Selina certainly didn't like the joke she'd played on Maria, when she made out that she'd heard bad news, saying it was cruel. Caroline apparently knew that Maria didn't really like things like astrology or fortune telling, yet she went ahead and booked it for all of them anyway.'

'It sounds like there was some friction there. Jealous of her friend being married before her, perhaps?' Burton speculated.

'Whatever it was,' Francis continued, 'Selina said that Barbara was particularly upset at Caroline's actions and got into an argument with her about it.'

'Yes, we noticed when we interviewed them that she took over and made herself the spokesperson,' Fielding recalled. 'Even her boss at the law practice said as much about her. Good worker, though, he told me.'

Simon Banks then informed them that he'd finished looking through the CCTV footage for the time Harry York had died.

'Unfortunately,' he said to them, 'there aren't any cameras at the rear of the building, but I've managed to see who I think is our latest victim coming out of a side street a block away.'

'Let's take a look at that,' Burton said, rising from his seat and walking over to Banks's desk. Fielding and Francis followed him.

All three stood behind Banks as he re-ran the video. The quality was far superior to what they'd hitherto seen in CCTV surveillance footage.

'Have they upgraded their systems or something?' Burton asked nobody in particular, eyes still on the monitor.

As they watched they saw their latest victim, Valerie Wilton, exiting from the alley in a hurry; it was about five businesses from York's estate agency. She then looked both ways before turning left and rushing away. Simon Banks froze the image there.

'So, she must have seen the killer?' he observed, quite rightly in Burton's opinion.

'And the killer must have also seen her and followed her.' Francis offered.

'But what about the bow; didn't we say that someone carrying one would have been spotted?' Fielding added.

'Then perhaps there was an accomplice, who followed Valerie while the archer either got rid of the bow or took it with them.'

'Should we check the back of the alley then boss?' Banks asked, and Burton thought that to be a good idea.

'I don't really think that they would have left the weapon behind for two reasons: one, it would have been spotted before now, and two, why leave it when you've just killed somebody with it? But there could very well be something there that they dropped accidentally. Yes, you and Jane head off there and see what turns up, will you? But before you go, start the CCTV up again and let's see if anyone followed her.'

Banks stayed on the camera fixed on the same spot. There was nothing for a few moments, and Burton was just about to tell him to call it a day, then they all saw a second figure emerging from the same alley.

'Stop it right there!' Burton called out and approached the monitor. He pointed his finger at the person, touching the screen as he did so. 'Can you enlarge this?'

As Banks zoomed in and cleared up the picture, none of them could believe what they were seeing. They couldn't make out the person's face, but it was their clothing that surprised them.

'It's not RAG week, is it?' Fielding asked, astonished at what she and the others were looking at. Both DCs informed her that it was not. 'Then what-'

'Isn't that a Royal Mail bag?' Burton interrupted, closely scrutinising the person's sack slung over their shoulder.

As Banks zoomed in even closer, the DI's supposition was confirmed; there was no doubting the clear and recognisable logo on it. But it wasn't just the mail sack that caught their eye. What concerned them more was the fact that whoever the person was, they were in full fancy dress and carrying a large bow.

***

'If that's a Royal Mail post person, then why is he dressed up like that? Who is he supposed to be anyway ... Robin Hood?' DC Francis surmised.

'So that's why nobody thought anything of it,' Fielding murmured. 'Harry York's killer didn't escape by car; they simply followed the person who'd witnessed it home. And that person appeared to be a postal worker. The piece of material that was found at Valerie Wilton's home must have come from that costume.'

'Banks, get onto the Royal Mail and see if any of their deliverers in central Manchester are wearing fancy dress for some unknown reason, will you?'

Taking Fielding to one side, Burton again apologised to her. 'I can't help it,' he said to her. 'Seven years as DI and I still think I'm heading up the case when I'm not.'

'It's okay, don't worry about it,' she reassured him, 'I'm not complaining in the slightest.'

'I know but-'

'Listen, I'm glad of the help right now; I feel like I'm failing.'

'You're certainly not doing that.' Burton so wanted to tell her about the sergeant's practical exam but couldn't as he was sworn to secrecy. He felt sure it would have helped her right at that moment.

Despite his words of comfort, Fielding felt otherwise, so decided to change the subject – well, not entirely, as it was still about the case.

'What do we think about this latest development? I don't for one moment believe that a postal worker is the killer.'

'Me neither, but I thought it best for Simon to check with the company. Anyone can copy a logo and stick it on a bag; it wouldn't be a hard thing to do.'

'That particular costume was carefully thought out, bearing in mind the symbol found on the body. It would also solve the problem of what to do with a bow simply by hiding it in plain sight. I wonder if the costume was hired; we could check local fancy dress suppliers to see if there were any recent rentals.'

'I could get one of the team onto that, or I could check it out if you like?' It was an offer Fielding couldn't refuse. It was great to have him back, albeit it only temporary. 'Have you heard back from Simmons yet; wasn't he checking out Norman Bishop's hotel?'

'No, not as yet. I asked him to take someone from SOCO with him to give the room a good going over.'

'The only problem I can see with that being the crime scene is, if Bishop was killed in his hotel room, then how did the murderer get him out of there? That's the only thing I'm having trouble with.'

'I agree,' Fielding nodded, 'but if they've planned ahead, then they must have accounted for all possibilities. Incidentally, what do you make of Louise's idea that the killer is killing multiple times to cover up the fact that only one person was the intended victim?'

'I'd say that's a distinct possibility,' he replied quickly, not needing to even consider it. 'If we're going to think on those lines, who would you say would be the intended target?'

'I'd say our first victim, Maria Turnbull.'

'For what reason?'

'I don't know, just a hunch,' Fielding said.

'Oh, so, *you're* going with hunches now!'

'I learned from the best,' she said graciously. 'Seriously though, despite the myriad of connections between all the others, I believe her to be the killer's main target. Maybe because there wasn't a sign left at the scene, maybe because she was the first victim, I just don't know. That's why I'm putting it down as a hunch.'

'We explained away the reason for there not being a sign left, so I just don't know with this one. Maria Turnbull seems to be the odd one out, that's all.'

'Exactly, and for that reason I think she's central to it all.'

Burton still wasn't sure, and Fielding knew that was unusual for him. His hunches were usually the basis for any, if not all, of his enquiries, so perhaps his mind was elsewhere on shadowing DCI Ambleton and his future role.

CHAPTER
TWENTY-NINE

Heaton Park is a magnificent 600-acre municipal area a few miles north of Manchester's city centre. Apart from the woodland area, the park boasts a wealth of outdoor attractions to cater for virtually every interest and age group. There's an 18-hole golf course and bowling green, as well as an observatory, a boating lake and an animal farm. It has just about everything anyone would want in order to escape from the hustle and bustle of busy northern city life, and temporarily imagine themselves in the heart of the countryside. For that reason, it is a very popular and well patronised spot in the summer months.

As dawn rose on what promised to be another warm, sunny day, the park's first influx of visitors began to arrive. The early morning sunshine brought with it the daily collection of pre-work joggers and early morning dog-walkers who normally appear on the scene long before anyone else, out there to exercising themselves, their pets, or, in some cases, both. It is also a favoured haunt of Sally Fielding who, having recently taken up jogging again simply to utilise the pair of trainers she'd bought on a whim, can be found here running up a sweat in rare moments of free time.

One such dog-walker out for early exercise was Mrs Mary Jones and her faithful Labrador, Mr Jinx. Having lost her husband some five years' previously, she acquired the rescue dog for companionship shortly afterwards, and their daily pattern was once around the boating lake and back home again via the ornamental gardens. Over the years she'd become a recognisable sight to other dog-walkers who walked the same route as she did, and they would wave to one another when seen in the distance. Mr Jinx was a placid dog, never barking at other dogs or trying to break free of his leash, and would happily and most loyally trot along at his owner's side. So, when he suddenly began acting strangely on this particular morning, Mary Jones was concerned. Looking around her, she couldn't see anything that could have sparked him wanting to suddenly break away and change his five-year spell of even-temperedness.

'What is it boy?' she looked down and asked him, not expecting a reply; but he kept barking and trying to pull away from her.

Going from five years of being impeccably well-behaved to this told her that there must be a strong reason for him wanting to do so, so she loosened the taut leash slightly and let him lead her in the direction of what was troubling him. His exuberance led them in the direction of the magnificent Old Town Hall Colonnade. The original Town Hall had been on King Street in the city centre; but the façade of the building, consisting of four Ionian columns set between two main turret-like sections, had been saved and moved to its new location in the park when the building was demolished in 1902. The Greek-style architecture, popularised in ancient Rome, set a new trend in architectural design which flourished over the centuries, and the Folly stands today in remembrance of that magnificent building and influential era.

When they reached the structure, the barking now turned to sniffing, and Jinx started at one end of the Folly and then moved around to the rear of it, muzzle down and dragging poor Mary with him. She was intrigued and curious as to what he could sense, especially as she could see nothing that could have possibly aroused this sudden interest.

'I don't know what's got you so worked up, Jinxy,' she said to him, but it was then that he started clawing at the ground. Deeper and deeper he went, taking off a clump of loose grass in the process.

'You'll get me in trouble, boy,' she declared, looking around to make sure there wasn't a park keeper patrolling the grounds.

Eventually finding what had brought him there, he sat down and cocked his head at his owner, tongue out and panting, with saliva drooling from his mouth from all the effort. It was as if he was urging her to look at what he'd found. Taking the hint, Mary moved forward and looked down at the ground; there was a clear polythene bag in the hole with something inside of it. Still holding onto Jinx's leash, she bent forward and worked it loose. His claws had caught on part of the bag while he was uncovering it and had torn a section open, revealing what was inside.

'Now what's that doing here?' she said to her pet as she looked at its contents. What she saw appeared to be a fancy-dress outfit, which she was just about to put back in the ground, but then noticed something peculiar about it. It could have easily been ketchup, or paint even, but something inside her told her that it was not, especially as it had been so carefully hidden.

'Is that blood, Jinx?' she murmured, to which Jinx responded with a bark.

***

On the walk home, Mary Jones racked her brains trying to think where the nearest police station to her home was, but realised that she didn't know. It made her wonder if, in fact, she'd ever known, and decided it to be highly unlikely. She did know, however, that if there was ever any reason to get in touch with the police, the best number to get them on was the 101 non-emergency number. So that was what she would do. She'd kept the item Mr Jinx had found in the park, and now felt it her civic duty to go and hand it in in person. As soon as she got back home, she let Jinx off his leash. As he lumbered dehydrated to the kitchen for a drink of water, she picked up the landline phone and dialled the police.

'My dog's found an item of clothing hidden in the park and I think it might have blood on it,' she began when connected, 'I think I should hand it in somewhere.'

The friendly girl who answered asked her for her postcode, and after a few moments told her that her nearest station was Harpurhey Police Station, which was on Upper Conran Street.

'Do you know where that is?' the advisor asked.

'Yes, I do,' Mary replied. 'I know the shopping centre, so I imagine it's not too far from there.'

'If you're driving, you need to go along Moston Lane, and the building is on the corner when you turn into Upper Conran Street.'

'Ah, that's probably why I didn't know it was there; I usually come in from the other end.'

'Is there anything else I can help you with?' the girl asked to which Mary replied that there wasn't. She thanked her for her help and ended the call.

Telling her dog that she was having to go out for a while, he sat and watched her with droplets of water still dripping from his mouth as she gathered up the package and her car keys and headed for the front door.

CHAPTER THIRTY

Mary found the police station without any difficulty, and parked in one of the visitor spaces next to the main entrance. She wasn't sure whether or not she should have worn gloves when bringing the package in, but then thought not as she'd already handled it. It made her wonder if they'd take her fingerprints to eliminate her from their enquiries. It was a term she'd often heard on TV crime dramas. But then again, the red stain may have only been what she'd first thought it to be, either ketchup or paint. She'd feel a bit stupid if it turned out to be the case. But the words of her late husband filled her head, 'better safe than sorry'; it was a motto of his, one he'd lived by, and it hadn't served him wrong. Even when he'd gone for a check-up after feeling a bit weaker than usual following a bout of the 'flu, he'd said his favourite words then. Little did he know that the illness he'd developed had already taken a firm hold and overwhelmed him. He died four months later.

Explaining to the sergeant on the main reception desk what she'd found, he took the package from her and asked her to take a seat, saying one of his colleagues would be along shortly to interview her. When a young man arrived, he took her into a private room off to the side. As he asked her a series of questions, he filled in the form he'd brought in with him. Had she seen the person who had left it there? What was she doing there so early in the morning? And other questions like that.

'Will you need to take my fingerprints?' she asked at one point, and he said that he would. She was waiting for the infamous words, but he just said it was to check with any prints they found on the bag or its contents.

'It was my dog who found it; do you need his prints too?' she joked, but the deadpan expression and response told her that it wasn't necessary. She felt silly, attempting a bit of humour at this point, but that was the sort of person she was. To her, humour always made a situation less serious, took the edge off, but it seemed that the young man wasn't having any of it. She decided not to try to make such a foolhardy remark again.

At the end of his questioning he asked her to read his report over and then sign it at the bottom where he'd placed a small 'x'.

'So, what happens now? Mary asked while signing it, and was told that it would be examined and further action would be taken if necessary. He went on to thank her for her diligence, and bringing the matter to their immediate attention. She felt as if it was a standardised reply in such circumstances.

'I don't need to do anything else, then?' she asked.

'No,' came the reply. And that was that.

When she returned home she felt a bit deflated by the whole thing. She knew that she had to hand it in, of course she did, but it didn't feel like any kind of achievement to her. She needed to know more about it, who had left it there, and why they were hiding it. So, when she turned on the television that evening, just as she was having something to eat, she was astonished to see the highlights of a press conference held that afternoon with the Manchester Police Force. The young girl leading the conference was appealing for anyone in the vicinity of the town centre the previous day between 12 and 1pm to come forward if they had seen a person in fancy dress and carrying a Royal Mail bag. If it hadn't appeared to be a very serious matter it would have sounded ludicrous. But then the girl went on to describe the costume the person was wearing, and that was when she picked up her phone and dialled the Freephone number on the television screen.

***

'Acting Detective Inspector Sally Fielding,' she announced to the caller who had been put through to her from the number displayed during the press and television conference.

'I saw you on the news,' Mary Jones said to her.

There was a momentary silence on Fielding's end of the line. Since the television stations had broadcast her meeting with the media, she'd had a grand total of twenty-five similar calls, none of which had amounted to anything concrete. In fact, they'd all been crank calls by attention-seekers; she had no reason to think that this latest one would be any different.

'Are you still there?' Mary asked anxiously.

'Yes, I'm here. How can I help you?'

As Fielding braced herself for another load of nonsense, the lady she was speaking to went on to describe the events of the morning, describing in detail what she'd found in the park.

'Well, it was Mr Jinx really,' she explained as Fielding grabbed a pen to jot it all down.

'Mr Jinx?'

'My dog, he's a Labrador, and he's normally so quiet but he just kept barking and barking you see so I knew that something was wrong. Then he led me to where it was buried.'

'And you didn't see anybody hiding it or running away from the scene?'

'No, there was nobody around, well not there anyway. There were other dog-walkers, the regulars like me, and of course there were a few joggers in the park too.'

'You said that you took it to the nearest police station; which one was that?'

'Harpurhey Police Station, on Upper Conran Street.'

'Did they give you an incident number?' Fielding asked, and Mary gave it to her.

'That's extremely helpful of you, Mrs Jones, and thank you for getting in touch with us.'

'It's my duty to, my dear.'

'Well, you'd be surprised by the number of people who would have just walked away from something like that.'

'Surely not!'

'Sadly yes.'

When Mary Jones ended the call she explained to her faithful dog what had just happened. Mr Jinx sat attentively listening, head cocking from side to side as his mistress related the story to him. He had no idea what she was talking about, of course, but she seemed very excited by it all.

CHAPTER
THIRTY-ONE

Sally Fielding looked up the number for Harpurhey Police Station and rang them. Quoting the incident number they'd given Mrs Jones, she was then put through to one of the detectives on duty.

'Yes, we have it here in storage,' he said to her.

'It's important evidence in an ongoing case and I'll need to come and get it straightaway.'

'We'll need confirmation from the officer in charge of the case before you can do that.'

'I'm in charge of the case,' Fielding stressed with some urgency. Surely she wasn't going to encounter a problem with red tape.

'Oh, I see. In that you'll need to email the request over to the evidence section and then we'll take it from there.'

Fielding was starting to become a bit impatient, but managed to calm herself down before replying. 'Can you let me have their email address then please?'

'Yes, of course.'

'And is the section manned 24-hours?'

'It isn't, but someone will be able to access the section for you.'

Keep calm, keep calm, she told herself. 'And can I send a copy to you; if it's not manned then I'll need someone to know about it and get if for me?'

Once she'd received the address for both the evidence section and for the young man she'd spoken to, she quickly typed in the request and sent if off. In it she said that the package was urgently required and that she'd be along to pick it up asap. Hopefully, that would do the trick and satisfy both the evidence department and the overly efficient police officer. Her admiration for Joe Burton grew even more, having to put up with this on a daily basis was something that she was going to have to get used to. Grabbing her belongings, she logged off from her computer and headed for Harpurhey Police Station. Hopefully, she'd return with what she was going for.

Thankfully, everything was in order by the time she arrived. After explaining the situation to the desk sergeant, he telephoned the officer in question and she waited for his arrival. She glanced at the clock above the desk; it was fast approaching 7pm, and she should have finished her shift and been home by now, but the people ringing in following the abridged television press conference had kept her busily writing their calls up. Joe had left at 6, and had offered to stay with her, but she'd told him to take the opportunity to get away when he could. Which is why she was now handling this one on her own.

DC Markham, the person Fielding had spoken to, appeared shortly after the call and greeted his superior officer in a manner a bit less officious than he had done before. Amazing what a Metropolitan Police email address could do, and a bit of status-checking. She knew that he would have also checked her out on the database in addition to the requisite official electronic letterhead he'd requested. She would have done exactly the same in his shoes.

'I'll take you to the evidence room now,' he said, happy to lead the way.

Fielding followed him downstairs to the basement. Opening the door, a long corridor was ahead them, and the overhead lights flickered into life as the sensors detected movement. He stopped by a door just after the third light had come on and scanned the panel on it with a key card. The red lights turned to green, and they entered.

'I came down as soon as I got your email,' he said, 'and already have it waiting for you over here.'

He'd already removed the package from its storage box and beside it was a clipboard with the release document on it. Quickly scanning what it said, she signed her name at the bottom of the sheet then picked up the costume still in its polythene bag.

'And this is exactly how it was brought in?' Fielding asked, looking at it.

'Yes,' he confirmed. 'I took the statement from the lady who brought it in, and she said that the tear in the bag was caused by her dog clawing at it to get at it in the ground.'

'That's fine,' she said, already having heard the story from Mrs Jones. She knew the tale about Mr Jinx's claw finding its way into the bag while he was digging.

'And here's your copy of the release form,' he said, handing it to her, 'and a copy of Mrs Jones's fingerprints, which she very kindly allowed us to take.'

'Good thinking,' Fielding said as she took them from him.

'Is there anything else I can help you with, detective inspector?'

Despite his willingness to help doubtlessly spurred on by her rank, Fielding had to tell him that there wasn't, and with that the DC locked up the room and she exited the basement clutching the evidence in order to get it over to her own division's forensic lab as soon as she could.

CHAPTER
THIRTY-TWO

Fortunately, the forensic unit at Fielding's station didn't close. Pressing the buzzer for attention, she recognised the girl who came to reception as one of the team who attended most of her investigations.

'Hello there,' Fielding said cheerily, 'they've got you working late I see.'

'I could say the same to you,' she laughed. 'Got something for us?'

'Yes, this,' the detective said, holding up the package.

The girl looked interested. 'I've been following the case; is that what I think it is?'

'I think it might very well be. Could be blood on there, could be something else, but I'd appreciate your team taking a look at it.'

'Not a problem.'

As she handed the bag over, Fielding also gave her Mary Jones's fingerprint sheet. 'From the lady who found the package, just to eliminate her.'

'That helps a lot, thank you. We'll let you know if and when we have something.'

Happy in the knowledge that she had done as much as she have done that evening, Fielding thanked her and decided to call it a day and head off home. Besides the cats, Joe Burton would also be waiting for her. The idea of someone making her something to eat when she returned home was still a bit of a novelty, but a welcome one nevertheless. She had been very surprised to discover that he was a bit of a whizz in the kitchen, as she was sure that his culinary expertise only extended to opening take-away cartons. How wrong she'd been. His creations had been surprising, and he even made allowances for her allergy to peppers by adapting recipes accordingly.

'So, that's where we are at the moment, Joe,' she said to her partner after they'd eaten a tasty concoction of rice, vegetables and noodles.

'Summers couldn't find anything in Norman Bishop's hotel room then?'

'Not a single thing. He said the SOCO officer went over it with a fine-tooth comb, but there wasn't any kind of evidence whatsoever.'

'Do you think the cleaning service had already tidied it up?'

Fielding shook her head. 'Jack spoke to the person on duty who had been assigned to clean the room, and they said that the room hardly needed cleaning at all. In fact, she'd told him it was spotless, which makes me think that if Bishop had been drowned in the bathroom, then whoever did it cleaned up after themselves – and did an excellent job of it.'

Burton agreed. 'It certainly sounds that way. Maybe you should get CCTV footage from the hotel for that day. If he was dead when he was taken from the room, it couldn't have been an easy operation to manoeuvre. I mean, how *do* you get a dead body out of a hotel room?'

'I just don't know, as you can't simply walk them out of the door now, can you? Out via a back way is a possibility, I suppose, but that would require in-depth knowledge of the hotel and the hope that nobody will see you while you're doing it. But don't worry, I've already requested the CCTV footage from that evening.'

'Of course you have, I should have known you'd be on the ball with this.'

'I'm really pleased that you're here tonight, Joe,' she said, curling up to him on the sofa. 'I don't know how you manage to keep yourself sane through all of this.'

'Well, you do the same job as I do when I'm dragging you around all the crimes scenes we've been to!' he laughed.

'Yes, I know, but being in charge of a case is a world away from being second-in-command.'

'Not so much; it's basically the same.'

'But the authority lies solely on your shoulders ...'

'Hey, listen,' he said, tilting her head up towards him, 'you're doing a great job and don't ever forget it. I know we're both going through a period of transition, but it'll all work out in the end, I can assure you on that score. I felt the same when Ambleton was promoted, but then you came along and all my worries were gone. I knew that you were more than capable, and your strength gave me strength.'

'That sounds like a rousing speech from a film!' she laughed, at which point he pulled her close to him and kissed her. Sooty and Sweep were both curled up and napping at the end of the sofa, and Burton's sudden action caused them to stir. They looked up at the embraced pair and scrutinised them with approving eyes before returning back to sleep.

'Did you bring an overnight bag with you?' Fielding asked when they parted.

He nodded.

'Good,' she said returning his kiss.

***

'I think we've got away with it; when can we meet up?' The text message read.

'I don't think we're clear yet.' Came the reply.

'But I've got to see you!'

'I feel we need to wait a bit longer.'

'It's killing me not seeing you.'

'We must be patient.'

'OK, but it's very hard.'

'It will all be worth it in the end.'

'I hope you're right.'

'You know that I am.'

***

As another day dawned, Sally Fielding awoke with a strong feeling that any information they gathered today would be crucial to the investigation. She hoped to hear that forensics would find DNA from the Robin Hood outfit that matched one of their suspects, and that the CCTV from the hotel Norman Bishop stayed in would reveal who removed him from the building. She just felt so positive about the whole thing, and that she and the team would make a breakthrough in the case, revealing one of the many suspects they had in their sights to be the actual killer. At least, that was what her optimism was telling her. She'd spent a wonderful evening with Joe Burton, and if that wasn't a reason to be overly happy then nothing was. She only hoped that the happiness of being with the man she loved wasn't clouding her judgement.

'What time is it?' Joe Burton asked, sensing she was awake.

Sally looked at the clock on the bedside table. 'Almost 5.30.'

He stretched and looked towards the window; the early-morning sunshine was already shining in through a gap in the curtains.

'Looks like it's going to be another warm day.'

'I feel very good about today,' she enthused, sitting up in the bed. 'I think something's going to break in the case.'

'Do you?' He turned on his side to face her.

'Yes. And I think it's going to come from that outfit that was found in Heaton Park.'

'Well, I hope it does. I'm going to be upstairs again, all day this time, so do let me know as and when something turns up. I feel confident if you feel confident.'

CHAPTER
THIRTY-THREE

Sally Fielding expected to be the first in when she arrived just after 8 o'clock, but found that it was not the case. Jack Summers was already seated at his desk and staring intently at his monitor as she entered.

'Oh, you're in early!' she exclaimed on seeing him.

'Yes,' he said, taking his eyes momentarily off the screen. 'I had a text message to say that the CCTV had come through, so I thought it best to get started on it. Hope you don't mind.'

'No, not at all. Good thinking.'

She already knew that Jack Summers had initiative from the time spent undercover with him. The work he'd done had been exemplary and well-received by the higher echelons in the force, and for that reason he'd been chosen to her new partner once Burton was promoted. She then went on to tell him about the outfit Mary Jones had found in the park.

'And with a bit of luck we should get something back from that later on in the day.'

DCs Francis, Preston and Banks had all been working on checking the suspects' backgrounds over the past few days – speaking to colleagues in places of employment, and to friends – and were expected to collate the summaries and present them to Fielding today. She hoped that what they'd discovered would shed light on a multitude of questions all waiting to be answered.

'I think it's coming together,' she said to Summers, repeating what she'd already told Burton earlier.

'I hope you're right,' he replied. 'This has to be one of our toughest cases yet.'

'I agree. Would you like me to take a look at some of the footage, there's nothing I can do until we get the results back from forensics?'

'Sure, that would be great.'

'Okay then, if you want to split the feed and send me half of it, I'll start straight away.'

Sally Fielding knew that there was nothing more boring than trawling through hours and hours of CCTV footage, but it had to be done. Thankfully, two sets of eyes are always less taxing than one pair having to strain at the feed. When Summers sent her the amended file, she found the recording was split onto four screens, which meant having to keep a close eye on each of the sections at the same time. The Premier Hotel housed a lot of corporate meetings, with people coming in from across the country to attend them. For this reason, it was a lot busier than most of the other hotels in the city. As Fielding watched, there was little or no action along the corridor which housed Norman Bishop's room, but the foyer and reception desk saw a lot of comings and goings during the course of the evening.

After about an hour of just sitting and watching, she was just about to take a break and go out for a coffee when she saw it. She immediately froze the recording, with the time stamp at the top of the quartered section reading 23:30:17, and called Summers over. As he came over and stood looking over her shoulder, she started the video up again. The luggage cart, which was frozen on the screen half-in and half-out of Norman Bishop's doorway, began to move again. But it wasn't just an empty cart; there was something covered up on it.

'This has to be it,' she said excitedly, and he saw exactly what she meant.

'That must be Bishop's body on there!' Summers could hardly believe what he was looking at.

'If you didn't know, you wouldn't know though, would you?'

This is it, Fielding thought; *we're going to see the killer face on.* But, of course, things were never that easy or simple. Logically, they should have seen who was pushing the trolley from the room, but they didn't. Whoever it was who was steering it must have known exactly where the CCTV camera was, because as they exited the room they immediately dropped their chin onto their chest so that only the top of their head could be seen.

'Dammit!' Fielding exploded, frustrated by the hours spent engaged on this for it all to come to nothing.

As they kept watching, the person turned the trolley to their right, closed the door behind them, and were gone. And that was it.

'But at least we know one thing, boss,' Summers said, trying to quell the anger and annoyance he knew that she must be feeling with the situation. 'We now know that there was only one person with Bishop and, by the looks of it, they were male.'

Fielding was still staring at the screen in disbelief when her phone rang. 'Acting DI Fielding,' she answered a little harshly than intended, which surprised the caller on the other end of the line.

'Oh, is everything all right?' a girl's voice asked her. 'This is Holly Benton from forensics with the test results of the item of clothing you handed in yesterday.'

Realising who she was, Fielding apologised profusely and felt obliged to explain her shortness with her. 'I'm sorry, I've just been watching CCTV hoping for a result, but it's fallen flat.'

'Well, I hope that what I have to tell you might be a bit of good news for you then.'

Fielding's interest was immediately sparked.

'The piece of torn cloth found at Valerie Wilton's house matched a tear in the sleeve of the outfit, so whoever wore it was there. As the lady who handed it in suspected, it *was* blood we found on the garment; but more than that, we've actually found DNA on it and you'll be pleased to hear that we've managed to trace it to someone in our system.'

It was great news to the detective, who now couldn't wait to hear who it was.

'It's from a Caroline Watkins; do you need her address, because it was from a number of years ago and she may no longer live there?'

But Fielding didn't need any further information, for she already knew where Ms Watkins lived. As she was thanking Holly for getting back to her so quickly, there was a reaction from Jack Summers who was still watching the CCTV stream at his desk.

'You have to see this!' he shouted over to her when she'd finished the call, and she hurried over to see what was exciting him so much. Just out of curiosity, he'd started up the video again while she was taking the call, and was very pleased that he had. Although they'd lost sight of both the trolley and the person pushing it, the camera was still focused on Norman Bishop's hotel room door. It had been closed by the unknown person, but then it opened again and a second figure emerged from it. The person was wearing a hoodie and a pair of sunglasses, but it was obvious from the size and shape of them that it was a woman.

CHAPTER
THIRTY-FOUR

Fielding picked up her mobile and dialled his number. This was far too important not to let him in on it.

'Can we get tech to work on the CCTV?' he asked, in response to her telling him that the woman's face in the video couldn't be made out. 'Get Peter Westerby onto it, I'm sure he'll come up with some programme or another that can help.'

She said that she would.

'And what about Caroline Watkins; have you checked to see why her DNA's in the system?'

'I just have,' she said, 'and it seems that a few years back she had to give a sample in a case. One of her clients saw something he perhaps shouldn't have and called her for help. Because she attended the scene, it was taken for elimination purpose and somehow it's remained in the system.'

'I'm surprised that we still have it, but that's a lucky break for us then.'

'Indeed.'

'In any case, I'm taking Jack with me to pick her up and bring her into the station. Jane, Phillipa and Simon haven't turned up anything untoward with regard to the other three suspects.'

'Did you get any further with looking into Madame Ortiz's background?'

'To tell the truth,' she admitted, 'I was going to this morning but then I gave Jack a hand with the CCTV.'

'Okay,' he said. 'Look, I'm going to be free in about fifteen minutes, so I can go and visit her again if you like?'

Fielding didn't really like, as she'd seen the way Ortiz was playing up to him the last time they'd visited her. But she knew Joe, and she knew that the woman's put-on charms wouldn't have any effect on him anyway, so she agreed and thanked him for offering.

'That's set then. We'll meet up afterwards to discuss our findings.'

After a quick call to Caroline Watkins's mobile, Fielding said her that she had some further questions for her and asked her where she was. When she replied that she was at work, the detective said that she'd come and meet her there. She didn't mention what the questions were, or that she and another detective would be taking her back to the station to ask them of her. As Caroline's DNA had been found on the costume, it all pointed to her having been the person wearing it and posing as a post person. How else could it have got there? She had known Harry York, as had Maria Turnbull, but what reason could she possibly have for killing Harry York, let alone anybody else? That was a question that needed to be asked at the police station and not at her place of work. If she was guilty of anything, Fielding didn't want her fleeing from the scene, although both she and Jack Summers could have easily prevented her from doing so. Interviewing her at the station meant that they had her secure and she wouldn't be going anywhere in a hurry if she felt inclined to do so.

'I have to be in court soon,' Caroline Watkins said to the two detectives as they were being shown into her office at the firm of solicitors where she worked. She was busily gathering together manila files from the filing cabinets and putting them into a large leather briefcase on the desk.

'I'm afraid that's going to have to wait,' Fielding said to her in no uncertain terms.

Caroline stopped and looked at her, the file in her hand half-in and half-out of the case. 'No, it can't wait, detective, I'm defending a client in very important case in about twenty minutes.'

'You'll either have to get someone to cover you or you'll need to get the case postponed.'

'I don't think so, detective.' She retorted.

'We're going to have to take you into the station for questioning.'

The solicitor appeared stunned. 'Questioning; for what reason?'

'We need to speak to you about the murder of Valerie Wilton.'

'Who? I don't know who that is.' She put the file onto her desk.

'That's what we need to speak to you about.'

***

Despite her initial objections, Caroline Watkins was well-versed in the law and had the sense to oblige with their wishes.

'I need to speak to my boss before I go,' she informed Fielding, who nodded her approval.

As Fielding waited in reception, Summers accompanied Caroline when she went to see one of the company's two partners, telling him that someone would need to take over her case, and suggested Paul Frost, another solicitor and who had apparently helped her with it. Her boss was as stunned as she was, and came out of his office to speak to Fielding.

'Are you sure this is really necessary?' he'd asked in a tone which the detective could hear was verging on anger that one of his team was being hauled in for questioning.

'Yes, I'm sure it's necessary, sir,' she said, not wishing to go into the fine detail of why.

'And exactly why are you taking her in?' he continued, not letting it go as easily as Fielding hoped.

'To help us with our enquiries.'

'And she can't help you here in the office?'

'I'm afraid not.' Fielding held her ground and stood firm. Burton would be proud, she mused.

'Very well, very well.' Like Caroline, he knew the law, but was far from happy with the fact that one of his team was being whisked away to a police station.

CHAPTER
THIRTY-FIVE

'Well, that's the strangest thing,' Caroline Watkins said as she looked at the garment on the table in front of her.

'And why's that?' Fielding asked coldly.

'I *used* to have an outfit like that, a while back, but then I think it ended up in a charity shop, you know, in one of those bags that are routinely put through your door.'

'Why on earth did you have a fancy-dress costume?' Summers asked of her, clearly puzzled why one of the city's top-notch solicitors, and someone who was so obviously fashion-conscious, would buy something like that.

'For a fancy-dress party, of course,' she said somewhat sarcastically, looking at Summers with an expression of bewilderment. 'Why else would I have it?'

'When exactly did you get rid of it?' Fielding felt completely deflated by this revelation. The DNA didn't lie, and she thought that she had the whole thing sussed out, well apart from the actual motive that is, and here she was back to square one again.

'Oh, I don't know, a few months back I suppose. I'd only worn it once, for a specific occasion and then got rid of it. Look, what's this all about, and who is ... what was that person's name again?'

'Valerie Wilton,' Summers obliged.

'Who is she?' Caroline pushed for an answer, and Fielding felt that she had no other option than to explain to her despite not wanting to.

'We think that she witnessed Harry York's murder and was followed home by somebody wearing a Robin Hood costume – your actual costume as it happens as it has your DNA on it.'

'How on earth did you get my DNA?' Caroline asked in horror.

'It was in the system, from when you visited one of your clients in his home following an incident two years' ago.'

'Why was it even in the system still?' The solicitor was furious, and Fielding could see her thoughts ticking over trying to recall. 'Yes I remember now,' she said at last, 'it was an incident involving one of my clients and that should have been destroyed when the case was resolved!'

'I know that, but somehow it wasn't.'

'I shall be raising a complaint about this at the highest level, detective.'

'I have no doubt that you will,' Fielding responded and left it at that. She could see it being an administrative nightmare of epic proportions, especially with the tenacious Ms Watkins on the case.

'You said that you gave it to charity, Ms Watkins?' Jack Summers asked hoping for some kind of lead here. 'Can you remember which one?'

Caroline Watkins gave him a withering look. 'Do you know how many charity bags come through the door over the course of a month?'

Summers actually did know how many, as he received a fair share of them himself. 'So, it was just a random bag then?'

'Yes.' Again, an expression designed to frighten clients and witnesses alike. She'd manage to perfect it, and obviously used it to her advantage in her career. As Summers had almost gone on to an acting career, he recognised somebody putting on a show for an audience – which on this occasion was himself and Fielding. He smiled to himself, which didn't go down too well with the undeterred Ms Watkins.

'Why are you smiling?' she asked angrily.

'I know an act when I see one,' he said to her, which seemed to temporarily cause a chink in her armour. Her manner changed, but then she bristled once again and sat upright in her seat.

'I am not putting on an act,' she declared defiantly, but Summers still smiled.

'Whatever you say,' was all he said, but it had the desired effect of quietening her.

Fielding could tell that this was going nowhere. Caroline Watkins had an answer for everything which, considering she was a solicitor, made a great deal of sense. She'd made a career out of having something to say. Under the circumstances, she had no other option than to end the questioning right there and allow her to leave.

'But we may need to question you again,' she added.

'Whatever for?'

'Well, for one thing, you knew all the victims here.'

'But, surely, that doesn't make me a person of interest?' The solicitor stood her ground firmly.

'Maybe not, but we may need to speak to you again.'

'Can I go now?' Caroline Watkins demanded, to which Fielding just nodded.

'So, what do we think?' Jack Summers asked when he and Fielding returned to the squad room.

Fielding shrugged her shoulders. 'I really don't know what to think about this. Okay, so supposing she's right and she did give her outfit to charity, isn't it a bit of a coincidence that it's turned up in a murder case, one in which she had multiple connections to?'

'I agree. And for that reason we can't just discard it.

'Absolutely. We'll wait to see what Joe Burton comes back to us with and get his take on it as well.'

***

Joe Burton knew that Fielding thought Madame Ortiz had been coming on to him on their visit, and perhaps she had, but that kind of thing wasn't going to either bother him or get in the way of the investigation. He'd called ahead, so was expected, but thought that, for Fielding's sake, he'd take heed of what she'd said to him. What they needed to know was who Ortiz knew amongst all the victims and suspects, and how she knew them. He knew for certain some of the connections, but wanted to hear it from the woman herself.

'Hello again,' Marilyn Parkinson greeted Burton at the front door and held it open for him to enter. Her faithful pooch was held tightly in her arms, which he was again grateful for. Although there hadn't been any kind of incident with the pet the last time he'd visited, he still worried about any dog he now encountered. The incident with his trousers and the over-enthusiastic hound had left an indelible mark upon his psyche.

Burton thought of Fielding, and the phrase 'into the lion's den' popped into his head. He smiled to himself, then thought to extend that smile to a greeting of his own so that it didn't look out of place. 'And you,' he said, stepping into the hallway. He again followed his host to the conservatory at the back of the house and sat down on a seat opposite her.

'Would you like a drink, detective?' Marilyn offered, but he declined, saying that he likely would only be a few minutes.

In stark contrast to the previous time he was there, she wore make-up, making her look more like her professional persona. The previous apparel of relaxed shirt and trousers had been replaced by a mid-calf length summer's dress with, yet again, a plunging front neckline. Was it for his benefit, he mused? If it was, it was lost on him. Perhaps Fielding had been right in her assumption after all. Yes, she was attractive, he couldn't deny that, but the only woman for him was his Sally Fielding. No other person could come near her, in his opinion, and certainly not some fancy fake Tarot card reader.

She uncrossed then re-crossed her legs somewhat provocatively, but Burton ignored it and delved into his pocket and produced his trusty elasticated notebook.

'Now, Ms Parkinson,' he began, 'I only have a few questions to ask you, but they are very important ones so I hope you can oblige with the answers.'

'Of course,' she purred. Burton ignored it.

'Please tell me how you know Harry York and Norman Bishop.'

Her eyebrows crinkled slightly. 'Well, I've heard about them on the news, of course.'

'But you've met them, haven't you?'

'Have I?' She answered the question with a question, but Burton didn't see it as a ploy to try to put him off. Did she genuinely not remember them, or was it a well put on front? He really wasn't sure.

'I believe that Harry York and the estate agency he worked for was instrumental with finding you your business property. Norman Bishop worked for the council and was one of the people who drew up your tenancy agreement.'

'My, you've been busy,' she smiled briefly. 'But it was a while ago and I didn't know that it was them. As you can imagine, I meet a lot of people, especially clients, and can't remember their names or faces, so I don't think you can fault me for not recall meeting those two particular people.'

'So, what about Caroline Watkins?'

'Caroline Watkins?'

'Yes, she was the one who organised the group meeting the other night, when Maria Turnbull died after leaving your workplace.'

'I only met her that night, detective.'

'She was the solicitor who drew up your initial and subsequent tenancy agreements.'

'Well, how am I supposed to know that!'

Burton could tell that she was starting to get a little annoyed with his line of questioning, but continued. 'You didn't meet her when you signed your agreement?'

'No, I did not. It was posted out to me and I returned it in the same way. Apart from Caroline Watkins, who you now tell me I met the other night, I have not personally met any of them. Even then, I had no idea that Ms Watkins had anything to do with my business affairs; I thought she was just someone who had booked a session with me, that's all.'

Burton felt disappointment. He'd hoped that this could be a great step forward in the investigation but, alas, it was not to be. Unless Ms Parkinson was lying, that is, and he really didn't think that she was judging by the way she'd answered him.

'Okay, thank you,' he said, closing his book and locking it shut with the elastic strap. 'I'm sorry, but I had to ask the questions as part of the enquiry.'

'I understand.' She was back to purring mode once again. 'Now, anything else you want to ask me, you know where I am.'

As Burton rose to go, he was grateful that the dog remained in his basket beside the patio door. However, there was one final question he just had to ask her, and there was no better way of asking it than just bluntly coming out with it.

'Just before I go,' he began, 'can you think of any reason why someone would want to frame you for murder?'

'I beg your pardon?' she asked, shocked by his question.

'We didn't mention it to you before, but we have evidence which seems to point us in your direction.'

'What?' Burton could see that Parkinson's reaction was genuine. She had no idea that she was in the frame for anything. 'I don't understand.'

'There are things that we've found which implicate you?'

'What kind of things,' she demanded.

'I'm afraid I can't disclose that to you, but it's clear that somebody wants us to be led back to you.

'Well, I can't think why, detective, I really can't. I'm not guilty of anything, let alone guilty of murdering anyone.'

'What about those odd letters you told me you'd been receiving; did anyone threaten you in any way?'

'Threaten me? No, well, not to that extent. I just put them down as people who were jealous of my talents and dismissed them as such.'

'Perhaps someone holding a grudge then, and who didn't like a reading you gave them? You might want to think about going through them again,' Burton suggested, 'look at them from a different perspective and let me know if anything stands out.'

'Okay, I will,' she said shakily as she walked with him towards the front door.

She remained standing in the doorway as he made his way down the path to the pavement. When he reached the car, he looked back at her; her face was as white as a sheet. It was only then that she closed the door and went back into the house.

CHAPTER
THIRTY-SIX

Burton felt as if he should have brought back something more concrete for Fielding but, sadly, that had not been the case. Unless she was putting on a very good act for him, he could find nothing wrong with the answers she'd given, and seemed to be genuinely shocked by the revelation that someone could be framing her for murder. But even so, it was still strange how she, and everyone else for that matter, was connected in one way or another to each other in the case. He wondered how Fielding had fared with the solicitor, Caroline Watkins. Surely the woman could not refute her DNA being all over the fancy dress clothing, so he hoped that she'd had more success than he had. In some ways, it looked like clear evidence for an arrest but, as he knew all too well, things didn't often turn out like they're supposed to. Far from it. Then there was the matter of motive. Like Marilyn Parkinson, what reason could she have had to kill, for none was evident for either of them?

Fielding and Summers were sitting deep in conversation with the other three detective constables when he entered the room.

Seeing him enter, Fielding called him over.

'Any luck with our clairvoyant?' she asked him, to which he simply shook his head.

'She seemed all dressed up to impress-'

'I told you!'

He smiled. 'Perhaps, but what she said made sense. She said that she'd never met them. Regarding her business property, she'd telephoned estate agents in the first instance; someone did show her around potential locations from Harry York's particular one, but she said that it was a woman. Following that, all the tenancy contract work was done by post, and she didn't realise that Watkins had been the solicitor working on it. In fact, she didn't know that any of the victims were linked.'

'And you believe her?'

'I have no reason not to,' he confessed, 'despite her trying to initially distract me with her low-cut dress!'

As the rest of the team laughed at his remark, Burton looked across at Fielding and mouthed 'she didn't succeed', followed by a wink.

'What about everybody else; what have you found out?' He addressed his remarks at the other three team members.

'Yes, everyone's been busy,' Fielding replied, but then let them tell him for themselves.

Simon Banks was the first to answer. 'I've been spending quite some time on CCTV, and I suddenly thought about the taxi cab the night of Maria Turnbull's death. I wondered if the cab company the party of women used had it in their vehicles, as I know that some firms do, and, on checking found that they did. So, while everybody else was out doing more background checks I paid a visit to the cab company to view the footage from that night.'

'And was there anything of any use on it?' Burton asked hopefully.

'They gave me a copy, which I'd like to show everybody now if I may? There is something of interest on it.'

While Simon set the playback up, Burton came around the desk and stood behind Fielding. Everyone else huddled in to watch. As they looked on, the video started with the interior of the cab just before all the women climbed into it. A few seconds in, Maria and Barbara entered first and sat together on the back seat, followed by Selena and Caroline, who sat on single seats facing them. Everyone appeared to be sitting quietly without speaking; there was obviously some kind of friction going on here.

'Is there any sound on this?' Burton asked.

'There is,' Banks said to him, 'but nobody appears to be speaking to one another.'

At that point the camera angle changed.

'Multiple cameras in the cab?' Burton speculated that the firm must have experienced problems in the past to invest in them, why else to go such trouble to keep an eye on their passengers.

Banks nodded. 'And this is the interesting point ... watch Maria.'

As they all sat looking at the first victim, she reached up touched the back of one hand against her forehead before leaning in towards the window and resting her head against it. Simon then fast-forwarded to the point when everyone else had got out of the cab and Barbara was left on her own with Maria. He had forwarded the playback a full fifteen minutes, and Maria hadn't moved in all that time. They heard Barbara speaking to her, telling her that she was home and was leaving the cab, but when there hadn't been a reaction had put a hand on her shoulder and gently shaken her. It was then that her body tipped sideways and fell onto the seat, with her head ending up on Barbara's lap. Banks froze the image there.

'So, she felt ill shortly after entering the cab by the look of it,' Phillipa Preston observed.

'And as she didn't move, she could have died any time from then,' Jane Francis added.

Burton stood with arms folded, deep in thought. 'It's a shame that the pathologist couldn't pinpoint the exact time of death, because looking at that footage I would have put my money on her having been poisoned just prior to her getting in the cab.'

'Which brings us back to the other three women as being our suspects,' Fielding reiterated. 'Louise Simmons did tell us that the psychology behind why people murder comes down to the basic reasons of revenge, money, and sex. A financial reason has already been hinted at with the death of Harry York, with him being on the board of governors at Thornton School.'

'But forensic accounting discounted that one,' Jack Summers spoke up.

'Yes, they did,' she agreed, 'so, perhaps not money then, although we can't discount it entirely.'

'How do the women know one another again?' Burton asked, arms still folded.

'Lifelong friends. They grew up together,' Fielding replied. 'Went to the same school, then off to different universities before meeting up again afterwards.'

'Hmmm.' The arms had unfolded and there was now one finger held to his mouth and tapping on his lips. Fielding recognised the action; it was one of his subconscious actions when he was thinking more deeply than usual. As she and the team watched, the tapping slowed down then came to a stop.

'Maybe,' he said, perhaps more to himself than to them, 'just maybe.'

There was a prolonged pause, with everyone hanging on to what might come next.

'Maria was the only married one of the group wasn't she, having only been wed last year?'

'That's correct. What are you thinking?'

'I'm thinking jealousy. One of the others was jealous of her perhaps?'

'Because she married first you mean? Surely it can't be as simple as that?'

'You said yourself that revenge, money and sex are all reasons why someone would murder.'

'I know I did,' Fielding admitted, 'but that would make it a little too obvious, wouldn't it?'

'I don't know, maybe it *is* as simple as that.' As she shared her life with a psychologist, Phillipa Preston had a fair understanding of the subject. Her partner had often thrown things by her when trying to get to grips with the human mind, and valued her take on things as a police officer. 'Should we get them in and interview them again?'

Fielding looked up at Burton and said, 'Yes, I think we should. Get them all in at the same time but interview them individually.'

He nodded his head in agreement, but said nothing. It was Sally Fielding's case after all.

CHAPTER
THIRTY-SEVEN

The plan was to invite them in five minutes apart, then have them all sit and wait in reception until called through. That way, Fielding and Burton could watch them on CCTV from another room to get their reactions on seeing one another. It was a technique they'd used before, and, as before, they hoped that it may cause one of them to act a little differently or strangely, thereby setting them apart from the rest. Of course, it was all conjecture, and none of them could have had anything to do with Maria Turnbull's death, but it was all they had to go on at the moment.

Then, with ten minutes before the first woman was due to arrive, Fielding had an unexpected call from the SOCO team.

'Detective Fielding?' the female voice asked, and was immediately recognised as Holly, the young girl she'd seen the other night when taking the Robin Hood outfit in for examination.

'Hello Holly. What can I do for you?'

The girl was thrilled that Fielding had remembered her name. 'I thought that I'd better let you know. We were going over the evidence again from Valerie Wilton's crime scene, and it seems that we have found a hair near to the front door which doesn't belong to the victim.'

'A hair? That's excellent news. When will you be able to test it for DNA?'

'Well, actually, that's why I'm calling. We are testing it now and hope to know more about it soon, hopefully within the next hour or so.'

Fielding couldn't believe their luck.

'Thank you, Holly, I really appreciate you calling.'

'Not a problem. I'll be back in touch as soon as we have something.'

'That sounded positive,' Burton said when she'd finished the call. 'Did I hear you right, a hair's been found somewhere?'

'Yes, that's right. SOCO found a hair at Valerie Wilton's crime scene and it's being tested as we speak.'

'Great news,' he began, but then noticed on the monitor that Selena Douglas had just arrived at the main enquiry desk. 'Ah, here we go, the first one's coming in now.'

As they recalled, Selena came across as a bit of a peacemaker, a pacifier who tried to keep order and calm between the friends. After approaching the desk and signing in she was asked to take one of the visitors' seats.

'It's good that we can hear so clearly,' Fielding remarked.

'We've got Peter Westerby to thank for that,' Burton said. 'He's managed to give the feedback a bit of "oomph", as he put it. It's not normally as clear as this.'

'Thank goodness for Peter Westerby then!'

After about five minutes of looking at her phone, Selena turned it off and placed it in her handbag. It was at that point that she looked up and noticed Barbara, who must have just appeared on the scene and was standing at the desk. She too, it seemed, had not initially seen her friend sitting down as she came in. Fielding could appreciate that. She'd often walk past someone she knew and, because she hadn't expected to see them there, had completely blanked them. In fact, she was infamous for it.

'Oh!' Selena said out loud, which made Barbara turn around as she recognised her voice.

'What are you doing here?' they said almost in unison.

'Well, it appears that none of them informed the other that they'd be coming in today,' Burton said as he continued to watch the screen.

'I was asked to come in,' Barbara explained to her friend.

'Me too,' came the reply.

As they sat down together and began chatting, speculating why they'd both been called in, the third friend walked in through the door. Caroline Watkins stopped in her tracks and lifted up her sunglasses.

'What's happening?' she asked, looking from one to the other before taking the glasses off and dropping them into her bag.

'We were asked to come along,' Selena replied.

'But at different times,' Barbara added, already having had the discussion with Selena.

'What time were you two asked to come in?' Caroline asked them.

When each confirmed their times, Caroline said that her appointment was five minutes after the last one.

'So why not ask us all in at the same time?' Barbara puzzled. She was even more confused by the fact they'd been asked at all. There was nothing more they could tell the detectives. Maria had been fine right up to the time she got into the cab – well, fine health-wise. Granted she'd had an argument with Caroline, which had involved all of them in the end, but that was somehow expected under the circumstances. Caroline should never have played that trick on her in the first place. If Caroline had any sense, or indeed been more aware of Maria's phobia for anything to do with mysticism or the supernatural, then she might not have done it. But Caroline had always been a bit like that, wanting to steal the limelight. Going away to university and meeting a whole new crowd of people had finally made Barbara realise that. It could also have been something to do with the fact that Maria had been the first to get married. Maria had been a bit of an ugly duckling in her early teens, the brainy one who wore dark-framed glasses and steel braces, but when she turned sixteen all that changed. She ditched the glasses in favour of contact lenses, and the braces had done their job and produced two rows of straight white teeth, and she began to style her hair differently. She even started experimenting with make-up. It was no wonder she had been the one to be snapped up first. She'd met her husband-to-be when she returned home to

Manchester, and all was rosy. Or it should have been, until she met her untimely death that is. Caroline was seeing someone, or at least she frequently hinted at the fact, but neither Barbara nor Selena knew who that was. She'd been very tight-lipped about a relationship, which made them both think that perhaps the man in her life was in fact married to someone else.

'They may ask us all in and interview us together like before,' Selena offered, but Caroline wasn't convinced and shook her head.

'I'm not convinced of that,' she said, 'especially if they've asked us to come here at different times.'

'So, what's your take on it?' Barbara asked her, 'I mean, from a legal point of view.'

'What do you mean?'

'Do you think they suspect us of having done something?'

Burton and Fielding's ears pricked up at this comment.

'Well, we haven't done anything wrong, have we?' Caroline retorted angrily, nostrils flaring to match her mood.

'Then why contact us at all?'

'Because our friend died. You know, our lifelong friend Maria!' Selena said with a raised voice. Maybe this was the time to get them into an interview room before they became even more aggravated by one another.

'Okay, I think we should step in,' Burton said, rising from his seat. 'I fear if we leave them any longer they'll be done for disturbing the peace.'

CHAPTER
THIRTY-EIGHT

'Jack, can you join us on this one please?' Burton asked his colleague. As he was soon to become Fielding's new partner, he thought it would be good experience to interview one of the three women on his own. If Summers took Selena, and Fielding, Barbara, then he'd tackle the seemingly self-inflated solicitor himself. He never flinched from any kind of challenge, and she appeared to be one by all accounts.

Jack Summers was thrilled to be given the opportunity. Burton knew that he was more than capable, plus a fresh pair of eyes couldn't do any harm. As all three detectives descended the stairs, the women all looked up. Caroline's stone-cold face gave nothing away, but the other two looked a bit worried by the sight of them.

'Ladies.' Burton acknowledged them as he approached the desk and asked if interview rooms one to three were available. It was all for show, of course, as he could have just gone there without involving the desk sergeant in any of the apparent subterfuge.

Fielding watched their expressions. Barbara and Selena exchanged glances and appeared to be concerned that each would be interviewed separately. Caroline, again, sat expressionless. Fielding could imagine the woman in court, posing a formidable figure as she defended or prosecuted, depending upon her role in the case. She would not like to be a witness being cross-examined by this one.

Burton turned to face them again. 'Right then,' he said. 'DS Summers, could you take Ms Douglas in please. Ms McKay, would you go with DI Fielding. And if you could come with me Ms Watkins.' He made it sound very formal, and intended to hopefully strike some kind of fear in them. If any of the women were guilty of anything, he was sure it would come out in the interviews, especially with the questions he and the team had prepared for them.

With Joe Burton leading the way, they all headed to the interview rooms. As he went into room number one, Fielding and Barbara McKay went into room two, with Summers and his charge going into the third door. None of the interviewees knew what the other one was being asked or saying, which was the way they wanted it. Burton was the first to start.

'So, Ms Watkins, could you please go over the events of the evening when Maria Turnbull was killed.' He used the word 'killed' not just for effect, as that was what had happened to her, and waited for a reaction to it.

'But I've already told you what happened that night.' It was said in a manner devoid of any emotion, which seemed to compound what they'd already suspected about her personality: cold and calculating. But the question was, was she cold and calculating enough to have deliberately murdered her long-standing friend?

'If you could just humour me and go through it once again please.' She wasn't going to be let off that easily.

Caroline Watkins sighed deeply and deliberately before answering.

'Like I said before ...'

Did Burton detect an eye roll?

'... I arranged the evening without saying where we were going as I thought it would be different enough for everyone to enjoy. Something unlike what we've done before; a few laughs, a bit of fun. How wrong I was about that!'

'It has sunk in that your friend died, hasn't it?'

Caroline looked at him strangely. 'Of course it has. What on earth do you mean by that?'

'It's just that you seem to be, well, a bit cold about it, that's all.'

'A bit cold!' she repeated his words. 'I've lost my best friend ... how dare you!'

'Well, your other two friends seem to be quite cut up about it, but you, you're very different to them.'

'Detective Burton, I based my career on keeping a cool, calm exterior. If I was to get hysterical every time I set foot in a courtroom I wouldn't be much good then, would I?'

'But this isn't about you, or about your work; this is about a woman, your friend, who has died on a night out that you arranged.'

'So, are you accusing me of having something to do with that?' she asked indignantly.

'Did you?'

'No, of course not!'

Burton made a mental note to himself not to go up against solicitors. Guilty or innocent, this one had a ready answer for everything which, when he thought about it, was to be expected. He decided to take another route.

'Can you tell me what you all drank that night?'

Caroline looked at him in what can be best described as disbelief. 'What?'

'Drink ... what did you all have to drink that night?'

'I heard you the first time, but what does that have to do with anything?'

This was the line of questioning he, Fielding and Summers had discussed beforehand. The medical examiner had confirmed that Maria Turnbull had ingested the poison, so it stood to reason that she must have been given it at some point. But the main question was, when was she given it? The doctor couldn't say exactly when that had been; it could have been minutes before she died, or it could have been days, but they were now working on the assumption that it had been in the few hours beforehand.

'Please just answer the question,' he urged.

'After we picked up Maria we went to a bar in town-'

'Which bar in town?'

Again the look before replying. 'We went to The Anthologist on St Peter Square.'

Burton wrote it down in his notebook. 'And what did you all drink?'

'Well, we had a couple of bottles of Prosecco between us.'

'So you had a table?'

'Yes. I don't usually sit at a bar drinking, detective!'

Burton could easily imagine that would not be her style. 'And did they arrive with the corks popped?'

'No, a waiter brought a bottle over in a cooler and popped it at the table.'

'The same with the second?'

'Yes.'

More note taking. 'And did anyone leave the table during the time you were there?'

'Well, I think we all did at some time, to go to the loo.'

'No-one was left alone with Maria then?'

It was then that it dawned on Caroline what Burton was getting at. 'Look, I don't like what you're getting at. Do you honestly think that one of us would murder our own friend?'

'I really don't know, which is why I'm asking the questions to try to find out.'

'Well let me tell you for certain. I DID NOT MURDER MY FRIEND! Now, if you wish to ask me any more questions then I must insist on having a solicitor in from my own firm.'

And with that she sat back in her seat and folded her arms. Burton had been challenged; the gauntlet was down, and there wasn't anything else he could do about it.

'That won't be necessary,' he said and sat back in his own chair, emulating her own movement by likewise crossing his arms.

CHAPTER
THIRTY-NINE

Leaving all three suspects in their respective interview rooms, Burton, Fielding and Summers met up in the corridor to discuss each of their outcomes.

'Caroline Watkins has cried wolf and asked for a solicitor from her own firm,' Burton said to them.

'Barbara has been co-operative and helpful throughout the interview. Says they went to a bar called The Anthologist and they shared a couple of bottles of sparkling wine before going to Madame Ortiz's.'

'Same here,' Summers said.

Burton suddenly had a thought. 'Did either of you ask if they had anything to drink at the clairvoyant's place, I know I didn't?'

When the other two both shook their heads Burton added, 'Then maybe we should.'

Back in the room with Caroline Watkins, Burton was met with the same stone-faced expression from her.

'Just one last question. When you were in Madame Ortiz's place was there anything to drink on the table?'

'Yes, a carafe of water,' she said after a few moments of keeping him waiting for an answer.

'Did Maria take a drink from it?'

'No, she didn't. None of us did.'

'And what about when you were in with Ortiz, was there any water in there?'

Burton could see her thinking back to the evening and trying to remember.

'I believe that there was. Yes, definitely, there was another carafe like the one in the waiting area.'

'So, it's possible that Maria might have taken a drink from that without you or any of your friends knowing?'

'It's possible, I suppose, but you'll have to ask Madame Ortiz that one as I didn't go in with her.'

Burton had every intention of doing so. Not wishing to incur either her deathly stare or the threat of bringing in a solicitor, he had no option but to let her and her friends go. After she left the room, he texted both Fielding and Summers telling them that they could do the same. After all the suspects had left, the three discussed their respective interviews with the women.

'Selena was quite distressed by the whole thing; says she is trying to come to terms with her friend's death and finds that she cannot until the whole matter is over with and her killer has been found,' Summers said.

'That doesn't sound like a guilty person to me,' Fielding looked at Burton, who nodded his agreement of her statement.

'I didn't get the impression that she was.'

'And I felt the same about Barbara,' Fielding said. 'Like Selena, she was really upset by it all, and I don't think she was putting it on. How about Caroline?'

'She's a hard one alright. I still can't make my mind up about her, but one thing's for sure she could be either lying or telling the truth and we'd never know which one it was. I think she's spent too long in the legal system to know right from wrong – and I know how cockeyed that sounds, but you know what I mean. If she's spending her life defending somebody who's guilty then maybe she could come to believe what she's saying.'

'So, is she still high up on our list?' Summers asked.

'I think so. Are they all agreed on the drinks?'

As Burton listened, the other two described things exactly as Caroline had told him – the two bottles of Prosecco they'd shared in the bar, and the water carafes at Madame Ortiz's. The next thing he wanted to do was to get a warrant to search Madame Ortiz's premises in order to examine the two carafes which had held the water. Although, if they had held anything they would by now have been washed out. Even so, forensics would still be able to work their magic on them and the property. He also considered getting a sniffer dog and handler in; he'd have to ask about poisons, and be specific about the type, but he was certain some would be trained to search for them. Although he hadn't yet fully excluded any of the girlfriends, Ortiz was now his number one suspect despite the clues on the body pointing to her. Surely, if she was guilty of anything, she wouldn't leave clues implicating herself ... or would she? That could easily be a ploy, a distraction just to confuse things.

'But that wouldn't prove Madame Ortiz guilty of anything,' Fielding argued when Burton told them of his plan. 'Any one of the women could have slipped something into Maria's water if she had any.'

'That's true, I know' he said, 'but at least we'd know the how and the when.'

'Why don't we just ask her first if we can take a look around?' Summers asked.

'If we just ask her without first going there, she can easily dispose of what it is we're looking for if she's guilty.'

'So, a warrant then?' Fielding asked, and Burton nodded his head.

***

'I could come along and open up this afternoon if you'd like?' Marilyn 'Madame Ortiz' Parkinson said to Burton when he rang her. 'Why exactly do you wish to look around my business premises, detective?'

'Just to get a feel of the place,' Burton lied. If he'd told her the real reason why he and a few of the SOCO team wanted to visit, then he felt that she'd beat them to it and clean everything up – presuming she was guilty of anything, that is. He'd produce the warrant when he was standing on the doorstep, preferably with one foot well and truly wedged in the door if need be.

'Well then, how about three o'clock?'

'Three o'clock it is then.'

'Right,' he said after the call ended, 'let's arrange for the warrant and also get onto SOCO to meet us at the Northern Quarter address.'

'Sorry, I appear to have taken over again,' he apologised to Fielding, as Summers set off to take care of the documentation they needed.

'Like I said to you the last time you did it, it's okay. But, please, don't do it again!' she said with a wink.

'I'll try not to!'

'I'm sure you can do better than try,' she laughed.

'All right, all right!' Burton held both arms up in the air in defeat. 'I'll *definitely* not do it again, okay?' He laughed.

CHAPTER FORTY

Despite Burton's attempts not to get involved, Fielding couldn't help but ask him to do so. He was temporarily free for a couple of days from shadowing DCI Ambleton, so she couldn't see any harm in him joining her and Summers. In fact, she had to admit that she welcomed it. When they pulled up close to the business premises of Madame Ortiz, they saw that the SOCO team were already waiting by the door in an unmarked van. They knew it was them as the van was a familiar sight at the crime scenes they'd visited over the years. There was also a police van, which Burton knew to contain the sniffer dog. As the teams alighted from their vehicles, so did the SOCO people, two men and one woman. Fielding recognised the woman in the group as Holly, and gave her a little wave of acknowledgement. She waved back. When they were all together outside the premises, including the dog and its handler, Fielding produced the warrant and gave them instructions as to what they needed them to do. She could see Burton was straining at the bit to say something, but he managed to bite his lip and let her get on with it. She knew it must have been hard for him to do so as, after all, he had spent the last seven years taking the lead and giving her the instructions. Things were now reversed, and would be changing dramatically going forward. She wondered just how often he'd be tempted to join the team and tag along on a case and not remain upstairs in an office on his own. Only time would tell presumably. But if he did, she'd be more than happy for him to do so.

'We're looking for water carafes,' she informed SOCO, 'and any traces of digitalis in them. We know that they've very likely been washed out by now, but if anything at all could be found we'd greatly appreciate it.'

'We'll also check the place thoroughly for any other traces of it,' the lead member of the team confirmed.

At which point Burton pressed the intercom button on the door and waited for an answer.

'It's Detective Inspector Joe Burton,' he said into the speaker when it was answered.

'Just come on up, detective,' Marilyn Parkinson said to him, completely unaware that it would not just be him entering the building.

As they were going up the stairs, Marilyn appeared on the landing smiling. However, her smile soon left her face. Instead of just Joe Burton, she was greeted by a whole host of people making their way towards her. Sally Fielding edged to one side of Burton and held up the warrant for her to see. To say she looked annoyed was greatly underestimating her expression.

'You tricked me,' Marilyn said in a scathing tone, staring hard at Burton.

'No, not really. I said that I wanted to speak to you at your business premises and that is still the case.'

For once, the astrologer was lost for words, and still facing him she backed along the corridor towards the reception area.

'And what is this?' she demanded of Fielding, pointing at the warrant.

'We need to check the premises for any signs of poison, Ms Parkinson,' the detective said matter-of-factly.

'For what? What do you mean you need to check for poison?'

'Exactly that,' Fielding continued. 'We believe that there may be toxic substances here and we have acquired a legal right to search for them.'

'You have to be kidding?' Marilyn said looking at Burton, but he stood resolute, unflinching from the task in hand. No low-cut dresses or shirts would ever distract him from his work, no matter how hard she may try. And yes, he had noticed that she was again displaying 'a little too much cleavage' for his benefit, as Fielding had not too delicately put it.

There were only three rooms on the first floor – the reception area, the consulting room, and a small kitchen. There was also a toilet, but could hardly be classed as a room on its own.

'We need the carafes,' Fielding instructed the SOCO team members, 'and a thorough search for anything suspicious looking.'

At this point, Marilyn Parkinson resolved herself to the situation she had found herself in and took a seat in the reception room. It was pointless arguing any further with the police as they had a court order to search for whatever it was they were looking for. She had no idea why they wanted to see her water jugs, but was helpless to resist.

Everyone was very thorough. Now and again they thought that the dog had discovered something interesting as it lingered at certain points for a little longer than it had at others, but then moved on again.

The SOCO team found three carafes in total, all in the kitchen and all had been cleaned. Although Burton had expected them to be, he was still upset that they were. Nevertheless, they began testing them in situ for any particle traces. He always remembered the words spoken by a forensic scientist in one of the compulsory training lectures in his early days on the force – trust science, because no matter how much an item has been cleaned, there's always something a forensic team can pick up.

As Fielding was keeping a close eye on what was going on, he kept a close eye on Ms Parkinson to make sure that she didn't make a runner, but he needn't have been worried as she just sat quietly on the chair and occasionally looked up as people came and went in the room. She didn't speak, and she didn't move. Burton couldn't tell if it was out of fear or complacence, or neither as she was very hard to read, but what he did pick up was the fact that she wasn't too bothered by them looking through her stuff. Guilty people tend not to be that laid back.

Being only a three-room property, the examination of it took less time than expected. Despite the words of Burton's former lecturer, the SOCO team didn't find anything on or in the carafes, nor did the sniffer dog find anything either. So, in

Fielding's mind, that only meant one thing: there was nothing to be found and perhaps never had been. In that case, how long before Maria Turnbull had ventured out for the evening had she been given what was to be a fatal dose of poison? They'd all witnessed her suddenly appearing ill on the surveillance video from inside the vehicle, but that didn't necessarily mean that she'd just been given the poison. Indeed, Doctor Mansfield had specifically said that the time of ingestion couldn't be determined, which made things even more complicated to determine.

When Fielding returned to the waiting room she called out to him, and he moved away from Marilyn Parkinson to be with her. 'There's nothing we can charge her with I'm afraid,' she said to him, to which he replied that he knew.

'So, what now?' she asked.

'Back to the station I fear.'

'I thought that you'd say that, and I agree. I also think that we'll have to look at things from a different angle.' Fielding didn't quite know at that precise moment what the different angle was, but she knew that it would mean all of the team having to go through every last little detail again and reassessing the situation.

Marilyn Parkinson still didn't look happy as she showed them out and took the opportunity to tell them so. 'You know you could have just asked to come and take a look around without having to go to all this,' she said acerbically from the top of the stairs as she watched them leave.

'Just following protocol,' Burton replied without looking back as he continued down the stairs.

'I think we've just made ourselves an enemy,' Fielding said when they were back in the car.

Burton just shrugged. 'I'm sure we've made plenty in our time, so one more isn't going to hurt.'

It was then that Fielding received another setback, this time from the young SOCO Holly. She informed the detective that the hair sample had been fast-tracked, but no information was on record as to whose DNA it belonged to.

CHAPTER FORTY-ONE

'We now need to look at this from a different perspective,' Fielding said to the team when she gathered them together back at the station. Burton would now be with them for a few days while Ambleton was away on annual leave, and although he'd said that she was still in charge of everything and to only consider him as another team-member, it was something she couldn't really do. She'd still look upon him as her go-to person and seek his advice when she needed to. Did this mean that she was unready to fulfil her new role then? Burton would say not, and that it was just a period of transition and the uncertainty surrounding it. He knew that she was ready, as did DCI Ambleton. She hoped for all their sakes that they was right.

'I know that we haven't got anything on Maria's friends or Madame Ortiz, and can't prove anything one way or another, but I still don't trust any of them,' Jack Summers said emphatically when they'd reassessed the situation.

'I agree,' Fielding replied. 'We still have to consider them as suspects thought.'

'Of course, there is one person we haven't properly questioned yet.' Fielding knew Burton so well, and knew that it wouldn't be long before he could resist a comment. 'Maria Turnbull's husband,' he continued.

'He was in no fit state to be interviewed when we saw him last.'

'I know, which is why I think we need to pay him another visit. If we can't find anything to link the others to the murder then he has to be a key suspect again.'

'Would you like me to ring him and make an appointment to go over?' Summers volunteered, to which Fielding replied that she would.

While he was doing that, Burton announced that there was to be another press conference that afternoon.

'Oh no, I don't think I could go through that again!' Although handling it fairly well, and the wannabe journalist's revelation at the end, Fielding didn't relish the prospect of another wrangle with the press and media.

'You don't have to,' Burton said, 'I can handle it if you like? If John Turnbull says it's okay to go over then you and Summers can just go by yourselves.'

'Are you sure?'

'Of course.

'Rather you than me,' she quipped, to which he smiled wryly.

'I could only get through to his mother,' Summers said upon returning. 'John is out picking up his in-laws from the airport and taking them back to his own house.'

'I'm surprised he's able to do that,' Burton remarked. He wouldn't have thought Turnbull would have been capable of going anywhere judging by how he'd been when he and Fielding had last seen him.

'Maybe he just needs to get out of the house,' Fielding offered. 'Plus, he's going to collect Maria's parents. I suspect that will be a hard meeting.'

'True. In that case, I'd still go to see the mother first.'

Fielding raised an eyebrow, which didn't go unnoticed by Burton.

'Just for some background information on him. How did he meet Maria, was their relationship okay, any worries, that sort of thing?'

'Okay. It can't do any harm, can it? You know, Joe, we're really struggling with this case. It seems that we're getting nowhere fast. If we could only pinpoint the time of Maria's death we'd be in a far better position than we are now.'

'I know we would. I think that's the one major problem we have with it. If you don't mind, I think I might give Mansfield a call and pop over to see him after the press conference and try to see if there's any way around that.'

'No, I don't mind at all. In fact, I'd be very happy if you did.'

'Right, that's done then.'

***

While Joe Burton was waiting for his meeting with the press, Fielding and Summers headed off to have a word with John Turnbull's mother. Hopefully, his father might also join in with the conversation this time, but judging by how he was when they saw him last, Fielding didn't hold out much hope. Unsurprisingly, the death of his daughter-in-law had hit him hard, and if retreating into himself helped him get through that then she couldn't really blame him for it. Different people react differently to death, and had their own way of coping with it. She'd seen it over and over again, and probably would do so for the foreseeable future. Some were like Mr Turnbull, whereas others veered to the other extreme. It was as if by coming to terms with their own mortality and fragility of their own lives they sought to enjoy themselves to the full. It was the whole 'eat, drink and be merry, for tomorrow we die' philosophy. Although not going to that extreme herself, she knew from personal experience that it was necessary to move on with your own life after the death of a loved one.

John Turnbull's mother welcomed them into her house.

'Come through, but I'm afraid John's had to go to the airport,' she said to them as she led them into her living room.

'Yes, I know. I believe you told my sergeant here that when he rang you.'

'Did I?' she asked vaguely as she turned to Summers.

Fielding could see that she was still in a state of shock about her daughter-in-law's demise, but wondered where her husband was as he wasn't sitting in the chair she remembered him being in.

'And your husband, where is he Mrs Turnbull?'

'He's having a bit of a lie down. Not feeling too well. I think he's coming down with something or other.'

Her speech was short and jerky and she was trying to carry on as normal, probably for both her son and husband, but seemed to be struggling with her own demons in an attempt to do so.

'Have *you* been to see a doctor, Mrs Turnbull?' Fielding asked considerately.

'Me ... see a doctor ... why on earth would I want to see a doctor?'

'Well, you've had a bit of a shock now, haven't you? It can't have been easy for any of you.' The detective was trying to be as sensitive as possible as in some ways it seemed that the reality of the situation hadn't quite sunk in yet.

'I'm fine, I'm fine,' she repeated, somewhat edgily. It was more than enough for Fielding to think that she wasn't fine at all. Despite the denial, the detective thought that underneath the increasingly agitated exterior there was a volcano waiting to erupt.

'Shall we sit down and have a little chat?' Fielding sat down on the sofa without waiting to be asked, and Summers followed suit. She hoped that her action would not appear rude and that Mrs Turnbull would do the same – which she did. It was only then that she appeared to let go of the forced put-on for the world.

'It's been such a shock,' she began, and Fielding could hear her voice beginning to break as she spoke. 'I know that we haven't known Maria that long, but we've both, my husband and I, grown to love her as part of the family. Well, she *was* part of the family. I can't imagine what John's going to do without her, I really can't.'

'Tell me how they met,' Fielding gently coaxed.

'Oh,' she wiped a tear from her cheek, 'they met at one of John's work's do's. He'd worked on and off with one of her friends, he said, something to do with the business side of things I believe, and Maria had come along to the party with her.'

'Can you recall the friend's name?'

'Carol, or something like that.'

Fielding and Summers exchanged quick glances.

'They just hit it off from the start. I have to say I was slightly surprised when he announced they were going to be married – we'd only met her a couple of times and there they were about to tie the knot. I suppose that's the way these days, not to hang around too long. Time's too short for the young ones. Back in my day it was a long spell of courting and asking parents for permission, but I guess it's all changed now.'

'And they got on okay?' Summers asked her.

Mrs Turnbull looked surprised at the question. 'Well, of course they did. That's an odd question to ask.'

'Just routine,' he explained.

'What about Maria's parents? Your son said that they'd retired early and gone to live abroad.'

'That's right. I'm not really sure what it was that they did, but it must have earned them a lot of money for them to be able to retire as early as they did.' She pulled a face at that last part, which Fielding picked up on.

'I sense something there; something you're unhappy about?'

Mrs Turnbull shuffled uncomfortably. 'Well, it's just ... we lost quite a bit of money about ten years ago. We used to be fairly well off, but then my husband was lured in by this investment company a friend of his told him about. I was a bit dubious at the time and told him to do more research on it, but he went ahead and invested in it anyway. Said it sounded almost too good to be true. As you can imagine, it was. We lost everything, absolutely everything, our house, our savings, the lot, and had to come and live here.' She waved a hand around at her surroundings as if embarrassed by them. 'We could never afford anything much after that. My husband felt so guilty about it, and we went through a very bad patch in our relationship, but when the money was gone it was gone, wasn't it? In the end I just resigned myself to the fact and tried to carry on and pick up the pieces as best as I could. We just don't talk about it these days.'

'Couldn't you have taken the company to court?' Summers asked her.

'Do you think we didn't try? Oh, we tried to, of course we did, but the company went into receivership and was declared bankrupt. Our solicitor said there was nothing we could do after that.'

'That's dreadful; I'm so sorry to hear that you had to go through that,' Fielding said to her. She couldn't even imagine how hard that must have been for them both.

'John took it very badly as I recall,' Mrs Turnbull continued, but then her voice just trailed off.

'Look, we don't want to keep you any longer, but how long will John be at the airport as we'd like to have a word with him too?'

'Oh, he's not coming back here. He said that he'd put Maria's parents up at his place. He's got the space, you see, and is able to accommodate them far better than we ever could.'

'I'm surprised he's able to get out of the house in order to do it, considering.'

'Our doctor prescribed him something,' she smiled, 'and it seems to have given him the will to live again.'

'Yes, medication can help.' Fielding remembered the death of her own father all those years ago, and how the family's doctor kept her mother afloat after tragedy struck. 'Thank you for your time, Mrs Turnbull, we appreciate it,' she continued, rising from her seat. Summers followed her lead.

CHAPTER FORTY-TWO

As John Turnbull hadn't arrived back from the airport by the time they got to his house, Fielding and Summers sat and waited outside in the car.

'I'm surprised he's able to function,' Summers said to her as they kept watch. 'I know I wouldn't be.'

'No, me neither.'

'I know Joe mentioned going to see Doctor Mansfield; do you think he might be able to pinpoint the death a little better?'

'I'd like to think so, but from what he told us before it doesn't seem very likely.'

'I wonder how he's getting on with the press conference?' Summers pondered.

Fielding grimaced. 'Please, don't remind me of that!'

'Not a pleasant thing, is it?'

'Rather him than me, but I suppose I'm going to have to get used to it in the future, both of us in fact.'

'I'm trying to train myself to see it as playing a part on the stage. I think it might help me to get through it a little better,' Summers confessed.

Fielding was surprised as he seemed to be taking it all in his stride the other day. 'So, your brave face was just an act then?'

'Of course,' he laughed. 'I was just as terrified as you were!'

'Well, you hid it very well,' she complimented him.

'Methinks that I should have been an actor on the stage then!'

'Maybe you should have!'

Just at that moment a car rounded the corner and came to a stop outside the house. The detectives could see John Turnbull in the driver's seat, with presumably his late wife's parents in the rear. Turnbull stared at them through the windscreen before turning off the ignition key and opening the door. Rather than come over to their car straight away, he opened the back offside door to allow the female passenger to exit then moved around to the back of the vehicle to the other one. Once out, the two passengers also looked towards the officers' car as Fielding and Summers started to alight from it. They spoke briefly to John as he gave them the keys to his house, then indicated that they should go inside before he joined the detectives waiting on the pavement for him.

'I wasn't aware that you were coming to see me; did you go to my parents' house first?'

'Yes, we did, as we assumed that you'd still be there,' Fielding said to him.

'No.' John Turnbull seemed a bit jittery to her, but then, he'd had just picked up his late wife's parents from the airport.

'Sorry, where are my manners,' he continued, 'please come inside, we can talk in there. I'm sure Maria's parents will want to hear what you have to say too.'

Fielding didn't like to tell him that he was a suspect in the case, even less so Maria's mother and father, so suggested to him that it might be best that they speak away from them.

'Perhaps we could talk on your driveway and not out here on the street?' she suggested, looking around her. It was quiet at the moment, but she could see a couple coming their way several houses down.

John Turnbull's frown said more than words ever could. He looked confused, but agreed to it.

'Now what is it you want to ask me?' He said when they were off the pavement.

Truth was, Fielding was uncertain where to begin, or even what to ask him. She couldn't very well come out and ask him if he killed his wife ... or could she? Could it be as simple as that, catch him off guard and see what his reaction is? She thought she'd try her luck.

'Did you kill your wife, Mr Turnbull?'

Not only was Turnbull taken aback, but Summers also looked at her in astonishment with a look that appeared to question his colleague's judgement.

'I beg your pardon?'

'I asked you if you-'

'I heard you,' he cut in, 'but I can't quite believe what I've just heard you ask me. I've just lost my wife, her parents have just come over here to bury her, and you're asking me a question like that? This is inexcusable, detective. Inexcusable.' The grieving widower obviously thought that Fielding had overstepped the mark with her off-the-wall idea.

'It's a question we have to ask, sir,' she quickly came out with. Glancing sideways at Summers, she could swear that his mouth was hanging open. Looking away, she concentrated on Turnbull again.

'I loved my wife. How could you even ask me a question like that?'

'Like I said, sir-'

Turnbull wouldn't let her finish. 'I'm going to get in touch with your superior. What's their name?'

Not wanting to involve DCI Ambleton in this, she gave him Joe Burton's name.

'I'll be getting in touch with him,' he said angrily, and stormed up to the front door of the house, leaving them standing on the drive. By this time the couple who had been walking up the street both stopped upon hearing the commotion and stared at both the detectives before moving quickly on.

'Do you think it worked?' Summers asked her.

'Let's hope so,' she said turning and heading back to the car. 'Nice acting by the way, you had me convinced you were shocked! Now I'd better get in touch with Joe before Mr Turnbull does.'

***

'So, you should expect a phone call from him,' Fielding said to Burton after telling him about her conversation with John Turnbull.

'Something to look forward to then,' he said, ironically. 'Do you think your idea worked?'

'It gave him something to think about, that's for sure.'

'We'll just have to wait and see.' He concluded.

'How did the press conference go?' She asked him, changing the subject.

'It went okay; easier than hoped for really. The press were, well, the press, but it's over with. After that I paid a visit to Doctor Mansfield. He said he'll have another look at the time of death. He's not promising anything, but he's going to ask one of his medical colleagues who specialises in poisons to have a look at the evidence and get his take on it.'

Fielding nodded, hopeful that it might come to something. It was the one thing they were lacking, something concrete about the time digitalis had been administered to Maria Turnbull. Without it they were just clutching at straws in the hope that somebody might slip up and give themselves away, which is why she posed the blunt, accusatory question at the husband in order to get some kind of reaction.

'Summers was great, by the way,' she said. 'I told you that he was heading for the stage at one point, didn't I?'

'Yes, you did. It came in handy then.'

'You know, I've been thinking,' Fielding continued, 'do you think it could just all be about the money?'

'Well, Maria's parents must have accumulated enough money over the years from their work for them to retire early, so perhaps if she died her husband John somehow inherited her wealth? If that's the case, I think we need to look into their background, find out what they did before they headed off to Spain.'

Fielding still looked pensive. 'But John has a very good job, hasn't he? I expect architecture pays good money, especially with the projects he's been involved with, so he'll have plenty money of his own from his lucrative employment.'

'True. Plus, we have to consider that, if money is the reason for Maria's death, how is it even related to the deaths of Harry York and Norman Bishop?'

They both fell silent, deep in thought about what the connection could be.

'You know,' Burton spoke first, 'we could be missing something.'

'Like what?'

'Like there's more than one thing going on here.'

Fielding looked puzzled.

'The deaths of Harry York and Norman Bishop may be part of it, yet not.'

Another confused expression from Fielding.

'Think about it,' he enthused, as if trying to work it out in his head as he was going along, 'all three deaths are related, they have to be, but what if, in the cases of York and Bishop, it was them either seeing or knowing something that they shouldn't have?'

'That's a very good point,' she agreed. 'But what? What could they both possibly have known that led to them getting killed?'

'I think we have to go back to the psychologist's line of thinking again, to the main reasons why killers kill: revenge, monetary gain, or to silence someone who is going to reveal a secret, for example, fraud or adultery.'

'Well, possibly monetary gain for John Turnbull. In the cases of Turnbull. York and Bishop, maybe they both knew something considered to be secretive and were going to reveal what that was.'

'In the case of the latter two, it can only be financial; but did they know something they shouldn't have, or done something they shouldn't?'

'It's Occam's Razor again,' Fielding said, reintroducing one of her favourite terms back into the thick of things. 'where the simplest answer is often the correct one.'

'Trust you!' Burton laughed, acknowledging her fondness for the theory. 'But I agree. For some reason, I think John Turnbull killed his wife along with York and Bishop, for either knowing something about it or relating to it. All we have to do now is prove it.'

CHAPTER FORTY-THREE

After briefing the team, everyone went through the evidence again to look at it from a different perspective. Burton now believed, as did Fielding, that John Turnbull was as guilty as hell.

'I need someone to look into Maria Turnbull's parents, what they did for a living, where they're living in Spain now, background stuff, that kind of thing.'

'I can get on that,' Summers volunteered, and was given the go-ahead to seek the information out.

'Okay, everybody else, go through statements again and see what everyone has in common.' Fielding once again took the lead, with Burton happy to step back be part of the team and not the main go-to person.

Over the course of the next few hours everyone concentrated on the task in hand, and by the end of it they had accumulated some very revealing information. But it was what Jack Summers found that sparked the most interest. Prior to their relocation abroad some ten years earlier, it appeared that the Richardsons had both been joint Directors of an overseas property investment company called Faraway Dreams. According to reports, the business had been a going concern until at some point it was subject to an official investigation and was forced to close. Seemingly, many of the company's investors had lost their life savings in bad investments, but according to the official police report it was a little more complex than that. The file which Summers had acquired seemed to suggest that the Richardsons had acted fraudulently, but before any proceedings had taken place, they'd fled the country. It appeared from this that they moved to Spain to avoid prosecution when the whole business went down the pan. Extradition had been applied for, but because Maria's parent had applied for Spanish citizenship by the time the Fraud Squad discovered their location, they couldn't just go in and arrest them. However, it had been noted in the files that Summers found that should they return to the UK for any reason they could still be held accountable. Both Burton and Fielding wondered if their daughter had known about the family business, and by the same token had she told her husband? But what, if anything, did that have to do with Maria's death, and the subsequent deaths of both Harry York and Norman Bishop? Those were the questions that needed to be answered.

'Should we alert the appropriate team that the Richardsons are back in this country?' Summers asked Fielding.

She looked towards Burton, but already knew what both of them were thinking.

'Yes, I believe that we should, under the circumstances,' she said, and Burton also nodded his head in agreement with that.

'Quite a catch for the Fraud Squad, I'd say,' he commented. He had a couple of friends on the team and suggested that he contact them straight away. Fielding thought that to be an excellent idea.

'We may not have caught a killer yet, but we've managed to find a couple of historic crooks,' Summers declared, overjoyed with his find.

'Good work, Jack,' Fielding gave praise where it was due.

'So, what did Harry York and Norman Bishop see or hear that got them killed?' Burton mused.

'Maybe it *was* financial,' Summers offered. 'Perhaps they both found out about Maria's parents and decided to do a bit of blackmailing?'

'Perhaps,' Burton mulled, but didn't sound too convinced by the suggestion.

'Yes,' Fielding jumped in, 'and Maria somehow mentioned it to Harry York.'

'That's assuming that she knew about her parents' affairs.'

'How could she not?'

'Well, I'm sure that parents can keep secrets from their children,' Burton came back with. 'They could have simply told her that they were retiring early and she'd be none the wiser, then headed off to the sun to escape prosecution.'

'So, if she didn't know about her parents then she couldn't have let it slip to Harry York.'

'Precisely.'

Fielding felt as if they were going around in circles. The only positive thing to come out of this was the fact that they'd discovered the current whereabouts of the Richardsons, who were still wanted for fraud even after ten years.

'At least we've solved another case,' Burton said placing a hand on Fielding's shoulder after seeing the look of desperation on her face. She knew he was right about that, although it was the present case that troubling her. She needed to know who had killed their three victims, and although it was now looking as if John Turnbull was their main suspect, there was little in the way of evidence or motive to support that. In fact, the same could be said of any of the other suspects. There was nothing concrete to support the finger pointing to either Caroline Watkins or Marilyn Parkinson. So, where did that leave them? They had the unexpected bonus of rooting out a criminal husband and wife team, but what they really needed was Doctor Mansfield's poisons expert to come back to them with something more definitive.

It was then that Fielding had an odd idea. 'You don't think that Maria could have poisoned herself, do you?'

'Whatever made you think that?' Burton asked her, surprised by the statement.

'I know that it wouldn't account for the other two murders, but what if she did?'

'But why would she do that?' Summers asked, as equally taken aback as Burton was. 'She appeared to have had a perfect life with an excellent job and a new husband?'

'Appearances can be deceptive,' Fielding said to him, 'We all know that's true. Maybe she found out about her parents; or maybe something else happened at home, like her husband abusing her?'

Burton exhaled a long, weary breath and looked around him at the other members of the team. 'What has everybody else found?'

DC Jane Francis spoke up first. 'I was concentrating on looking into Caroline Watkins's background. As expected, she'd completely clean; however, some of her legal decisions might be considered questionable, bearing in mind who some of the firm's clients appear to be.'

Burton was curious. 'Like whom?'

'Well, Jimmy Fitzpatrick for one.'

Summers let out a long whistle. Jimmy Fitzpatrick was a known businessman in the city who was rumoured to have links with some of London's big crime families, although that 'fact' had never been proven and probably wouldn't be with solicitors like Watkins to defend him.

'Well, that's interesting,' Burton declared. 'I wonder if Jimmy Fitzpatrick knew Maria Turnbull's parents?'

'I don't think all criminals actually know one another personally,' Fielding remarked, although she could see where he was going with that reasoning.

'No, but it would be interesting to know, wouldn't it?'

'And how can we go about finding that out?' Summers asked.

'We go and ask him.'

***

Jimmy Fitzgerald's place of business was a high-end car dealership on the A6 just south of the city. Fielding thought back to a previous case and another 'car dealer' she'd had dealings with in the person of one Gabriel Reyes, the smooth-talking South American who'd taken a shine to her during the course of the investigation. Fitzgerald was well-known to the police as he'd been watched on a number of occasions when his link to London had been discovered, but the man had never left himself exposed or put a foot wrong in that respect. If it hadn't been for the known connection, then nobody would have been any the wiser.

They hadn't called ahead so as to give the element of surprise, although if Fitzpatrick was as careful as they expected him to be given the information they had, then their arrival wouldn't even raise an eyebrow with him. So, when they parked up near the front entrance, the only sign that there was something else going on here was the sight of a man in a black suit and tie wandering around inside the glass-fronted showroom. He looked completely out of place amidst the other salesmen, who were all jacketless and had their sleeves rolled up, and would have looked more at home outside a nightclub. The man in black caught sight of them as they alighted the car and immediately pulled a phone from his pocket. If he'd intended to be discreet doing it then he'd fallen way short of the mark; it was obvious that he was phoning his boss to give him the heads-up.

'Interesting,' Fielding remarked.

'Well, in a few seconds Fitzpatrick will know that the police are here,' Burton laughed. Although both he and Fielding were both plain-clothed, the fact that they were police officers must have been written across both their foreheads.

'I didn't think that we were that obvious,' Fielding retorted.

'We must be.'

'I would have easily taken us for a couple looking to get a new car.'

Burton held the door open for her to enter then followed in behind, whereupon they were immediately pounced upon by one of the eager bare-forearmed sales team.

'Hello there and welcome to Fitzpatrick's. How may I be of assistance?' he asked them with a wide beaming grin, which might have been appreciated by a genuine punter to the salesroom. Before the detectives could answer, Mr Burly Black Suit quickly appeared behind him and interrupted his pre-emptive sales pitch.

'It's all right, Jake,' he said to the young man, 'I think they're here to see Mr Fitzpatrick himself and not to purchase a new vehicle, am I right?' The latter question addressed to Burton and Fielding.

'Yes, that's correct,' Burton said, bringing out his warrant card. Fielding did the same. 'It's only a courtesy call, and to ask him for a little advice.'

Fitzpatrick's bouncer looked surprised. It seemed that he was expecting to be shown a search warrant and was taken aback by the officer's request for a chat. At that point, his phone rang and he answered it. He listened and didn't say a word before replacing it in his pocket, after which he told them that the showroom's owner would be more than happy to see them.

Burton looked around him, scanning the premises for cameras, as that would have been the only way Fitzpatrick would have known what they'd come for. Probably had audio too, he didn't doubt.

They followed behind as the bouncer led the way, taking them through to the rear of the showroom and then up a flight of stair to the first floor. He stopped beside a door and knocked, waiting for a response. Only when he heard 'Come in' did he open the door and let them through.

'Detectives Burton and Fielding,' he announced, before exiting and closing the door behind him.

The two police officers hadn't crossed paths with Jimmy Fitzpatrick before but had heard many stories about him and his underworld connections. He'd never been caught for anything, but everybody knew that whatever he was into he was in it right up to his neck. Only the evidence was absent. But that wasn't why they were here today; all they were after was finding out what, if anything, he knew about the Richardsons and their former less-than-genuine overseas property company.

Fitzpatrick stood up and came around from behind his desk to greet them. He was a short man, no taller than 5'6" or 5'7", but was immaculately dressed. Fielding thought of the Hercules Poirot character from the Agatha Christie novels, such was the way he carried himself with his styling and manner. All that was lacking was a neatly maintained moustache.

'And how may I help the officers of the law?' he asked, extending a hand to each in turn. Burton couldn't tell if he was being sincere or sarcastic in the manner in which he addressed them.

'We'd just like to ask you a couple of questions, sir.' Burton said.

'Please sit.'

Burton and Fielding sat on the two chairs set out in front of the man's desk. There were several monitors on his desk with their backs towards them, some of which had evidently captured their arrival and heard what they'd said. This was made evident by what he said next.

'I understand you are after a bit of advice?' he laughed gently. 'It's not often the police come to me asking for advice.'

The man had, it seemed, no qualms about hiding his true nature or his nefarious connections.

'Yes,' Fielding thought that it was time she joined in with the conversation. 'We were wondering if you'd ever met a Mr and Mrs Turnbull, Brian and Margaret, who owned a company called Faraway Dreams? This would have been over ten years ago.'

Fitzpatrick sat back in his chair. 'And why do you think I would know them?' he asked.

It was a fair question, and one which neither of them had a ready answer for. Burton improvised.

'It's just ... how can I put this? ... it's just that they did a bit of a runner to Spain a decade ago, and we know that you might know a number of people over there.'

Fitzpatrick laughed heartily. 'Very delicately put, detective,' he complimented Burton on his tact. It was a risk on Burton's part and he knew it, however, the businessman didn't seem fazed by what he was suggesting. Fielding, though, was horrified. The last thing she wanted was to be stuck in an office with a known gangland associate without any form of backup.

'I like you!' Fitzpatrick added, 'and your lady friend there. Well, let me think. Ten years is a long time, you know, but let me see what I can remember for you. Brian and Margaret Townsend ... Faraway Dreams ...'

He seemed to drift off for a moment in an attempt to recall, during which time Burton and

Fielding exchanged glances. His was one of success, but hers was one of fear. Seeing this, he reached across and gently squeezed her hand, which wasn't unnoticed by Fitzpatrick, despite his concentrated attempts at recollection.

'More than just police partners, then?'

Burton didn't feel comfortable disclosing anything about his personal life, so just gave the man a smile.

'Okay, yes, I have heard of them,' he said at long last. 'I believe that they packed up and left to go and live in Spain?' As Burton nodded, he continued. 'They had a lot of unhappy customers. I hear they swindled a lot of people out of a lot of money.'

'How much money, do you know?' Fielding asked.

'It must have been quite a lot for them to leave the country like that.'

'And did you have any direct dealing with them?' she continued.

'You mean like selling them a new car?'

Fielding looked wryly at Burton. 'No, and you know what I mean, sir.'

'Mr Fitzpatrick,' Burton took over at this point, 'we're not here about you, in fact at this precise moment in time we're not bothered about you in the slightest – no offence. All we want to do is to find out a little more about the Richardsons and their background.'

Fitzpatrick pouted his lips. 'You've hurt my feelings, detective,' he said, feigning sadness.

'Come on,' Burton retorted, 'we all know about your connections and, like I said, that's irrelevant at this moment. The couple's daughter's just been murdered, and all we want to know is could it somehow be related to her parents' criminal activities.' He chastised himself as soon as he said it. He hadn't wanted to reveal as much as that to the man, but it was far too late now to take it back now.

'Okay,' Fitzpatrick said, once again sitting back in his seat. 'I knew the Richardsons indirectly. Heard about their business and why they left for sunnier climes. Rumour was that the daughter didn't know a thing about it. Was away at university, I believe, when it all went down.'

'So that couldn't have got her killed, in your opinion?'

'No, I don't think so. Why would anyone want to kill her for her parents' wrong doing?'

It was a fair question, and one the detectives agreed with. They too couldn't see a connection, but they had to hear it from someone who appeared to know all there was to know about the country's criminal undertakings.

'While we're here,' Burton began, and Fitzpatrick seemed to flinch slightly as he wondered what might be coming next. 'Your solicitor is Caroline Watkins, isn't she?'

'She is employed at the firm of solicitors who work on my behalf, that's correct.'

'What can you tell us about her?'

Fitzpatrick laughed. 'What's Caroline gone and done now? She's a feisty one, that one, and I wouldn't be surprised in the least if she's overstepped the mark this time!'

'Is she known for overstepping the mark then?' Fielding asked.

'She will do what she needs to do in order to get the work done.'

'Meaning?'

'Meaning just that. She fights hard for a client and will manage to dig up all kinds of juicy information on their behalf. She's a fighter; maybe she should come and work for me!'

'Do you think that she would go as far as murder?' Burton had to ask to question he'd wanted to ask from the start.

Fitzpatrick looked shocked. 'Murder?' He shook his head. 'She's a hard one alright, but murder, no I certainly wouldn't take her to be someone who would extend herself to doing that. The only murderous thing about her is her tongue, and works by words and not actions, that's why she's so successful.'

'Okay then.' Burton rose from his seat, followed by his partner. 'Thank you for your time,' he said, 'we really appreciate it.'

'As do I. It's nice not to have a search warrant waved in my face by the boys in blue. Or the girls in blue either,' he added, smiling at Fielding as he said it.

CHAPTER FORTY-FOUR

'He wasn't as bad as I thought he'd be,' Fielding declared when they were back in the car.

'Looks can be deceiving,' Burton reminded her.

'I guess, but he was helpful enough considering we just walked in and asked to speak to him.'

'Probably like he said, he was happy that we didn't barge in and wave a search warrant in his face.'

'I've heard of him, of course, the rumours and everything. Funny that we've never crossed paths with him before now though.'

'Not our patch, I guess. I think the Fraud guys have a big file on him, and pay him visits now and again, which is probably why he thought we'd be producing a search warrant, but as far as I know he's never been involved with murder.'

'As far as we know,' Fielding said.

'Yes, that's true. But despite everything, he didn't seem like much of a threat.'

'That's probably because *we* weren't threatening *him*.'

'Again, true.'

'So, what about Caroline Watkins?' Fielding mused. 'She certainly seems to be the determined one.'

'Especially if the company has people like Fitzpatrick on their books.'

'But determined enough to kill, and if so, for what reason?'

It was indeed a question to be asked, as the suspect spotlight now veered back and forth between her and John Turnbull. When they got back to the station the place was alive with excitement.

'What's going on?' Burton asked Phillipa Preston, but then spotted Summers talking to his friend from the Fraud Squad. 'Hey, Mark,' he called over to him.

The man excused himself and came over, grinning ear from ear as he shook Burton's hand vigorously.

'Good call, mate,' he said to him. 'You only gone and led us to a pair of criminals we've been trying to land for a decade!'

'The Richardsons you mean?'

'Yes, the Richardsons!' he repeated excitedly. 'We've got them banged up right now, but we've had to call a duty doctor in to take a look at them.'

'Oh, why was that?' Fielding asked, at which point Burton apologised and introduced her to his old friend.

'Pleased to meet you,' Mark said holding out his hand to her, which she shook. 'Yes, they were both complaining of feeling queasy, which we thought to be a ploy under the circumstances, but then the doctor said that he needed to do a few tests in-depth on them as he felt they weren't putting it on.'

Burton and Fielding exchanged questioning glances.

'Why, what's wrong?' the Fraud Squad detective asked them on seeing their expressions.

'Do me a favour, Mark,' Burton said urgently, 'get your doctor to do a test for poisoning, will you?'

'Poison? Whatever for?'

'Just call it a hunch.'

'Okay, will do,' Mark said, immediately reaching in his pocket for his phone. They knew one another well enough to know that if a concern was raised it was a valid one.

'And tell them to specifically look for digitalis,' Burton added.

While Mark was making the call, Fielding, like Burton, felt that they'd made a huge breakthrough.

'This could be what we've been waiting for,' she said.

It's funny how, when the ball is set in motion, things seem to escalate very quickly. Simon Banks excitedly caught Burton's and Fielding's attention and called them over to his desk.

'Yes, what is it?' Burton asked, standing behind his chair. Fielding joined him.

'Among other things, I've been searching for photographs of Marilyn Parkinson online which might show her with a boyfriend and I came across this,' he said, pointing at the image on the monitor from a local newspaper. 'It was taken just over a year ago, and was at a reception held at the Town Hall.'

As Burton and Fielding looked closer, they could clearly see Parkinson and John Turnbull in the background, looking a little closer than just casual acquaintances.

'That's great, Simon!' Burton couldn't contain his excitement. 'This is just what we've been looking for. Print if off, will you? Well done!'

At the same time, DC Phillipa Preston took a call from dispatch. The call came in from the hairdressing salon next door to Madame Ortiz's business premises, and the person on the other end of the phone reported a disturbance in the astrologer's place of work, bad enough, it seemed, to initiate a call to the police.

'Did they say what it was?' Burton asked, grabbing his jacket as he spoke.

'Only that there appeared to be raised voices and the sound of things being broken,' Phillipa said to him.

'Okay, thanks for that,' he said to her, as he sprinted out with Fielding not too far behind him.

***

By the time they got to Madame Ortiz's business address, there was already a police car with its lights still flashing parked up outside the premises.

'I'll go and have a word with the person who reported it,' Fielding said to him, 'to hear what they have to say.'

As she went next door, Burton bounded up the stairs to where he could hear raised voices coming from the reception area. Both Marilyn Parkinson and Caroline Watkins were being restrained by two uniformed officers, while a third was making a call. Despite the restraint, each was trying to break away and get to the other. Burton noticed scratches on the women's faces, and what looked like the start of a black eye on Parkinson. Both looked as if they'd been involved in one hell of a brawl.

'What's going on?' Burton asked the constable who was on his phone.

'I'm calling for back-up, sir,' he said, 'these two are not going to go away quietly.

'Can you get any sense out of them?'

'Not a thing. By the time we got here they were well into a scrap. Took all my colleagues' powers to even part the two of them. Oh, and we found a couple of syringes on the floor over by the door there, so not sure if this is a drugs thing or not. We left them where we found them, mainly because we knew it would be best to, and also that we had our hands full with the two women.'

Burton sensed that it was not a 'drugs thing' in the way that the constable had meant. But two syringes? That seemed to imply that each one of them had tried to attack the other with one. But why, and, perhaps more importantly, where had they obtained them from? He took a poly bag out from his pocket and slipped on a pair of nitrile gloves. Walking over to the door which led into Madame Ortiz's consulting room, he bent down and picked up both the syringes. Both were almost full so, assumingly, neither had carried out that which they'd intended.

'What do you think's in them?' the constable continued.

'If it's what I think it is, then I believe it could well be the resolution of the case my team's working on.'

CHAPTER FORTY-FIVE

Marilyn Parkinson sat in Interview Room 1, right next to Interview Room 2 where Caroline Watkins likewise sat. Both were battered and bruised; both were tight-lipped about what had actually happened in the former's business premises. Neither was speaking, and neither showed any emotion about their current situation.

'What is going on with those two?' Fielding asked, standing in the corridor alongside her partner.

'I thought they'd at least say something, anything really. Of all people, Caroline Watkins should know how this looks.'

'I'm surprised she hasn't asked for a member of her law firm to come in to try and get her released.'

'I'm not sure what either of them are guilty of, apart from assault, that is.' Burton ran a hand through his hair, a well-known habit of his when something was puzzling him. 'The syringes look damaging, and I suspect we know what they contained, but until their contents are analysed then we've got nothing.'

'We can still hold them though, until we get that information through.'

'Yes,' he said defiantly, 'and we will.'

It was decided that Fielding, along with Jack Summers, should conduct the interviews with the two women. Burton would watch the proceedings from the observation area between rooms 1 and 2. After ringing the squad room and asking acting DI Summers to join them, the two detectives waited outside the rooms until he arrived. Summers was thrilled to have been asked as it meant he was again being handed more responsibility. He'd certainly need it for his future role with Fielding.

Waiting until Burton entered the adjoining room, Fielding then opened the door to room number 1. Parkinson looked up from her seat behind the desk. She looked scared and afraid, and seemed to be a little uncertain of what was actually happening. Fielding nodded to the female constable on duty inside the room, who knew the gesture to mean that she was temporarily released from her watch and to wait outside until called back in again. When the door closed behind her, Fielding and Summers both took seats opposite, and Fielding opened the manila folder she was holding.

'I'm sorry I'm not looking my usual self,' Parkinson said with a very slight smile as she attempted to tidy her dishevelled hair, still disorderly from Caroline Watkins's attack on her.

'Can you tell me exactly what happened at your business premises tonight, Ms Parkinson?' Fielding kept it professional, completely dismissing the woman's comments on her appearance and got straight down to the point of questioning her.

Marilyn Parkinson immediately stopped trying to sort her hair out. She could see the serious look in the detective's face, and knew that this was no time for light-hearted conversation.

'Well,' she began. 'that woman, Caroline Watkins, who I remembered from that dreadful thing that happened with that poor girl, got in touch with me.'

'Maria Turnbull,' Fielding said to her.

'Sorry?'

'Maria Turnbull. That's the name of the young woman who died.'

'Yes, yes of course,' Parkinson continued. 'I thought that she wanted to speak to me regarding her friend's death.'

'How did she get in touch with you?'

'Via a message on my website along with her telephone number.'

'Why did you think that she wanted to speak to you about it?' Summers asked. Fielding was glad that he was getting himself involved in the interview so soon. She thought back to her early days with Joe Burton as her partner; she would jump in and ask relevant question and recalled him praising her for it. Summers would make a good partner, but she already knew that from her stint with him on a previous case.

'I just thought that she needed somebody to talk to, you know, somebody separate from her friends. I find that sometimes it can be easier to have a heart-to-heart with somebody you hardly know, somebody who's completely impartial.'

'Didn't you think that a little strange?'

'Well, I did, a little bit, but she sounded so upset when I rang that I felt I had to meet up with her to try to see if I could be of some help.'

'So, she was the one who suggested coming to you?' Fielding asked this time.

'Yes.'

'Then what happened?'

'She told me when she'd arrive, so I went over there early and waited. She was prompt, and I let her in and invited her upstairs. We were just chatting, and then she just went into her bag and brought out a syringe and that was when I got worried. I managed to run into my back room, the one where I do my readings, and grab my phone from the table. I called 999, but she forced her way in and tried her best to try and stick the needle into me. I'd dropped the phone by then but the line was still open and they could hear what was going on, which I guess that is how the police came so quickly.'

'And that's how you both got all your cuts and bruises?'

'Yes!' Parkinson seemed indignant that she'd been asked such a question. 'The woman was trying to stick goodness knows what into me; I wasn't going to hang around and let her do that, would you?'

'And how many syringes did you see her with?'

'How many?'

'Yes.'

'Why, just the one, of course.'

'Are you absolutely certain?' Fielding pushed.

'Yes. She was only holding one. Are you suggesting that she had more than one?'

Fielding didn't respond, but instead brought a photo out of the file and slid it across the desk.

'Do you know who this person is?' she asked, showing her the shot of someone exiting Norman Bishop's room on CCTV at the Premier Hotel in Blackburn.

Parkinson looked puzzled. 'No, I can't see their face. Why, who is it?'

Fielding noted her reaction to it; she didn't see any shock on her face, which might have been present had she been the person in the shot. Without saying anything, she closed the file in front of her and thanked her for her time. As she and Summers rose, Marilyn Parkinson asked them what was going to happen next.

'Just sit tight and we'll get back to you as soon as we can.'

'Can I press charges against her?'

'We'll see. Just give us time to ask more questions.' And with that the two detectives exited the room, allowing the constable to enter and resume her position watching over the suspect.

CHAPTER FORTY-SIX

As they left the room, Joe Burton was already waiting for them in the corridor. He exhaled a long breath.

'Do we believe her?' he asked.

'I don't think she has any reason to lie to us, do you?'

'I just don't know,' came the response. Like Fielding, he couldn't see what Parkinson would have to lie about, but then she wouldn't be the first suspect to pull the wool over their eyes during questioning.

'What I don't get is why she agreed to invite a complete stranger to come around to speak to her?' he continued.

'Not exactly a complete stranger, I guess, as she had visited her as a client.'

'But even so.'

'I agree,' Fielding said to him. 'As she said, she just thought that she needed to talk to somebody who was there the night her friend Maria died.'

'That sounds a bit strange to me, doesn't it you?'

Fielding nodded. 'A bit. I didn't see a guilty reaction when I showed her the photo, did you?'

'No, I didn't. Well, maybe we should just keep an open mind with her. Let's see what Watkins has to say for herself, should we?'

As Burton resumed his position in the viewing area, this time overseeing interview room number 2, Fielding and Summers went in to see the solicitor. Like the other female constable, the one watching now Watkins was dismissed for the duration of the interview.

Caroline Watkins sat back in her chair when they entered, adopting the defensive pose of crossing her arms over her chest. She looked at them sternly in an 'if looks could kill' kind of way. Unlike Marilyn Parkinson, who looked scared and afraid at their entrance, Watkins appeared completely in control and unmoved. Despite the subliminal message, Fielding was unfazed. She'd seen it so many times before that she was immune to things like this.

'Now Ms Watkins,' Fielding began as she and Summers took a seat, 'I'd like you to tell me about what happened between yourself and Ms Parkinson that led to you both being here.'

Watkins looked her straight in the eye and took a long breath. 'And I'd like to tell you that I want to speak to my solicitor.'

It wasn't the answer Fielding had expected. If Caroline Watkins had wanted a solicitor, why hadn't she asked for one as soon as she arrived in the station?

From his vantage point in the adjoining room, Burton's frustration with the woman reached boiling point, and he slammed both his fists down hard on the table beside the two-way mirror. Fielding and Summers both heard it, as did Watkins, who sat with a one-sided smirk on her face. The two detectives rose from their seats. They would now have to wait until her legal representative arrived, would doubtlessly be a member of her own law firm.

'We could all hear you through the glass,' Fielding scolded Burton when they were in the corridor. But he didn't apologise for his actions.

'I don't know if I don't care for the woman because she's a solicitor, or it's the fact that she has this supercilious air about her. Either way ...' his voice just trailed off. Fielding knew that Burton had two pet hates: the press, and solicitors. Any one of the two could push his buttons to the point where he would get into a state and slam his fists down in despair or, when anything solid was absent, swear prolifically. As on this occasion he could be heard, she was glad the former was his choice of relief. Joe Burton didn't often swear as a rule, but when he did he certainly didn't hold back.

'Let her call her solicitor then and see just what she has to say to them,' he resumed after a while. 'I'm surprised Marilyn Parkinson hasn't asked for one as well.'

'Or she hasn't because she doesn't think that she needs one,' Summers offered.

'She definitely didn't seem to think that she did.' Fielding agreed with him.

Right then a call came through to Burton's mobile. 'Okay, that's good news. Thanks for your help.'

As Fielding looked at him questioningly, Burton said that the call was from Mark at the Fraud Squad and the poison found in the Richardsons *had* be analysed as digitalis.

'Right then,' he announced, feeling a tad more cheerful than he had a few moments earlier, 'let's go and pick John Turnbull up. Jack, can you come with us just in case he decides to resist arrest? But can you first go up and see one of the others and get them to arrange Watkins's call to her solicitor then wait for them to arrive.'

***

When the three detectives arrived at John Turnbull's residence they immediately saw that his car was not on the driveway.

'Oh no,' Burton declared on seeing its absence. Surely the man hadn't done a runner, had he?

'See if you can get around the back,' he said to Jack as they scrambled out of the vehicle, 'and we'll check the front.'

After sprinting up the driveway and pressing the doorbell several times it became apparent from the lack of response that Turnbull was not at home.

'Anything back there?' Burton asked as Summers reappeared through the gate to the rear of the house.

He shook his head. 'The place looks empty. Unless he's hiding on the premises somewhere.'

'No. I think we should take it that he's gone, especially if his car's not here,' Burton said to him.

'We could try his parents' home,' Fielding suggested, which was agreed upon.

'John? No he isn't here,' Mrs Turnbull said when they arrived at her house. 'Why? Whatever is wrong?'

'Have you any idea where he might have gone?' Burton was becoming agitated again. They had to move quickly. John Turnbull must know by now that the Richardsons had been picked up by the police, and if he wasn't at home then the chances were he was trying to make some kind of a getaway.

'What is it? Mr Turnbull senior called from a room inside the house before appearing in the hallway and making his way towards them. It was the first time they'd seen him out of his chair.

'It's the police,' his wife explained to him as he joined her in the doorway. 'They're wanting to know where John is.'

'Well, he went to pick up Maria's parents from the airport, didn't he?' Mr Turnbull senior explained.

'He did that and they're here, but now we're trying to find him.'

'He'll be at home then,' the father continued.

'No, we've just been there and he's gone.'

'Maybe he's showing them around then?' Mrs Turnbull offered.

Burton hadn't intended to tell them that the Richardsons were now in hospital under police supervision but felt it necessary to say something. 'I'm afraid that here's been a bit of an accident.'

Mrs Turnbull's hands went straight up to her mouth and her face drained of all its colour as she imagined the worst. 'Are they okay? Is our John all right?'

'The Richardson are hospitalised, but it's John we're trying to find,' Fielding stepped in to try and calm the woman down.

'Has he discharged himself or something?' the father asked. John's mother was still standing aghast. 'Maybe he's in shock and wandered off?'

'So, you've no idea where he would be if he wasn't at home?' Burton continued, his face now showing the anguish he was trying so hard to hide.

'Is he in some kind of trouble?' Mrs Turnbull had overcome her initial shock to ask the one question the detectives hoped that neither she nor her husband would.

'We just need to speak to him, that's all.' Burton felt like screaming. He wanted to scream out that yes, their son could be in trouble; that their son was the prime suspect for murdering his wife and poisoning his in-laws. But he didn't. He kept his calm, as best as he could, waiting for some kind of clue from John Turnbull's parents as to where he could have gone.

'Well, he did ask for his passport the other day. We kept it here, see. We just thought that maybe after the funeral he was thinking about going over to Spain to spend some time with Maria's folks,' the father said. 'It would probably do him the world of good.'

Burton felt this to be the breakthrough that they were looking for. Quickly thanking Mr and Mrs Turnbull for their assistance, he and the other two detectives turned tail and headed back to the car, leaving the parents stunned by their sudden departure and still wondering about the welfare of their son.

CHAPTER FORTY-SEVEN

'Who did you get to wait for Caroline Watkins's solicitor?' he asked Summers who was sitting in the back seat.

'Jane,' came the reply.

'So are Simon and Phillipa free right now?'

'Yes, they are.'

Burton didn't waste time getting on the phone to the remaining team members. Dialling Fielding's extension and it was picked up by Simon, who was immediately brought up to speed and instructed to get on to Manchester Airport in the hope that John Turnbull may not have already fled the country.

'What if he's driven to another airport?' Simon logically asked.

'I'm hoping that he hasn't. But if Manchester can't locate him then we'll have to consider contacting the next nearest ones. Can you do that immediately please Simon?'

'Okay, I'm on it.'

Burton drove back like a man possessed. Despite his tangible anxiety of the situation, Fielding knew for a fact that this was exactly the sort of thing he'd miss when he was promoted to DCI. A more desk-based job just didn't suit him or his nature, but a promotion was a good thing and always aspired for by any police officer. She felt pleased for him in that respect, but sorry that he'd miss the hands-on graft that he enjoyed so much. Things exactly like this.

By the time they reached the office, Simon and Phillipa had everything well in control. A call had just come in from the transport police at the airport just prior to Burton and the others' arrival, and John Turnbull had been reported to have checked in to a flight to the Costa Del Sol. His parents had been correct in their assumption that their son might wish to visit his late wife's parents' house, it just wasn't in the way that they'd imagined it.

'They're going in now to pick him up,' Simon announced to a delighted Burton.

'Great. Has Caroline Watkins's solicitor arrived yet?'

'Jane rang up before you came in to say that he's on his way but hasn't arrived yet.'

'Right, that's fine. I have a plan for when John Turnbull is brought in.'

***

'That's the front desk,' Simon answered the call that he'd been waiting for. 'Turnbull's just come in, and they're holding him down there until you go and get him.'

'That's great, Simon. Thank you for your help with this.'

Burton picked up the file they had on Turnbull. 'Right. Are we all set with the plan?'

Fielding and Summers both nodded.

'Okay then, here we go.'

While they were waiting, Burton, together with Fielding and Summers, had formulated a plan which they aimed to put in action even before they'd manoeuvred John Turnbull into the interview room. Summers was to go ahead and wait facing them just outside room number 3. Jane would already be sitting in with Caroline Watkins awaiting the arrival of her solicitor, and Phillipa would be in with Marilyn Parkinson completing a release form. Summers would tap on each door as he passed so that they could be opened in preparation. As John Turnbull walked along the corridor, it was hoped that he wouldn't be able to resist looking into an open door. Summers was to watch his reaction on seeing the women sitting in the rooms, and the two detective constables were to watch both women's reactions upon seeing him brought into custody.

John Turnbull was far from happy when he saw Burton and the other two detectives approaching.

'What is going on, Burton?' he demanded, which immediately got Burton's back up.

'That's Detective Inspector Burton,' he said in the same tone he'd been spoken to.

'Detective Inspector then. Why have I been hauled into here like some common criminal?'

Burton bit his lip. He wasn't going to say what he was thinking, as he didn't yet know for certain what he was surmising despite believing it to be the case. What he needed was the man to slip up once he was in the interview room.

'We just have a few more questions for you before you leave the country.'

'Could it not have waited until I got back? I was just going over to get Maria's parents some things they'd forgotten to bring with them for the funeral.'

'No, I'm afraid that it could not.'

'Well, I'll be expecting a refund for my flight that I've missed.'

Burton chose to ignore that remark, trying to keep it as low key as possible as to not spook the man as to the real intention for bringing him in. 'If you'd like to come along with us; we'll take you to somewhere a little more private where we can have a chat.'

Turnbull rose. Although not happy to do so, he'd go along with the annoying detective to get this stupidity over as quickly as possible in order to catch the next available flight to Spain.

As they'd pre-arranged, when they approached the interview rooms Summers went ahead, tapped on each door, then waited outside room number 3 in order to watch Turnbull's reaction when he passed rooms 1 and 2. As hoped, Turnbull did indeed glance into the rooms as he passed. Walking behind him, Burton and Fielding noticed a slight hesitance as he passed room number 1 which housed Marilyn Parkinson. But it was when he passed room number 2 that they noticed something more definitive. He momentarily stopped, and his shoulders stiffened before continuing on. They already knew from the evidence already collected that John Turnbull had met both of the women in the line of his business, but what they'd just witnessed seemed to reveal something a little more than simply an occasional working relationship between each of them.

As Turnbull approached room 3, Summers indicated with a wave of his hand that he should enter. Doing as he was told he walked in and took a seat on the far side of the table. Burton and Fielding then followed him in and sat down opposite. Summers had also been asked to attend, and stood near the door after he'd closed it. The two detectives had barely sat down before Turnbull announced that he wasn't prepared to say anything to them without first having a word with his solicitor. Burton couldn't believe what he was hearing, but the sight of the two women must have really spooked the man. He really should have just walked out without saying anything, but couldn't resist saying as he headed out of the door that 'both women had told them everything'. He then left Turnbull to mull that comment over.

CHAPTER FORTY-EIGHT

John Turnbull used his call to a solicitor to ring Caroline Watkins's law firm. He was informed that somebody was already on their way to see her, and that they visit him afterwards.

In the meantime, Burton spoke to Phillipa and Jane to get their take on the women's reaction to seeing Turnbull being brought in. They reported that they'd both reacted with surprise, more so with Marilyn Parkinson, and the DCs both suspected there to be a more intimate familiarity there too. Parkinson had then gone on to also request the services of a solicitor.

'So that's all three of them lawyering up then!' Burton was dismayed, but hopeful that something good would eventually come out of it. 'Let's hope that their legal representatives persuade their clients to tell the truth.'

The solicitor sent from Caroline Watkins's law firm was a young man. Far too young, in Burton's opinion. In fact, he looked like an office junior, but he knew that looks could be very deceiving. After spending some time with Watkins then with Turnbull, the solicitor announced that neither of his clients were willing to say anything further. If Burton wished to charge them with something, then he suggested that he do so. Otherwise, he requested that they be released immediately. Burton felt himself slipping into despair again, but then as he watched the man walk away, help came to him from an unlikely source.

The door to interview room 1 opened, and Marilyn Parkinson's solicitor walked through it. He came to a stop when he saw Joe Burton standing there.

'I have advised my client against it,' he began, closing his briefcase, 'but she says that she will speak to you now and tell you everything she knows.'

Burton's spirits rose. *When one door closes another one opens*, *quite literally*, he thought to himself. Fielding and Summers had returned upstairs, but he rang for them to come down again.

'We've had a breakthrough,' he said.

Marilyn Parkinson had been crying. Her eyes were red-rimmed, and an overly used paper tissue was balled-up in one hand. She sat up straight in her seat and dabbed at her face when the three detectives entered. Summers once again assumed his observational position from behind Burton and Fielding, still feeling privileged to be included in the proceedings.

Parkinson gave a nervous laugh when the door closed behind them.

'I've been advised not to say anything,' she said, 'but, quite frankly, I can't see the point in that.'

'We appreciate you doing this,' Burton said to her. 'So, what is it that you have to tell us?'

She gave a deep sigh before proceeding. 'I first met John at one of his office parties. As I'd just signed a contract for the lease on my business property with his company I was asked if I'd like to come along. I said yes. I took a fancy to him, I'll admit it. I don't usually let myself get so involved so easily, but John was, well, I thought that he was different.'

It was then that Burton produced a copy of the photograph Simon had managed to find from one of Turnbull's parties. Parkinson reached across and took it.

'Ah,' she smiled, 'so you already knew.'

'We didn't really know any more than the fact that you both knew one another,' Fielding admitted. 'I guess it was a little more than just that?'

'Yes, it was. For me, at least. We saw one another for a few months. We were discreet, although I couldn't really see the reason for us being so careful as neither of us was attached. Or so I thought. John then told me that he was ending our relationship. Said he'd met somebody else and it was serious. I thought that *we* were serious! The next thing I heard was that he was married. I felt so cheated. I saw him out and about with his new wife a short while afterwards. At least I thought it was his new wife, but I later found it wasn't. So, not only did he drop me like a ton of bricks, but he also found himself a wife and was cheating on her too. I have to admit that I followed him a few times, making sure that he couldn't see me doing so. I was still in love with him even though it was evident that he wasn't with me. I'm not entirely sure he loved his wife either after having seen him with this other woman on his arm, the pair of them all lovey-dovey and laughing together. I couldn't believe it the day his wife Maria and her friends made an appointment to come and see me, the day she died. I recognised Maria as soon as I saw her, but I also recognised Caroline Watkins. She was often in the papers, some big solicitor or something, always representing this one or that one, but the main reason I recognised her was the fact that she was the woman I saw out and about with John – the one he pushed me aside for.

'So how did you feel about that, Marilyn?'

'How did you think I felt? I felt angry, and annoyed, and cheated. The way any woman in love would feel if she saw the man she loved walking hand in hand with somebody else.'

Fielding really couldn't disagree with that. If she and Joe Burton were to split up for any reason, and she were to see him around town with another woman, she knew for a fact that it would break her heart. So she could relate to what she was saying.

'So tell us about the two syringes?'

'What two syringes? Like I said before I only saw one, the one that woman tried to attack me with. If she had two, then perhaps she brought it to give me two doses of whatever was in it.'

Fielding believed her. She'd been up-front and honest since speaking with her solicitor, so had no reason to believe that she wasn't being so now. So why did Watkins bring two syringes with her? Was it, as Parkinson said, as an extra precaution to make sure, or perhaps it was in case one syringe got broken?

'Okay,' Burton announced with a sigh, 'I think we have all we need for the moment. We'll get a statement drawn up for you to sign.'

As all three detectives left the room, Fielding knew that Burton had something up his sleeve. She knew him well enough to know that he wouldn't end an interview just like that and had something else planned even though Parkinson had told them all she could – or all she was willing to tell them.

'What's the plan then?' she asked once the door behind them had closed.

'I've got an idea,' he announced, before heading towards the next interview room door.

Fielding stopped him by putting a hand on his arm. 'But her solicitor told us she wouldn't say anything.'

'I'm not going in; I'm just going to stick my head through the door to tell her something, not to ask her a question. She doesn't even have to open her mouth and speak, which makes it a whole different story, doesn't it?' he said with a wink.

What was he up to, Fielding wondered? She was intrigued. When Burton opened interview room 2's door, Caroline Watkins looked up and frowned angrily when she saw who it was. She wanted to say something to him, to remind him about what her solicitor had said, but knew that she couldn't. She'd been advised to say nothing and not interact any further with the police. So why was he now trying to antagonise her?

'Just the let you know,' he said, half-in and half-out of the door, 'that both Marilyn Parkinson and John Turnbull have told us everything. The game's over, I'm afraid.' And with that he shut the door. Moving on to the room where John Turnbull was sitting, he did the same thing with him.

'What now?' Fielding asked when he'd finished his little game with them.

'Now we wait,' he smiled smugly.

CHAPTER FORTY-NINE

As things were taking a little longer than he'd expected following his fabricated statement, Burton was getting a little bit anxious, especially as he saw Fielding's questioning expression. Had he made a mistake, he wondered? Despite both parties consulting with their solicitors, he'd expected the statement would make them want to put their side of things forward and override their decision not to say anything further. After all, they wouldn't know that only Marilyn Parkinson had spoken to them. But, so far, nobody was speaking. Had he perhaps taken things one step too far and his plan had backfired? If this were to come out in court proceedings then he'd be in deep trouble.

But then Burton's phone pinged with a text message. Phillipa Preston informed him that

Caroline Watkins wanted to speak to him. He felt relieved in more ways than one.

'Right,' he said to Fielding, 'here we go. I know you think that was dangerous move, but it seems to have paid off. Watkins wants to talk.'

'I think you're very lucky,' she said. 'You took a big risk with that one.'

'I know, and I was beginning to think that this was the biggest mistake of my career. But let's see what she has to say for herself, shall we?'

Caroline Watkins was a changed woman. Gone was the air of superiority and the sanctimonious arrogance, to be replaced by something more akin to defeat.

'I don't know what they've told you,' she began. 'but perhaps I should tell you my side of the story. If I stay quiet then that's almost tantamount to admitting guilt.'

Gone was the crossed arms defensive stance, to be replaced by both of her hands placed palm down on the table. There were beads of sweat on both them and also on her forehead. The woman was worried, of that Burton was certain.

'I think that would be a good idea,' he said to her.

'I met John through work. My firm had had legal dealings with his, contracts and things like that. I found him charming, and he was very much the flirty type. Perhaps I should have realised and shouldn't have been so silly, but I found myself falling in love with him. Before we got together, I'd seen him at some of the works evening events with a woman. I later found out who she was: Marilyn Parkinson, or to give her her professional name, Madame Ortiz. I got jealous, and the next time I saw John I started to flirt with him too. It paid off as the next thing I knew we were a couple. I didn't ask him about his previous girlfriend as I didn't want him to know that I knew who she was. That would have made my actions look contrived. I know that they were, but I didn't want him to know that.

'I understand,' Burton continued.

'Do you?' Watkins asked sorrowfully.

'Yes, I think so.'

Watkins then continued. 'Then I made the mistake of asking Maria along to one of the works events. I even introduced him to her. I never for one moment thought that he would do to me what he'd done to Marilyn, in that he'd dump me and go off with Maria. When I challenged him about it, John told me that he had a reason why he wanted to get to know her better. I just thought that he was spinning me a line. Then when they got married quickly I thought that perhaps she was pregnant or something; I mean, nobody gets married that quickly, do they, unless they are? I didn't see her after that, not until the night we all went out together. The other girls had seen her and told me that she wasn't pregnant, so I wondered why there was this almighty rush to get wed.'

'Perhaps they'd genuinely fallen in love with one another,' Fielding said to her.

Watkins laughed. 'I suspected that it wouldn't last, I mean, he seems to be a ladies' man who just wants what he can take and to hell with the women he casts aside.'

'But you still loved him, right? And you'd do anything for him, even now?'

She hung her head and said, barely audibly, 'Yes, I suppose so.'

'So tell us about the syringes. What was all that about?' Burton resumed his cross-examination.

'It was John, he told me to do it.'

'To do what, exactly?'

'To inject her with it. But I only had the one syringe. She must have had one as well from him. I guess we were both set up.'

This was an interesting statement, the detectives thought. Had Turnbull orchestrated the whole event by providing each with a syringe in order for them to do away with the other? In a strange, sick way it almost made sense.

'And do you know what was in the syringe you had?'

'He didn't say precisely, but he said that she was pestering him and that it would make her sick for a while. I guess he told her the same thing.'

'Not exactly,' Burton said. 'They contained poison, digitalis, to be precise.'

'What?' She looked genuinely shocked. 'No, no, no, that can't be right. He would never ask me to do something like that?'

'You think not? We think, in fact we know, that Maria was injected with digitalis some time just before she died.'

'You mean that he ... that he killed her? No, I don't believe it; that can't be right, it just can't!'

If Caroline Watkins was indeed innocent then she was putting up a very good show. Still, neither of the detectives could truly determine if she was telling the truth or not. Was it that her career as a solicitor had prepared her well to quick-wittedly respond to any form of questioning, or was it all a ruse to get her side of things across, genuine or not, before Turnbull had a chance to? In their minds she was definitely not out of the woods yet. Maybe now was the best time to speak to the main man himself, to see what story he would come up with.

CHAPTER FIFTY

As they opened the door to interview room number 1, John Turnbull looked more relaxed than any other suspect they'd ever had in their custody. He was either innocent of all charges, or he was so mentally prepared for any question they chose to throw at him that nothing could possibly faze him. It could be either, or both. But then again, hadn't he been into acting at school? Burton recalled the photograph of him in his parents' home. It showed him performing in a school or college play. As it was displayed in a prominent place, it must have had a great deal of importance to both him and his family. Like Summers, who'd actually considered going to study at RADA rather than becoming a police officer, perhaps he could psyche himself up to act out a convincing scene? Playing the grieving husband when he, in fact, was quite the opposite: a cold-blooded, calculating killer, of not only his wife, but of two other people as well. The truth of the matter was, whatever he said to them now, could they really believe it to be the truth?

As the constable on duty in the room was dismissed, Burton and Fielding sat down on the seats opposite Turnbull. He straightened himself up in his seat.

'You wanted to speak to us?' Burton asked him, to which he nodded.

'I don't know what those two women have said to you, but I wanted to put whatever story they've told you straight.'

'Why do you think they've said anything to us about you?'

'Then why are they here?'

'Actually,' Burton admitted, 'we brought them in because they were involved in a disagreement which ended in physical violence.'

'What, were those two scrapping, over me?' He gave an arrogant laugh, the kind a person gives when they consider themselves the centre of attention. Pure narcissism.

'We didn't say it was over you, Mr Turnbull,' Fielding corrected the man's self-centred assumption.

'Oh?' he seemed disappointed. 'Okay then.'

'So what do you have to tell us?' Burton was becoming impatient.

'Yes, I knew both women, intimate with them even. But like every relationship, one ends and another begins. You know what it's like.'

'Go on.' Burton said. Neither he nor Fielding were going to be drawn into a personal conversation, especially not from a murder suspect.

'When I finished with Marilyn she became overly jealous and kept pestering me.'

'Pestering you?' Fielding was curious to hear what Turnbull's definition of the word was.

He sighed, as if bored by the recollection of it. 'She'd ring me, text me, that kind of thing. I made it quite clear that I was not with her anymore and was with somebody else, but she kept on contacting me.'

'Some people would think that flattering.'

'Not when it's all day and all night. Anyway, I'd met Caroline by then and knew that she was the one I wanted to be with.'

'Until Maria Richardson came along,' Fielding reminded him.

'What can I say,' Turnbull laughed, 'I'm a red-blooded male, I like to play the field.'

'We heard that you had an underlying motive for marrying her; is that true?'

Turnbull's whole expression changed when he heard Burton's question.

'Which one of them told you that?' he demanded, although he was in no position to do so.

So there was something in what Caroline Watkins had said, Burton thought, otherwise why would he have reacted the way he just did? 'It doesn't matter,' he continued. He wasn't going to give the man the satisfaction of knowing that. At least Watkins wasn't lying about that little gem. 'Just answer the question please.'

'I'm afraid that I can't, detective.'

'Why not?'

'I think I need to speak to my solicitor again, if you don't mind?'

Burton did mind, but what else could he do. If he couldn't get an answer out of Maria's husband, then perhaps the person who had told him that snippet of information in the first place might.

Caroline Watkins had been forthcoming before, so he hoped that she would be so again. That is, if she was to be believed in the first place. As far as he knew, all three of them could be in it together, covering for one another and making up stories as they went along just to confuse things.

'So, Caroline, tell me exactly why John married Maria,' he asked as he and Fielding again sat in with Watkins.

A half-smile crossed her lips. 'Won't he tell you?' she asked.

Burton shook his head.

'I'm not surprised, although I am surprised that he's talking to you. I suspect he thought that he'd got away with it and would blame either me or Marilyn for everything.'

'And what is everything?'

'The deaths ... all of them. He did them all, you know. Him alone. Oh, I knew all about them, but I didn't actually kill anybody.'

'But he wasn't alone; we know that for a fact that he had an accomplice. Are you admitting to being an accessory?' Burton couldn't believe she was saying as much as she was, especially with her being a solicitor and all. But love can be a strange thing, and have a strange effect upon people, especially if they've been spurned by the one they love as she had.

'We all are, I guess, if you look at it like that. Has John told you exactly why he wanted to marry Maria? It wasn't for love, you know.'

Burton wanted to push her on that last comment, but sensed there was something wrong here. She seemed to be far too relaxed; her almost glazed eyes seemed to be looking at some distance point behind him and was slurring her words slightly.

'Are you all right, Ms Watkins?' he asked her, noticing that there was now an even larger build-up of sweat particles on her forehead.

'Actually ... no ... I ... don't ... feel ...'

Then everything happened quickly. Caroline Watkins slid from the chair and fell awkwardly onto the floor behind the table, banging her head on the floor as she did so. Burton was up in an instant and ran around to her side. It looked to him like she was having some kind of a fit as she was convulsing uncontrollably.

'Quick, Sally, ring through for a medic!' he shouted to his partner. Not being medically trained, he was unsure what to do for the best in a situation like this, but thought the one thing he could do for her was to try to stop her head from crashing against the ground, so he cradled it on his lap.

As Fielding ran out into the corridor, alarm bells started to ring throughout the station, making everyone aware that there was an emergency situation. The lights also dimmed in the interview room and went onto emergency lighting, with a single flashing red one over the door pulsating to the sound of the siren. Within minutes, the station medical team arrived and they set to work on Ms Watkins. Burton left the room to find Fielding.

'There's an ambulance on its way,' she informed him. 'What just happened in there?'

'I don't know,' he said, rubbing his neck. 'But that's a little bit more than a fit, I think.'

'What are you thinking?'

'I'm thinking that she could have been poisoned.'

'But how?'

Burton shrugged. He'd never had a suspect die whilst in his custody, and he sincerely hoped that Caroline Watkins wouldn't be the first.

EPILOGUE

All Burton could really do with the remaining two suspects was to charge them. He felt that he had heard enough from them to do this as they had all, essentially, admitted to a degree their involvement in it. Despite initially thinking the Marilyn Parkinson was an innocent victim in all this, from what Caroline Watkins had said prior to her taking ill, he believed that they may have all had some part to play in the deaths of not only Maria Turnbull but also Harry York and Norman Bishop. Perhaps John Turnbull was the puppet master here, and was playing his suitors off one against the other. He still didn't know who had actually done the killing – it could have been John Turnbull and Marilyn Parkinson, Turnbull and Caroline Watkins, or all three together; either option was possible. But what he did know was all three of them were involved in some way, regardless of any protestations, and that was enough for him to make the arrests. He only hoped

Watkins survived in order to say more, as the one thing he really wanted to know was why – why did Maria have to die in the first place?

While he was waiting to hear the news regarding Watkins's condition, Burton's friend Mark from the Fraud Squad rang him to say that the Richardsons had both pulled through, thanks mainly to Burton's suggestion to screen them for digitalis poisoning. They had both been charged whilst on the recovery ward, and had now been moved to private rooms with a police presence in attendance until they could be sent to prison.

'I think what we found out might just be of interest to you, Joe,' Mark said, and he continued to tell him what he and his team had discovered about Faraway Dreams, the company the Richardsons had been directors of prior to its collapse and their abscondment to Spain.

'We managed to get a list of all the people the company did out of their savings in order to urge them to press charges, and there was a name on the list we thought that you'd like to be made aware of.'

'Oh?' Burton asked, intrigued.

'Yes, it's Tim Turnbull, John Turnbull's father.'

Burton couldn't believe what he was hearing. This was the answer he'd been looking for, the reason why John Turnbull must have done the things he'd done. He'd apparently married the Richardsons's daughter for one reason and one reason alone, to kill her in order to get them back to the UK. When interviewing the parents Mark had discovered that Maria had fallen out with her family a bit when they'd decided to pack up and leave. As she was attending university, with a career all planned out for herself, she hadn't wished to join them, and this had caused some friction. She remained in touch with them, but didn't wish to go out to Spain to visit them simply because they told her that they didn't want to return back to the UK ... for anything. She took that to be her included. The reason for that was now quite clear: they feared they'd be arrested as soon as they set foot in the country. John's reason for marrying her was cold and calculated, and not based in the slightest on love. It was based upon revenge for what her parents had done to his.

'Thank you, Mark, that's answered quite a few questions, and solved the case for us,' Burton said to his long-time friend. 'We'll compile the facts for a jury to decide all their fates.'

'Glad I could help. It's the least I could do for what you did for me.'

***

Whenever the team closed a case, they spent that evening in their local having a celebratory drink, and this evening would be no different to any that had gone before. Their choice of pub being one just around the corner from the station. Not only did the team want to mark the end of yet another case, but also wanted to celebrate the promotions of Joe Burton, Sally Fielding and Jack Summers.

'Why don't we make an evening of it and book a table for the two of us at that restaurant we were talking about the other day?' Burton said to Fielding just before they were leaving.

'You mean the Italian one in the Northern Quarter?'

'Yes. You said that you'd like to try it.'

'I did. So yes, I'd love to.'

'Good. I'll go ahead and book it then.'

What Sally Fielding didn't know was Burton had a specific reason for suggesting the restaurant, one which she'd find out later that night.

At 7.30pm, the two detectives called for a cab and excused themselves from the team's celebrations and made their way to the restaurant. Once there, they were shown to a quiet table near the rear and away from everyone. Although not overly busy, the restaurant still had a fair number of patrons.

'It's nice to get a bit of peace and quiet!' Fielding laughed, having spent the last few hours in a busy public house with the rest of the team, and most of the time having to shout over the noise to be heard.

'Yes, I know what you mean.'

'This is really nice,' she said, looking around her at the décor. It was modern, but with a hint of old-world charm, with photographs of famous Italian landmarks adorning the walls.

Burton was becoming more nervous by the second, but managed to contain it well. At least, well enough for Fielding not to suspect anything.

'I took the liberty of ordering us a bottle of champagne, to celebrate both our promotions,' he said as he saw a waiter approaching from behind her with a bottle and a wine cooler in hand.

'Oh, Joe, that sounds lovely!' Fielding exclaimed. It had been a long time since she'd had a real bottle of champagne, usually only buying the cheap fizz from the local supermarket. Not that there was anything wrong with her Pink Fizz as she called it, as she was partial to it now and again.

'Well, it is a bit of a special night, isn't it?' He declared confidently, despite fighting back his jitters.

When the waiter arrived, he set the cooler and its stand on the floor and popped the cork from the bottle, pouring only an initial small amount in each of the two flutes.

'Cheers!' Burton said, picking up his glass and chinking it on the side of hers. The sound of the two crystal flutes meeting rang out a clear, pleasant tone.

'Oh, wait!' he suddenly declared, putting it down again. 'I think there's something in your glass, right at the bottom. Here, let me get it out for you.'

Fielding hardly had time to see what it was before he'd taken the glass from her and stuck his fingers right into it. Feeling a bit embarrassed by this movement, she looked up at the waiter and wondered what he must be thinking, but he only looked down at her and smiled.

It was then that she looked back at Burton. He rose from his seat and pushed his chair back away from him, at the same time the waiter pulled the wine cooler back a short way away from the table. Walking around to her, Burton got down on one knee and held something up in his hand. As she focused on it, she saw that he was holding a diamond ring.

'Joe ... what's ...' she began, but before she could say any more, he shushed her into silence.

'Alice Sally Fielding,' he began, gulping hard as he said it, 'would you do me the greatest pleasure of agreeing to become my wife.'

Fielding didn't know what to say at first as she was still reeling from the shock of seeing him finger-deep into her champagne glass, but then said, 'Yes, yes, of course I will, Joe!'

At this point, the whole of the restaurant erupted, with staff and customers alike applauding to celebrate two people publicly and unashamedly declaring their love for one another. Burton was relieved, and also delighted that his plan had worked without too much stress. He was also thrilled that the love of his life had agreed to marry him. It was a wonderful moment for both of them, as far away from the horrors of their job as they could get.

But their happiness was to be short-lived. Little did they both know that the seeds of their next case were being sown right at the very moment of Joe Burton's proposal. Long-hidden secrets, lies and shame had emerged which would lead one individual to enact their revenge, and in doing so test the team to their limit and change some of their lives forever.

ABOUT THE AUTHOR

Pamela Murray is from the North East of England, and is the author of The Manchester Murders book series featuring detectives Burton and Fielding.

She began writing in her teens, when she and her school friend used to write short stories for one another. The writing continued on and off over the years, but was only reignited within the last decade when the same school friend introduced her to the local writers group she was in.

She had intended to enter journalism after leaving school but found herself going to work in a public library instead, so there's always been more than a passing interest in books, writing, and literature.

Printed in Dunstable, United Kingdom